"{Ross Macdonald} carried form and style about as far as they would go, writing classic family tragedies in the guise of private detective mysteries."

—***The Guardian***

➡

"Most mystery writers merely write about crime. Ross Macdonald writes about sin."

—***Atlantic***

"Ross Macdonald gives to the detective story that accent of class that the late Raymond Chandler did."

—**Seymour Korman, *Chicago Tribune***

➡

"Macdonald should not be limited in audience to connoisseurs of mystery fiction. He is one of a handful of writers in the genre whose worth and quality surpass the limitations of the form."

—**Robert Kirsch, *Los Angeles Times***

➡

"Reveals a disturbing segment of California coastal society. . . . As always, Mr. Macdonald's persons and environment enrich his schema."

—***Book Week***

ALSO BY ROSS MACDONALD

The Moving Target
The Chill
The Galton Case
The Blue Hammer
The Way Some People Die
The Far Side of the Dollar

Published by
WARNER BOOKS

December 1990
Hope this keeps you happy for a couple of hours! I love you, Meg

PRAISE FOR

BLACK MONEY

and Ross Macdonald

"A beautiful job . . . rich in plot and character. . . . The denouement is both surprising and shocking and the whole is up to Mr. Macdonald's own extraordinarily high standards."

—***New York Times Book Review***

"Let's be honest: Ross Macdonald remains *the* grandmaster, taking the crime novel to new heights by imbuing it with psychological resonance, complexity of story, and richness of style that remain awe-inspiring. Those of us in his wake owe a debt that can never be paid."

—**Jonathan Kellerman**

"Ross Macdonald is an important American novelist!"

—***San Francisco Chronicle***

more. . . .

"It was not just that Ross Macdonald taught us how to write; he did something much more, he taught us how to read, and how to think about life, and maybe in some small, but mattering way, how to live. . . . I owe him."

—**Robert B. Parker**

"A more serious and complex writer than Chandler and Hammett ever were."

—**Eudora Welty**

"Without in the least abating my admiration for Dashiell Hammett and Raymond Chandler, I should like to venture the heretical suggestion that Ross Macdonald is a better novelist than either of them."

—**Anthony Boucher**

"Ross Macdonald must be ranked high amongst American thriller-writers."

—***The Times Literary Supplement* (London)**

"Ross Macdonald's work has consistently nourished me. . . . I have turned to it often to hear what I should like to call the justice of its voice and to be enlightened by its wisdom, delighted by its imagination, and, not incidentally, superbly entertained."

—**Thomas Berger**

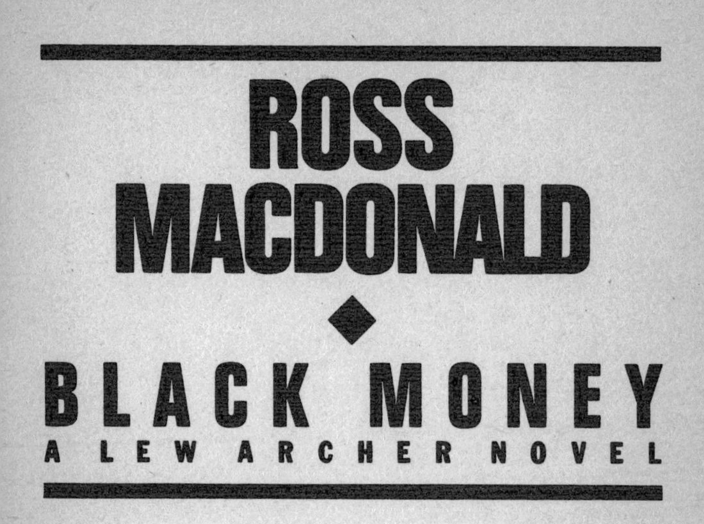

A Warner Communications Company

To Robert Easton

WARNER BOOKS EDITION

This Warner Books Edition is published by
arrangement with Alfred A. Knopf, Inc., 201 East 50th Street,
New York, N.Y. 10022

Cover design by Jackie Merri Meyer
Cover illustration by Gary Kelley

Warner Books, Inc.
666 Fifth Avenue
New York, N.Y. 10103

A Warner Communications Company

Printed in the United States of America

First Warner Books Printing: August, 1990

10 9 8 7 6 5 4 3 2 1

I

I'D BEEN HEARING about the Tennis Club for years, but I'd never been inside of it. Its courts and bungalows, its swimming pool and cabanas and pavilions, were disposed around a cove of the Pacific a few miles south of the Los Angeles County border. Just parking my Ford in the asphalt lot beside the tennis courts made me feel like less of a dropout from the affluent society.

The carefully groomed woman at the front desk of the main building told me that Peter Jamieson was probably in the snack bar. I walked around the end of the fifty-meter pool, which was enclosed on three sides by cabanas. On the fourth side the sea gleamed through a ten-foot wire fence like a blue fish alive in a net. A few dry bathers were lying around as if the yellow eye of the sun had hypnotized them.

When I saw my prospective client, in the sunny courtyard outside the snack bar, I recognized him instinctively. He looked like money about three generations removed from its source. Though he couldn't have been out of his early twenties, his face was puffy and apologetic, the face of a middle-aged boy. Under his carefully tailored Ivy League suit he wore a layer of fat like easily penetrable armor. He had the kind of soft brown eyes which are very often short-sighted.

When I approached his table he got up quickly, almost knocking over his double malted. "You must be Mr. Archer."

I acknowledged that I was.

"I'm glad to see you." He let me feel his large amorphous hand. "Let me get you something. The Monday hot lunch is New England boiled dinner."

"Thanks, I had lunch before I left Los Angeles. A cup of coffee, maybe."

He went and got it for me. In the creeping fig that covered one wall of the court, a pair of house finches were discussing family matters. The male, which had a splash of red on its front, took off on an errand. My eye followed him across the framed blue sky, then out of the frame.

"It's a beautiful day," I said to Peter Jamieson. "Also this coffee is good."

"Yes, they make good coffee." He sipped dolefully at his malted, then said abruptly: "Can you get her back for me?"

"I can't make your girl come back if she doesn't want to. I told you that on the phone."

"I know. I put it wrong. Even assuming she doesn't come back to me, we can still save her from ruining her life." He rested his arms on the table and leaned towards me, trying to imbue me with crusading fervor. "We can't let her marry this man. And I'm not talking out of jealousy. Even if I can't have her, I want to protect her."

"From the other man."

"I'm serious, Mr. Archer. This man is apparently wanted by the police. He claims to be a Frenchman, a French aristocrat no less, but nobody really knows who he is or where he comes from. He may not even be Caucasian."

"Where did you get that idea?"

"He's so dark. And Ginny is so fair. It nauseates me to see her with him."

"But it doesn't nauseate her."

"No. Of course she doesn't know what I know about him. He's a wanted man, probably some kind of a criminal."

"How did you find that out?"

"From a detective. He caught me—I mean, I was watching

the house last night, waiting to see if Ginny came home with him."

"Do you make a practice of watching Martel's house?"

"Just this last weekend. I didn't know if they were coming back from the weekend."

"She went away for the weekend with him?"

He nodded dismally. "Before she left she gave me back my engagement ring. She said she had no further use for it. Or me."

He fumbled in his watch pocket and produced the ring, as if it was evidence. In a way it was. The diamonds that encrusted the platinum band must have been worth several thousand dollars. Its return meant that Ginny was serious about Martel.

"What did the man say?"

Peter didn't seem to hear me. He was absorbed in the ring. He turned it slowly so that the diamonds caught and refracted the light from the sky. He winced, as if their cold fire had burned his fingers.

"What did the detective say about Martel?"

"He didn't actually say anything outright. He asked me what I was doing there sitting in my car, and I told him I was waiting for Martel. He wanted to know where Martel came from, how long he'd been in Montevista, where he got his money—"

"Martel has money?"

"He seems to have. He certainly flings it around. But as I told the man, I don't know where it came from or where he came from. Then he tried to ask me some questions about Ginny—he must have seen her with Martel. I refused to discuss her, and he let me go."

"Was he a local detective?"

"I don't know. He showed me some kind of badge, but I couldn't see it in the dark. He got in the car beside me all of a sudden and started talking. He was a very fast talker."

"Describe him. Young or old?"

"In between, around thirty-five or so. He had on some kind of a tweed jacket, and a light gray hat pulled down over his eyes. He was about my size, I think—I'm five-foot-ten—but not so heavy. I really can't describe his face, but I didn't like the sound of him. I thought at first he was some kind of crook trying to hold me up."

"Did he have a gun?"

"If he had, I didn't see it. When he finished asking me questions, he told me to be on my way. That was when I decided to buy a detective of my own."

There was a touch of arrogance in the phrase, reminding me that he was in the habit of buying things and people. But the boy was a little different from some other rich people I'd known. He heard himself, and apologized:

"I'm sorry. I didn't mean that the way it sounded."

"It's all right, as long as you realize that all you can do is rent me. What kind of a girl is Ginny?"

The question silenced him for a minute. The ring was still on the table, and his brown eyes focused on it until they crossed. I could hear the clatter of pans and conversation from the snack bar, interspersed with the sweeter notes of the finches.

"She's a beautiful girl," he said with a dreamy cross-eyed expression, "and really quite innocent. Undeveloped for her age, in spite of her brains. She can't possibly realize what she's getting into. I tried to show her the pitfalls, marrying a man with no real information about his background. But she wouldn't listen. She said she intended to marry him no matter what I said."

"Did she say why?"

"He reminds her of her father, that was one thing."

"Is Martel an older man?"

"I don't know how old he is. He must be thirty at least, maybe older than that."

"Is money one of the attractions?"

"It can't be. She could have married me, in fact we were due to be married next month. And I'm not poor." He added, with the caution of old money: "We're not the Rockefellers, but we're not poor."

"Good. I charge a hundred dollars a day and expenses."

"Isn't that quite a lot?"

"I don't think so. Actually it's just enough to get by on. I don't work all the time, and I have to maintain an office."

"I see."

"I'll take three hundred dollars advance from you." I knew from experience that very rich people were the hardest to collect from after the event.

He shied at the amount, but he didn't object. "I'll write you a check," he said, reaching into his inside breast pocket.

"First, tell me just what you expect in return for your money."

"I want you to find out who Martel is and where he came from and where his money came from. And why he came here to Montevista in the first place. Once I know something about him, I'm sure I can make Ginny see reason."

"And marry you?"

"And *not* marry him. That's all I hope to accomplish. I don't suppose she'll ever marry me."

But he carefully put the engagement ring away in the watch pocket of his trousers. Then he wrote me a check for three hundred dollars drawn on the Pacific Point National Bank.

I got out my little black book. "What's Ginny's full name?"

"Virginia Fablon. She lives with her mother, Marietta. Mrs. Roy Fablon. Their house is next door to ours on Laurel Drive." He gave me both addresses.

"Would Mrs. Fablon be willing to talk to me?"

"I don't know why not. She's Ginny mother, she's interested in her welfare."

"How does Mrs. Fablon feel about Martel?"

"I haven't discussed him with her. I think she's taken in, like everyone else."

"What about Ginny's father?"

"He isn't around any more."

"What does that mean, Peter?"

The question bothered him. He fidgeted and said without meeting my eyes: "Mr. Fablon died."

"Recently?"

"Six or seven years ago. Ginny still hasn't got over it. She was crazy about her father."

"You knew her then?"

"All my life. I've been in love with her since I was eleven."

"How long is that?"

"Thirteen years. I realize it's an unlucky number," he added, as if he was collecting signs of bad luck.

"How old is Ginny?"

"Twenty-four. We're the same age. But she looks younger and I look older."

I asked him some questions about the other man. Francis Martel had driven his own black Bentley into Montevista about two months ago, on a rainy day in March, and moved into the Bagshaw house, which he leased furnished from General Bagshaw's widow. Old Mrs. Bagshaw had apparently got him into the Tennis Club. Martel seldom appeared there and when he did appear he hid himself in his second-floor cabana. The hell of it was that Ginny had taken to hiding there with him, too.

"She even dropped out of school," Peter said, "so she could be with him all the time."

"What school was she going to?"

"Montevista State. She was majoring in French. Virginia has always been crazy about French language and literature. But she dropped it, just like that." He tried to snap his fingers: they made a sad squeaking sound.

"Maybe she wanted more of the real thing."

"You mean because he claims to be a Frenchman?"

"How do you know he isn't?"

"I know a phoney when I see one," Peter said.

"But Ginny doesn't?"

"He has her hypnotized. It isn't a normal healthy relationship. It's all mixed up with her father and the fact that he was part French. She flung herself into this whole French business the same year that he died, and now it's coming to a head."

"I don't quite follow."

"I know, I don't express myself too well. But I'm

worried sick about her. I've been eating so much I've given up weighing myself. I must weigh over two hundred." He palpated his stomach, cautiously.

"Roadwork would help."

He looked at me in a puzzled way. "I beg your pardon?"

"Get out on the beach and run."

"I couldn't, I'm much too depressed." He sucked up the last of his malted, making a noise like a death-rattle. "You'll get to work on this right away, won't you, Mr. Archer?"

II

MONTEVISTA IS a residential community adjacent to and symbiotic with the harbor city of Pacific Point. It has only one small shopping center, which calls itself the Village Square. Among its mock-rustic shops the Montevistans play at being simple villagers the way the courtiers of Versailles pretended to be peasants.

I cashed Peter's check at the Village branch of the Pacific Point National Bank. The transaction had to be okayed by the manager, a sharp-eyed young man in a conservative gray suit whose name was McMinn. He volunteered that he knew the Jamieson family very well; in fact the older Peter Jamieson was on the bank's board of directors.

McMinn seemed to take a dim but lofty pleasure in mentioning this, as if money conferred spiritual grace, which could be shared by talking about people who had it. I enhanced his pleasure by asking him how to get to the Bagshaw house.

"It's away back in the foothills. You'll need a map." He rummaged in the bottom drawer of his desk and produced a map, on which he made some markings. "I suppose you know that General Bagshaw is dead."

"I'm sorry to hear it."

"We were devastated here at the bank. He always did his local banking with us. Mrs. Bagshaw still does, of course. If it's Mrs. Bagshaw you want to see, she's moved into one of the cottages at the Tennis Club. The house is leased to a fellow by the name of Martel."

"You know him?"

"I've seen him. He does his banking at our main office downtown."

McMinn gave me a quick suspicious look. "Are you acquainted with Mr. Martel?"

"Not yet."

I drove back into the foothills. The slopes were still green from the rains. The white and purple flowers on the brush gave out a smell like the slow breath of sunlight.

When I stopped my car at the Bagshaw mailbox, I could see the ocean below, hung on the horizon like unevenly blued washing. I had climbed only a few hundred feet but could feel the change in temperature, as if I had risen much nearer to the noon sun.

The house sat alone in its own canyon head, several hundred feet above the road. It looked almost as tiny as a bird-house. A blacktop driveway hairpinned up to it from where I was parked.

A convertible with a snarl in the gearbox was toiling up behind me from the direction of town. It passed me, an old black Caddie, gray with dust, and stopped in front of my car.

The driver got out and came toward me. He was a middle-sized man wearing a hound's-tooth jacket and a good-looking pearl gray fedora, which he wore at a cocky slant. He moved with a kind of quick embarrassed belligerence. I had no doubt that he was Peter's "detective," but he didn't look like a detective to me. An air of desperate failure hung about him like a personal odor.

I got out my black book and made a note of the Cadillac's license number. It had California plates.

"What are you writing?"

"A poem."

He reached through the open window for my notebook. "Let's see it," he said in a loud unimpressive voice. His eyes were anxious.

"I never show work in progress."

I closed the book and put it back in my inside breast pocket. Then I started to turn up the window on his arm. He yanked his arm away and pressed his face against the glass, blurring it momentarily with his breath.

"I want to see what you wrote about me." He took a miniature camera out of his pocket and rapped on the window with it, foolishly and frantically. "What did you write about me?"

It was the kind of situation I liked to avoid, or terminate quickly. As the century wore on—I could feel it wearing on—angry pointless encounters like this one tended more and more to erupt in violence. I got out on the right-hand side and walked around the front of the car toward him.

As long as I was in my car, he had been yelling at a machine, a Cadillac yelling at a Ford. Now we were both men, and he was shorter and narrower than I was. He stopped yelling. His whole personality changed. He wiped his mouth with the back of his hand, as if to disclaim the evil spirit that had invaded him and made him yell at me. Self-doubt pulled at his face like a surgically hidden scar.

"I didn't do anything out of line, did I? You got no call to write down my license number."

"That remains to be seen," I said in a semi-official tone. "What are you doing here?"

"Sightseeing. I'm a tourist." His pale eyes glanced around at the sparsely inhabited hills as if he had never been out in the country before. "This is a public road, isn't it?"

"We've had a report of a man who was representing himself as a law officer last night."

His glance lighted briefly on my face, then jumped away. "It couldn't be me. I never been here before in my life."

"Let's see your driver's license."

"Listen," he said, "we can get together on this. I don't

have much with me but I got other resources.'' He drew a lonely ten from a worn calfskin billfold and tucked it in the breast pocket of my jacket. ''Here. Buy something for the kids. And call me Harry.''

He smiled with conscious charm. But the charm he was conscious of, if it had ever existed, had dried up and blown away. His front teeth glared at me like a pair of chisels. I removed the ten from my pocket, tore it in half, and gave him back the pieces.

His face fell apart. ''That's a ten-dollar bill. You must be a kook to tear up money like that.''

''You can put it together with Scotch tape. Now let me see your license before you commit another felony.''

''Felony?'' He said it the way a sick man pronounces the name of his disease.

''Bribery and impersonating an officer are felonies, Harry.''

He looked around at the daylight as if it had betrayed him, again. A little pale moon hung in a corner of the sky, faint as a thumbprint on a windowpane.

A fiercer light flashed down the canyon above us and almost dazzled me. It seemed to come from the head of a man who was standing with a girl on the terrace of the Bagshaw house. For a second I had the impression that he had great round eyes and that they had emitted the flashing light. Then I realized he was watching us through binoculars.

The man and the girl with him were as small as figures on a wedding cake. Their height and distance from me gave me a queer feeling, as if they were somehow unattainable, out of reach, out of time.

Harry Felony scrambled into his car and tried to start the engine. It turned over slowly like a dead man turning over in his grave. I had time to open the far door and get in on the gnawed leather seat.

''Where are we going, Harry?''

''Nowhere.'' He turned off the ignition and dropped his hands. ''Why don't you leave me alone?''

''Because you stopped a young man on this road last night and said you were a detective and asked him a lot of questions.''

He was silent while his malleable face went through new adjustments. "I am a detective, in a way."

"Where's your badge?"

He reached into his pocket for something, probably a dimestore badge, then changed his mind. "I don't have one," he admitted. "I'm just a kind of amateur dick, you might say, looking into something for a friend. She"—he swallowed the pronoun—"they didn't say anything about this kind of trouble."

"Maybe we can make a deal after all. Let me see your driver's license."

He got out his worn billfold and handed me a photostat.

HARRY HENDRICKS
10750 Vanowen, Apt. 12
Canoga Park, Calif.
SEX M COLOR HAIR brn COLOR EYES blu HEIGHT 5′9″
WEIGHT 165 MARRIED no DATE OF BIRTH Apr 12 1928
AGE 38

From the lower left-hand corner a photograph of Harry grinned at me. I took down the address and the number of the license in my notebook.

"What do you want all that stuff for?" he said in a worried voice.

"So I can keep track of you. What do you do for a living, Harry?"

"Sell cars."

"I don't believe you."

"*Used* cars, on commission," he said bitterly. "I used to be an insurance adjuster but the little fellows can't compete with the big boys anymore. I've done a lot of things in my time. Name it and I done it."

"Ever do time?"

He gave me a hurt look. "Of course not. You said something about a deal."

"I like to know who I'm dealing with."

"Hell, you can trust me. I've got connections."

"In the used car business?"

"You'd be surprised," he said.

"And what do your connections want you to do to Martel?"

"Nothing to him. I'm just supposed to case the joint and find out who he is if I can."

"Who is he?"

Harry spread his hands on top of the steering wheel. "I only been in town less than twenty-four hours, and the local yokels don't know a thing about him." He peered at me sideways. "If you're a cop like you say—"

"I didn't say. I'm a private detective. This area is strictly patrolled." The two facts were true, but unrelated.

Harry related them. "Then you should be able to get the information. There's money in it, we could split it two ways."

"How much?"

"A hundred I could promise you."

"I'll see what I can find out. Where are you staying in town?"

"The Breakwater Hotel. That's on the waterfront."

"And who is the woman who put you up to this?"

"Nobody said anything about a woman."

"You said 'she.' "

"I must have been thinking of my wife. She's got nothing to do with this."

"I can't believe that. Your driver's license says you aren't married."

"I am married, though." The point seemed important to him, as if I'd denied him membership in the human race. "That's a mistake on the license. I forgot I was married that day, I mean—"

His explanation was interrupted by the smooth mutter of a car coming down the winding driveway above us. It was Martel's black Bentley. The man behind the wheel wore rectangular dark glasses which covered the upper part of his face like a mask.

The girl beside him had on dark glasses, too. They almost made her look like any Hollywood blonde.

Harry got out his miniature camera, which was hardly bigger than a cigarette lighter. He ran across the road and planted himself in the entrance to the driveway, holding the camera concealed in his right hand.

The driver of the Bentley got out facing him. He was compact and muscular, dressed in English-looking sports clothes, tweeds and brogues, which didn't go with his own swarthy sleekness. He said in a controlled, faintly accented voice: "Can I help you in any way?"

"Yeah. Watch the birdies." Harry raised the camera and took his picture. "Thanks, Mr. Martel."

"You are not welcome." Martel's fleshy mouth became ugly. "Give me that camera please."

"Nuts. It's worth a hundred and fifty bucks."

"It's worth two hundred to me," Martel said, "with the film in it. I have a passion for privacy, you see." He pronounced the word 'passion' with a long nasal 'o,' like a Frenchman. But he was dark for a Frenchman.

I looked at the blonde girl in the car. Though I couldn't see her eyes, she seemed to be looking back across the road at me. The lower part of her face was immobile, as if she was afraid to react to the situation. It had the dead beauty of marble.

Harry was calculating in his head, almost audibly. "You can have it for three hundred."

"*Tres bien,* three hundred. That should include a—what is the word?—receipt, with your signature and address."

"Uh-uh." I had a quick impression of Harry's whole life: he didn't know how to stop when he was winning.

The girl leaned out of the open door of the Bentley. "Don't let him hold you up, Francis."

"I have no intention of that."

Martel moved suddenly on Harry and plucked the camera out of his hand. He stepped back, dropped it on the asphalt, and ground it under his heel.

Harry was appalled. "You can't do that!"

"But I have. It's a *fait accompli.*"

"I want my money."

"No money. *Pas d'argent. Rien du tout.*"

Martel got into the black car and slammed the door. Harry followed him yelling:

"You can't do that to me! That camera doesn't belong to me! You've got to pay for it."

"Pay him, Francis," the girl said.

"No. He had his chance." Martel made another sudden movement. His fist appeared at the window, with the small round eye of a gun peering over his index finger. "Listen to me my friend. I do not like to be bothered by *canaille*. If you come this way again or trespass on my privacy in any way, I will kill you." He clicked his tongue.

Harry backed away from him. He backed to the edge of the driveway, lost his footing, and almost fell. Unimpeded by false shame, he came up like a sprinter and ran for the Cadillac. He got in wheezing and sweating.

"He almost shot me. You're a witness to that."

"You're lucky he didn't."

"Arrest him. Go ahead. He can't get away with that. He's nothing but a cheap crook. That French act he puts on is as queer as a three-dollar bill."

"Can you prove it?"

"Not right now. But I'm gonna get that dago. He can't get away with smashing my camera. It's a valuable camera, and it wasn't mine, either." His voice was aggrieved: the world had let him down for the thousandth time. "You wouldn't just sit there if you were a security cop like you say."

The Bentley rolled out of the driveway into the road. One wheel passed over the broken camera and flattened it. Martel drove away sedately toward town.

"I've got to think of something," Harry said more or less to himself.

He took off his hat as if it limited the sweep and scope of his mind, and held it on his knees like a begging bowl. The printing on the silk lining said that it came from The Haberdashery in Las Vegas. The gold printing on the leather sweatband said L. Spillman. Harry stole his hat, I thought. Or else he was carrying a false driver's license.

He turned to me as if he had heard my unspoken accusation. With carefully rationed hostility, he said: "You don't have to feel you have to stick around. You've been no help."

I said I would see him later at the hotel. The prospect didn't seem to excite him much.

III

LAUREL DRIVE ran deep between hedges like an English lane. An immense green barricade of pittosporum hid Mrs. Fablon's garden from the road. On the far side of the garden a woman who at a distance looked like Ginny's sister was sitting with a man at an umbrella table, eating lunch.

The man had a long jaw which hardened when I appeared in the driveway. He stood up wiping his mouth with a napkin. He was tall and erect, and his face was handsome in a bony pugnacious way.

"I'll be shoving off," I heard him say under his breath.

"Don't hurry away, I'm not expecting anyone."

"Neither was I," he said shortly.

He flung his napkin down on top of his half-eaten salmon mayonnaise. Without speaking again, or looking at me, he walked to a Mercedes parked under an oak, got in, and drove out the other side of the semi-circular driveway. He acted like a man who was anxious for an excuse to get away.

Mrs. Fablon stayed at the table, looking quite composed. "Who on earth are you?"

"My name is Archer. I'm a private detective."

"Does Dr. Sylvester know you?"

"If he does, I don't know him. Why?"

"He rushed off in such a hurry when he saw you."

"I'm sorry about that."

"You needn't be. The luncheon was no great success. Don't tell me Audrey Sylvester is having him followed."

"Possibly. Not by me. Should she have?"

"Certainly not to my doorstep. George Sylvester has been my family doctor for ten years, and the relationship between us is about as highly seasoned as a tongue-depressor." She smiled at her own elaborate wit. "Do you follow people, Mr. Archer?"

I looked at her eyes to see if she was kidding. If she was, they didn't show it. They were pale blue, with a kind of pastel imperviousness. I was interested in her eyes, because I hadn't seen her daughter's.

They were innocent eyes, not youthful but innocent, as if they perceived only pre-selected facts. Such eyes went with the carefully dyed blonde hair whipped like cream on her pretty skull, with the impossibly good figure under her too youthful dress, and with the guileless way she let me look at her. But under her serenity she was tense.

"I must be wanted for something," she said with a half smile. "Am I wanted for something?"

I didn't reply. I was trying to think of a tactful way to broach the subject of Ginny and Martel.

"I keep asking you questions," she said, "and you don't say anything. Is that the way detectives operate?"

"I have my own ways of working."

"Mysterious ways your wonders to perform? I was beginning to suspect as much. Now tell me what wonders you're bent on performing."

"It has to do with your daughter Ginny."

"I see." But her eyes didn't change. "Sit down if you like." She indicated the metal chair across from her. "Is Virginia in some kind of trouble? She never has been."

"That's the question I'm trying to answer."

"Who put you up to it?" she said rather sharply. "It wasn't George Sylvester?"

"What makes you think it was?"

"The way he ran off just now." She was watching me carefully. "But it wasn't George, was it? He's quite infatuated with Virginia—all the men are—but he wouldn't expose himself—" She paused.

"Expose himself?"

She frowned with her meager out-of-place eyebrows.

"You're drawing me out and making me say things I don't want to." She caught her breath. "I know, it must have been Peter. Was it?"

"I can't go into that."

"If it was Peter, he's even more hopeless than I supposed. It was Peter, wasn't it? He's been threatening to hire detectives for some time. Peter is mad with jealousy, but I had no idea he'd go this far."

"This isn't very far. He asked me to look into the background of the man she's planning to marry. I suppose you know Francis Martel."

"I've met him, naturally. He's a fascinating person."

"No doubt. But something happened in the last hour which makes it seem worthwhile to investigate him. I saw it happen, in the road below his house. A man tried to take a picture of him. Martel scared him off with a gun. He threatened to kill him."

She nodded calmly. "I don't blame him at all."

"Does he make a habit of threatening to murder people?"

"It wouldn't be murder, it would be self-protection." She sounded as if she was quoting somebody else. "There are reasons for what you saw, I'm sure. He doesn't want his identity to be known."

"Do you know who he is?"

"I'm pledged to secrecy." She touched her red lips with a finger tipped with the same red.

"Who is he," I said, "the lost Dauphin of France?"

Without trying, I had succeeded in startling her. She stared at me with her mouth open. Then she remembered that it looked better closed, and closed it.

"I can't tell you who he is," she said after a while. "There could be very serious international repercussions if Francis were discovered here." Once again she seemed to be reciting. "I'm sure you mean well in what you're doing—I'm not so sure about Peter—but I'm going to ask you to cease and desist, Mr. Archer."

She wasn't kidding me now. Her voice was grave.

"Are you trying to tell me Martel is a political figure?"

"He was. He will be again, when the conditions are ripe. Right now he's an exile from his native country," she said dramatically.

"France?"

"He's a Frenchman, yes, he makes no secret of that."

"But his name isn't Francis Martel?"

"He has a right to use it, but it isn't his actual name."

"What is his name?"

"I don't know. But it's one of the great names of France."

"Do you have evidence to support all this?"

"Evidence?" She smiled at me as if she had superior knowledge piped in directly from the infinite. "You don't ask your friends for evidence."

"I do."

"Then you probably don't have many friends. I can see you have a suspicious nature. You and Peter Jamieson make a good pair."

"Have you known him long?"

I meant Martel, but she misunderstood my question, I think deliberately. "Peter has been underfoot in our house for twenty years." She gestured toward the rambling one-story house behind her. "I swear I've been wiping his nose for at least that long. When Peter's mother died, I sort of took him over for a while. He was just a little boy. But little boys grow up, and when he did he fell in love with Ginny, which he had no right to do. She doesn't care for Peter in that way, doesn't and didn't. He simply wore down her resistance because there was nobody else."

She sounded fond of Peter in spite of herself. I said so.

"Of course, you get fond of anyone if you see him every day for twenty years. Also I detest him, especially at the moment. My daughter has a brilliant chance. She's a beautiful girl"—she lifted her chin as if Ginny's beauty belonged to both of them, like a family heirloom—"and she deserves her chance. I don't want Peter, or you, fouling it up."

"I don't intend to foul anything up."

She sighed. "Can't I persuade you simply to drop it?"

"Not without some further checking."

"Will you promise me one thing then? Will you try to handle yourself without spoiling matters for Ginny? The thing she has with Francis Martel is very bright and shining, and very new. Don't tarnish it."

"I won't if it's real."

"It's real, believe me. Francis Martel worships the ground she walks on. And Virginia's quite mad about him."

I thought I could hear a self-fulfilling wish in what she said, and I threw her a curve:

"Is that why she went away for the weekend with him?"

Her blue eyes, impervious till now, winced away from mine. "You have no right to ask such questions. You're not a gentleman, are you?"

"But Martel is?"

"I've had about enough of you and your innuendos, Mr. Archer." She stood up. It was a dismissal.

IV

I WENT NEXT DOOR to the Jamieson house. It was a great Spanish mansion, grimy white, which had the barren atmosphere of an institution.

The woman who answered the door, after repeated ringing, wore a striped gray dress which might have been a uniform but wasn't quite. She was handsome and dark, with the slightly imperious look of the only woman in a big house.

"You didn't have to keep ringing. I heard you the first time."

"Why didn't you answer the first time?"

"I've got better things to do than to answer the door," she said tartly. "I was putting a goose in the oven." She looked down at her greasy hands, and wiped them on her apron.

"What did you want?"

"I'd like to see Peter Jamieson."

"Junior or senior?"

"Junior."

"He's probably still down at the Tennis Club. I'll ask his father."

"Maybe I could talk to Mr. Jamieson. My name is Archer."

"Maybe. I'll see."

I waited in the dim hallway on a high-backed Spanish chair which Torquemada had made with his own hands. The housekeeper returned eventually, and said with some surprise that Mr. Jamieson would see me. She led me past closed oak doors to an oak-paneled library whose deeply embrasured windows looked out on the mountains.

A man was sunk in an armchair by the windows, reading a book. His hair was gray and his face was very nearly the same colorless color. When he took off his reading glasses and peered up at me, I could see that his look was faint and faraway.

Half of a highball stood on a low table beside him, and close at hand on a larger table were a bottle of bourbon and a pitcher of water. I caught the housekeeper glaring at the highball and the bottle as if they represented everything she hated. She had violent black eyes, and she looked like a good hater.

"Mr. Archer," she said.

"Thank you, Vera. Hello, Mr. Archer. Sit down, here." He waved his hand at an armchair facing his. His hand was almost transparent against the light. "Would you like a drink before Vera goes?"

"Not so early in the day, thanks."

"I don't often drink so early myself." I noticed that the book in his hands was upside down. He hadn't wanted to be found just drinking. He closed the book and laid it on the table. "*The Book of the Dead,*" he said. "Egyptian stuff. You may go, Vera. I'm perfectly competent to entertain Mr. Archer myself."

"Yessir," she said in a dubious voice, and went out closing the door sharply.

"Vera is a powerful woman," Jamieson said. "She's the bane of my existence, but also the blessing. I don't know how this household would function without her. She's been like a mother to my poor boy. My wife has been dead for many years, you know." The flesh around his eyes seemed to crumple, as if the blow of her death was about to fall again. He took a long sip of his highball to ward it off. "Sure you won't have a drink?"

"Not while I'm working."

"I understand you're working for my son. He asked my advice about hiring you. I told him to go ahead."

"I'm glad you know about it. I won't have to beat around the bush. Do you think Francis Martel is an impostor?"

"We all are, to some extent, wouldn't you say? Take me, for instance. I'm a solitary drinker, as you can see. The more I drink, the more sorely I am tempted to conceal it. The only way I can preserve any integrity at all is by drinking openly, and facing the music with Peter and of course with Vera."

"You got that off your chest," I said smiling, "but it doesn't tell me much about Martel."

"I don't know. Anything I've learned about people I've had to learn by examining myself. It's a slow painful process," he said with an inward look. "If Martel is an impostor, he's taking some big chances."

"Have you met him?"

"No. But sequestered as my life is, I do get bulletins from the world of men. Martel has aroused a good deal of local interest."

"What's the consensus?"

"There are two camps. There always are. That's the

worst thing about democracy; there have to be two opinions about every issue.'' He talked like a man who needed a listener. ''Those who know Martel and like him, mainly the women, accept him at his face value as a distinguished young Frenchman of independent means. Others think he's more or less a fraud.''

''A con man?''

He raised his transparent hand. ''Hardly that. There's not much question that he's a cultivated European.''

''And no question that he has independent means?''

''I'm afraid not. I happen to know that his initial deposit at the local bank was in six figures.''

''I understand you're on the board of the bank.''

''So you've investigated me,'' he said with some resentment. ''You do me too much honor.''

''I got it accidentally from Mr. McMinn, when I cashed a check. Can you find out where Martel's money came from?''

''I suppose I can try.''

''It could be borrowed money,'' I said. ''I've known con men who used borrowed money, sometimes borrowed from gangsters, to get local status quickly.''

''For what possible purpose?''

''I know of one who bought a municipal bus system on terms, cannibalized it, then moved out and left it bankrupt. In the last few years they've even been buying banks.''

''Martel hasn't been buying anything that I know of.''

''Except Virginia Fablon.''

Jamieson wrinkled his forehead. He picked up his highball, saw that it was nearly gone, and got up to make himself another. He was tall, but thin and frail. He moved like an old man, but I suspected he wasn't much older than I was—fifty at most.

When he'd made his fresh drink and comforted himself with part of it and resettled himself in his leather armchair, I said:

''Does Ginny have money?''

''Hardly enough to interest a confidence man. She isn't a girl who needs money to interest any kind of a man—in fact she's probably turned down more advances than most young women dream of. Frankly, I was surprised when she accepted Peter, and not so very surprised when she broke the engagement. I tried to tell him that last night. It was safe enough when they were high school kids. But a beautiful young wife can be a curse to an ordinary man, especially if he loses her." The flesh around his eyes was crumpling again. "It's dangerous to get what you want, you know. It sets you up for tragedy. But my poor son can't see that. Young people can't learn from the misfortunes of their elders."

He was becoming faintly garrulous. Looking past him at the mountains, I had a feeling of unreality, as if the sunlit world had moved back out of reach.

"We were talking about the Fablons and their money."

Jamieson visibly pulled himself together. "Yes, of course. They can't have a great deal. The Fablons did have money at one time, but Roy gambled a lot of it away. The rumor was that that was one reason he committed suicide. Fortunately Marietta has her own small private income. They have enough to live comfortably, but as I said, certainly not enough to tempt a fortune-hunter. Let alone a fortune-hunter with a hundred thousand dollars in cash of his own."

"Is a hundred grand in the bank all that Martel would need to get into the club?"

"The Tennis Club? Certainly not. You have to be sponsored by at least one member and passed on by the membership committee."

"Who sponsored him?"

"Mrs. Bagshaw, I believe. It's a common enough practice, when members lease their houses in town here. It's nothing against the tenant."

"And nothing in his favor. Do you accept the idea that Martel is some kind of political refugee?"

"He may very well be. Frankly, I didn't discourage Peter from hiring you because I'd like to satisfy my curiosity. And I'd also like him to get this business of Ginny out of his system. It's hurting him more than you perhaps realize. I'm his father, and I can see it. I may not be much of a father to him, but I do know my son. And I know Ginny, too.''

''You don't want Ginny as a daughter-in-law?''

''On the contrary. She'd brighten any house, even this one. But I'm very much afraid she doesn't love my poor son. I'm afraid she agreed to marry him because she felt sorry for him.''

''Mrs. Fablon said very much the same thing.''

''So you've talked to Marietta?''

''A little.''

''She's a much more serious woman than she pretends. So is Ginny. Ginny has always been a very serious young woman, even when she was a child. She used to sit in my study here whole weekends at a time, reading the books.''

''*The Book of the Dead?*''

''I wouldn't be at all surprised.''

''You mentioned that her father committed suicide.''

''Yes.'' Jamieson stirred uneasily, and reached for his highball, as if the little death it provided was homeopathic medicine against the big one waiting. ''The decimation among my friends these last ten years has been horrendous. Not to mention my enemies.''

''Which was Roy Fablon, friend or enemy?''

''Roy was a friend, a very good friend at one time. Of course I disapproved of what he did to his wife and daughter. Ginny was only sixteen or seventeen at the time, and it hit her hard.''

''What did he do?''

''Walked into the ocean with his clothes on one night. They found his body about ten days later. The sharks had been at it, and he was scarcely identifiable.'' He passed his hand over his gray face, and took a long drink.

''Did you see the body?''

''Yes. They made me look at it. It was a very humiliating experience.''

''Humiliating?''

''It's dreadful to realize how mortal we are, and what time and tide will do to us. I can remember Roy Fablon when he was one of the best-looking men at Princeton, and one of the finest athletes."

"You knew him at Princeton?"

"Very well. He was my roommate. I was really the one who brought him out here to Montevista."

I rose to leave, but he held me at the door. "There's something I should ask you Mr. Archer. How well do you know Montevista? I don't mean typographically. Socially."

"Not well. It's rich for my blood."

"There's something I should tell you, then, as an old Montevista hand. Almost anything can happen here. Almost everything has. It's partly the champagne climate and partly, to be frank, the presence of inordinate amounts of money. Montevista's been an international watering resort for nearly a century. Deposed maharajahs rub shoulders with Nobel prize-winners and Chicago meat packers' daughters marry the sons of South American billionaires.

"In this context, Martel isn't so extraordinary. In fact when you compare him with some of our Montevista denizens, he's quite routine. You really should bear that in mind."

"I'll try to."

I thanked him and left.

V

THE HEAT OF THE DAY was waning with the sun. Approaching the Tennis Club, I could feel a cool wind from the ocean on my face. The flag on top of the main building was whipping.

The woman at the front desk informed me that Peter was probably in the showers. She'd seen him come up from the beach a few minutes ago. I could go in and wait for him by the pool.

The lifeguard's blue canvas chair was unoccupied, and I sat in it. The afternoon wind had driven away most of the sunbathers. On the far side of the pool, in a sheltered corner behind a plate-glass screen, four white-haired ladies were playing cards with the grim concentration of bridge players. The three fates plus one, I thought, wishing there was someone I could say it to.

A large boy in trunks who didn't look like a possible audience came out of the dressing rooms. He disposed his statuesque limbs on the tile deck near me. His smooth simple face was complicated by a certain wildness of the eye. His blond head had not been able to resist the bleach bottle. I noticed that his hair was wet and striated as if he had just been combing it.

"Is Peter Jamieson inside?"

"Yeah. He's getting dressed. You got my chair, but that's all right. I can sit here." He patted the tiles beside him. "You a guest of his?"

"I'm just meeting him here."

"He was running on the beach. I told him he better take it easy. You got to work up to it."

"But you have to start somewhere."

"I guess so. I don't run much, myself. It wears down the muscles." With quiet pride, he glanced down at his bronze pectorals. "I like to look like a typical California lifeguard."

"You do."

"Thank you," he said. "I put a lot of time and work into it. Like surfing. I took this job here on account of the surfing opportunities. I go to college, too," he added.

"What college?"

"Montevista State College. The one here."

"Who runs the French department?"

"I wouldn't know. I'm studying business ad and real estate. Very interesting." He reminded me of the dumb blondes who had cluttered up the California landscape when I was his age. Now a lot of them were boys. "You planning to study French, mister?"

"I just want to get the answers to a few questions."

"Maybe Mr. Martel could help you. He's a Frenchman."

"Is he here?"

"Yeah, I just been talking to him—he talks English, too, just like you and I."

He pointed toward the second-floor cabana nearest the sea. Through its open front I could see a man moving in the shadow of the awning. He was carrying a multicolored armful.

"He's moving his things out," the lifeguard said. "I offered to help him but he didn't want me messing with his personal stuff."

"Is he leaving?"

"He's giving up the cabana anyway. The beauty of it is, he said I could have the furniture he bought for it. It's outdoor furniture but it's practically brand new and it must of cost him a fortune. It'll look swell in my apartment. All I have is a sleeping bag right now. All my money goes to keep up the cars."

"Cars?"

"I have a wagon for surfing," he said. "And me and my buddy have a sports car for out-of-town trips. You can save a lot of time with a sports car."

The boy was driving me crazy. The trouble was that there were thousands of him, neo-primitives who didn't seem to belong in the modern world. But it came to me with a jolt that maybe they were better adapted to it than I was. They could live like happy savages on the beach while computers and computer-jockeys did most of the work and made all the decisions.

"Why is Mr. Martel moving out of the cabana? It looks like a good one."

"The best. You can see down the coast as far as the surfing reef." He flung out his muscled arm. "Mr. Martel used to sit there and watch us surfing. He told me once he did some surfing himself in his younger days."

"Did he say where?"

"On that same reef, I think."

"Has he been here before?"

"I wouldn't know about that. Not in my time, anyway."

"And you don't know why he's leaving the cabana?"

"He didn't like it here. He was always complaining about something, like the water in the pool being fresh—he thought it should be salt. And he didn't get along with some of the members." The boy fell silent. His mind rubbed two facts together and struck a brief spark. "Listen, don't tell Peter Jamieson that Mr. Martel is giving me his furniture. He wouldn't like it."

"Why not?"

"He's one of the ones that didn't get along with Mr. Martel. A couple of times they almost had a fight."

"Over Ginny Fablon?"

"I guess you know all about it, eh?"

"No, I don't."

"I better not tell you, anyway. Peter Jamieson will find out and I get called on the rug for talking about the members."

He was embarrassed by all the talking he had already done. One of the bridge players rescued him from my questions. She called across the pool:

"Stan, will you bring us four coffees? Black?"

He rose and trudged away.

I put on sunglasses and in their sudden twilight climbed the wooden stairs to the second-floor deck and walked along to the end. A rattan table in the middle of Martel's cabana was piled with things: bathing suits and robes and beach outfits for both men and women, flippers and masks, bottles of bourbon and brandy, a small electric heater, a bamboo cane. Martel came out of one of the two inner dressing rooms carrying a miniature television set which he put on the table.

"Moving out?"

He looked sharply. Now I was wearing sunglasses and he wasn't. His eyes were very dark and bright, focusing the dark-bright intensity of his face. He had a long nose, slightly curved, which appeared both self-assertive and inquisitive. He didn't appear to recognize me.

"What if I am?" he said in a guarded tone.

"I thought I might take it over."

"That won't be possible. I have it leased for the season."

"But you're not going to use it."

"I haven't made up my mind yet."

He was talking to himself more than to me. His dark gaze had moved past me down the coast. I turned and followed it. A blue wave crumbled white on the reef. Further out a dozen boys knelt on their boards like worshippers.

"Ever do any surfing?"

"No."

"Skin diving? I notice you have some equipment there."

"Yes, I've done some skin diving."

I was listening carefully to him. He still had an accent but it was much less pronounced than in the argument with Harry Hendricks, and he wasn't using any French words. Of course he was less excited now.

"Ever try skin diving in the Mediterranean? They say skin diving originated in the Mediterranean."

"It did and I have," he said. "I happen to be a native of France."

"What part?"

"Paris."

"That's interesting. I was in Paris during the war."

"A great many Americans were," he answered dryly. "Now if you will excuse me I have to dispose of these things."

"Can I help?"

"No. Thank you. Good day."

He bowed curtly. I wandered away along the deck, trying to analyze my impression of him. His tar-black hair and smooth solid face and the unblunted sharpness of his eyes placed his age at not more than thirty. He had the controlled force and reticence of an older man. I didn't know what to make of him.

I found my way into the labyrinth of the downstairs dressing rooms. School was out by now and a gang of small boys were snapping towels at each other's legs and emitting shouts of menace and horrible laughter. I told them to shut up. They waited until I was out of sight, and laughed more horribly than they had before.

Peter was tying his tie in front of a steam-fogged mirror.

He caught a glimpse of me in it and turned with a smile, the first I'd seen on his face. He was shiny and red.

"I didn't know you were here. I was running on the beach."

"Good," I said. "I've just been talking to Martel. He's moving the stuff out of his cabana. He may be planning to skip."

"With Ginny?"

"I didn't think I'd better ask him that. Under ordinary circumstances I wouldn't have approached him at all. It's not a good way to operate. But we may be running short of time."

I'd wiped out Peter's smile and started him biting his mouth. "I was hoping you could do something to stop him."

"I haven't quit. The trouble is I don't know what questions to ask. I've never been to France, and I don't remember much of my high school French."

"Neither do I. I took a freshman course from Professor Tappinger, but he flunked me."

"Was this at the local college?"

"Yes." He felt called upon to explain that he had been supposed to go to Princeton, and failed to make the grade. "But I did graduate from Montevista State last year."

"And Ginny was supposed to graduate this year?"

"Yes. She took a couple of years out. She was a receptionist at Dr. Sylvester's clinic, but she got sick of that and went back to school last year."

"Was your man Tappinger one of her professors?"

"He taught most of her French courses."

"Is Tappinger good at his subject?"

"Ginny thought so, and she was one of his best students."

"Then he should be willing to help us out."

I told Peter to make an appointment with the professor, for this afternoon if possible, and said I would meet him in the parking lot. I didn't want Martel to see us leaving together.

VI

"MR. JAMIESON just left," the woman at the front desk said. "I don't know how you missed him."

She had a gently modulated voice, and she sounded real concerned. I took a closer look at her. She was a subdued young woman dressed in a brown tweed suit. Her dark hair framed an oval, piquant face. She was too heavily made up, but that was occupational.

"I talked to Mr. Jamieson inside, but don't mention it to anyone."

"Why should I mention it to anyone?" she said.

"Somebody might ask you."

"I never discuss the goings and comings of the members and their guests. Besides, I don't remember your name."

"Archer, Lew Archer."

"I'm Ella Strome." The nameplate on the desk in front of her said: Mrs. Strome, Club Secretary. She saw me looking at it and added in a neutral tone: "I'm not married at present."

"Neither am I. What time do you get off for dinner?"

"Tonight I don't. We're having a dinner-dance. But thank you."

"Don't mention it."

In the parking lot by the tennis courts, Peter was waiting for me in his Corvette. The place was surrounded by massed green clouds of eucalyptus trees, and their faintly medicinal scent flavored the air. Only one of the half-dozen courts was in use: a pro in a "Tennis Club" sweatshirt was showing a very small girl how to serve, while her mother watched from the sidelines.

"Professor Tappinger isn't in his office and he isn't at

home,'' Peter said. ''His wife said he should be on his way home.''

''I can use a little more time here. I understand Mrs. Bagshaw lives at the club.''

''She's in one of the cottages.'' He gestured toward the trees at the back of the lot.

''Have you asked her any questions about Martel?''

''No.''

''But you know Mrs. Bagshaw?''

''Not that well. I know everyone in Montevista,'' he added without enthusiasm. ''And they know me, I guess.''

I went through the eucalyptus grove and through a gate in a picket fence which enclosed an expanse of lawn next to the pool enclosure. A dozen or so gray-painted brick cottages were dispersed around the lawn, shielded from their neighbors by patio walls and flowering shrubs. A small Mexican in a khaki coverall was manipulating a hose among the shrubbery.

''*Buenos días.*''

''It is a fine day,'' he said with a white flash of teeth, and turned the stream from his hose toward the sky, like a fountain. ''You looking for somebody?''

''Mrs. Bagshaw.''

''That's her cottage there.'' Its roof was half-hidden by a purple avalanche of bougainvillea. ''She just came back a couple of minutes ago.''

Mrs. Bagshaw turned out to be one of the poolside bridge-players, the one who had ordered the coffee. She was an alert-looking seventy or so.

''Didn't I see you talking to Stanley just now?'' she asked me at the door.

''I was, yes.''

''And then to Mr. Martel?''

''Yes.''

''And now you come to me. It's an interesting progression.'' She shook her white curls. ''I don't know whether to be flattered or discomfited.''

''Don't be either, Mrs. Bagshaw. My name is Archer, and I'm a detective, as you may have guessed.''

She let me into a sitting room which contained too much

furniture. The Oriental rug on the floor was so good I hated to step on it. She noticed my noticing it.

"It doesn't go with this place at all. But I couldn't bear to leave it behind." Without changing her tone, she said: "Sit down. I suppose you're engaged in the current village sport of prying into Francis Martel's affairs."

"It's my profession, not my sport."

"Who brought you here?" she said brusquely.

"A local family."

"Marietta Fablon?"

"She's interested in the outcome of my researches, yes."

"Researches is a glossy word for what you do, Mr. Archer. You're driving Mr. Martel out of town. Is that your purpose?"

"No."

"I wonder about that. He's leaving, you know. He told me so not fifteen minutes ago."

"Is Ginny Fablon going with him?"

She lowered her eyes to her lap. "Miss Fablon was not discussed. She is in any case a young woman of twenty-four—at her age I had been married for five years—and she's perfectly capable of looking after herself and making her own choices." Her voice, which had faltered for a moment, regained its strength. "More capable than most young women, in my opinion."

"So you think she's going with him."

"I don't know. But this is a free country, I believe."

"It is for people who know what and who they're dealing with. You can't make valid choices without facts."

She shook her curls. Her face remained unshaken, like cement. "I don't wish to be lectured at. I brought Francis Martel into Montevista—ah—circles, and I feel perfectly sanguine about doing so. I like him. It's true I can't provide you with a copy of his genealogical tree. But I'm sure it's a good one. He's one of the most distinguished young Frenchmen of my acquaintance."

"He is a Frenchman, then?"

"Is there any doubt of that?"

"There's always doubt, until the facts are established."

"And you are the great arbiter of the facts, are you?"

"In my own investigations I naturally tend to be."

It was a fairly sharp interchange, and it made her angry. She resolved her anger by laughing out loud at me. "You talk up, don't you?"

"I might as well. I'm not getting anywhere anyway."

"That's because there's nowhere to get. Merely because Mr. Martel doesn't look like other people, they assume there's some dark secret in his past. The trouble with my neighbors is a simple one. They haven't enough to do, and they live like the Scilly islanders by taking in each other's dirty linen. If there isn't enough dirty linen to go around, they manufacture it."

She must be uncertain, I thought, or she wouldn't be talking so much and so well. Martel was in some degree her responsibility. She said into the silence between us:

"Have you found out anything against him?"

"Not really. Not yet."

"You imply that you expect to."

"I don't know. How did you become acquainted with him, through a real-estate broker?"

"Oh no, we have friends in common."

"Here in Montevista?"

"In Washington," she said, "more precisely, in Georgetown. General Bagshaw and I once lived in Georgetown."

"And you met Martel there?"

"I didn't say that. He knew some old neighbors of ours—" She hesitated, looking at me doubtfully. "I don't believe I ought to give you their name."

"It would help if you did."

"No. They're very fine and gentle people, and I don't want them bothered with this sort of thing."

"Martel used them as a reference. They might not approve of that. They may not even know him."

"I'm sure they do."

"Did they give him a letter of introduction?"

"No."

"Then all you have is his word?"

"It seems—it seemed to be enough. He talked very freely

and fully about them." But the doubt with which she regarded me was spreading and deepening, undercutting her confidence in her own judgment. "Do you seriously believe he's some sort of impostor?"

"My mind is open on the subject. I'm trying to open yours."

"And pry a name out of me," she said rather grimly.

"I don't need the name if you'll help."

"How can I help?"

"Call your Georgetown friends and ask them what they know about Martel."

She lifted her head. "I may do that."

"Please do. They're the only real lead I have."

"I will. Tonight."

"May I check with you later then?"

"I suppose you may."

"I'm sorry if I've upset you."

"You haven't. It's the moral question, really. Did I do right or wrong? Of course if we stopped to consider the possible consequences of everything we do, we'd end up doing nothing."

"How soon is he leaving?"

"Immediately, I think. Today or tomorrow."

"Did he say why?"

"No. He's very reticent. But I know why. Everyone's suspicious of him. He's made no friends here."

"Except Ginny."

"He didn't mention her."

"Or say where he was going?"

"No."

VII

PETER MET ME at the gate in the picket fence. Professor Tappinger was home now, and would see us.

He lived in the adjoining harbor city, in a rather rundown tract whose one obvious advantage was a view of the ocean. The sun, heavy and red, was almost down on the horizon now. Its image floated like spilled fire on the water.

The Tappinger house was a green stucco cottage which except for its color duplicated every third house in the block. The cement walk which led up to the front door was an obstacle course of roller skates, a bicycle, a tricycle. A girl of six or seven answered the door. She had a dutch bob and enormous watching eyes.

"Daddy says that you can join him in the study."

She led us through the trampled-looking living room into the kitchen. A woman was bowed over the sink in a passive-aggressive attitude, peeling potatoes. A boy of about three was butting her in the legs and chortling. She paid no attention to him and very little to us. She was a good-looking woman no more than thirty, with a youthful pony-tail, and blue eyes which passed over me coolly.

"He's in the study," she said, and gestured with one elbow toward a door.

It let us into a converted garage lined with bookshelves. A fluorescent fixture hung on a chain over a work table cluttered with open books and papers. The professor was seated there with his back to us. He didn't turn around when Peter spoke to him. The implication seemed to be that we were interrupting important brainwork.

"Professor Tappinger?" Peter said again.

"I hear you." His voice was impatient. "Excuse me for another minute, please. I'm trying to finish a sentence."

He scratched at his head with the blunt end of his pen, and jotted something down. His coppery brown hair had a frost of gray at the edges. I saw when he eventually got up that he was a short man, and at least ten years older than his handsome wife. He had probably been handsome, too, with his sensitive mouth and clean features. But he looked as if he had had a recent illness, and the eyes behind his reading glasses were haunted by the memory of it. His handshake was cold.

"How are you, Mr. Archer? How are you, Peter? Forgive me for keeping you waiting. I snatch these precious moments of concentration from the Bergsonian flux. With a twelve-hour teaching load and all the preparation it entails, it isn't easy to get anything written. I envy Flaubert the luxury he had of spending whole days in search of the right word, *le mot juste*—"

Tappinger seemed to have the professional habit of non-stop talking. I interrupted him: "What are you working on?"

"A book, if I can ever get the time to do it. My subject is the French influence on modern American literature—at the moment I'm studying the vexed question of Stephen Crane. But that wouldn't interest you. Peter tells me you're a detective."

"Yes. I'm trying to get some information about a man named Francis Martel. Have you run into him?"

"I doubt it, but his name is certainly interesting. It's one of the ancient names of France."

"Martel is supposed to be a Frenchman. His story is that he's a political refugee."

"How old is he?"

"About thirty." I described him: "He's a man of medium height, trim and fast on his feet. Black hair, black eyes, dark complexion. He has a French accent which varies from strong to weak."

"And you think he's putting it on?"

"I don't know. If he's a phoney, he's fooled quite a few people. I'm trying to find out who and what he really is."

"Reality is an illusive thing," Tappinger said sententiously.

"What do you want me to do—listen to his French and pronounce on its authenticity?"

He was only half serious, but I answered him seriously: "That might be a good idea, if we could work it out. But Martel is on the point of leaving town. I thought if you could provide me with a few questions that only an educated Frenchman could answer—"

"You wish me to prepare a test, is that it?"

"With the answers."

"I suppose I can do that. When do you need it? Tomorrow?"

"Right now."

"That's simply impossible."

"But he may be leaving any minute."

"I can't help that!" Tappinger's voice had risen womanishly. "I have forty papers to read tonight—those bureaucrats at the college don't even provide me with a student reader. I have no time for my own children—"

I said: "Okay, we'll skip it. It wasn't a very good idea in the first place."

"But we have to do something," Peter said. "I'll be glad to pay you for your time, professor."

"I don't want your money. All I want is the free use of my own days." Tappinger was practically wailing.

His wife opened the kitchen door and looked out. Her face was set in a look of concern which somehow gave the impression that it had been blunted by use.

"What's the trouble, Daddy?"

"Nothing, and don't call me Daddy. I'm not that much older than you are."

She lifted and dropped one shoulder in a gesture of physical contempt and looked at me. "Is something the matter out here?"

"We seem to be getting on your husband's nerves. This wasn't a good time to come."

Tappinger said to his wife in a quieter tone: "It's nothing that need concern you, Bess. I'm supposed to prepare some questions to test a certain man's knowledge of French."

"Is that all?"

"That's all."

She closed the kitchen door. Tappinger turned to us: "Forgive the elevation of the voice. I've got a headache." He pressed his hand to his pale rounded forehead. "I suppose I can do this work for you now—I've expended twice the energy just talking about it—but I don't understand the hurry."

Peter said: "Martel is taking Ginny with him. We have to stop him."

"Ginny?" Tappinger looked puzzled.

"I thought you told him about her," I said to Peter.

"I tried to, on the phone, but he wouldn't listen." He turned back to Tappinger. "You remember Virginia Fablon, professor?"

"Naturally I do. Is she involved in this?"

"Very much so. She says she intends to marry Martel."

"And you're in love with her yourself, is that it?"

Peter blushed. "Yes, but I'm not doing this merely for selfish reasons. Ginny doesn't realize the mess she's getting into."

"Have you talked to her about it?"

"I've tried to. But she's infatuated with Martel. He was the reason she dropped out of school last month."

"Really? I thought she was ill. That was the word that went around the college."

"There's nothing the matter with her," Peter said. "Except him."

"What is her opinion of his Frenchness?"

"She's completely taken in," Peter said.

"Then he probably is French. Miss Fablon has a fair grasp of the language."

"He could be both a Frenchman and a phoney," I said. "We're really trying to find out if he's the cultivated aristocrat he pretends to be."

For the first time Tappinger really looked interested. "That should be possible. Let me try." He sat down at his cluttered table and picked up his pen. "Just give me ten minutes, gentlemen."

We retreated to the living room. Mrs. Tappinger followed us from the kitchen, trailed by the three-year-old.

"Is Daddy all right?" she asked me in a little-girl voice so thin and sweet it sounded like self-parody.

"I think so."

"He hasn't been well, ever since last year. They turned him down for his full professorship. It was a terrible disappointment to him. He tends to take it out on—well, anybody available. Especially me." She made her shoulder gesture. This time her contempt seemed to be for herself.

"Please," Peter said in embarrassment. "Professor Tappinger has already apologized."

"That's good. He usually doesn't. Especially when his own family is involved."

She meant herself. In fact it was herself she wanted to talk about, and it was me she wanted to talk about herself to. Her body leaning in the doorway, the blue side glances of her eyes, the drooping movements of her mouth more than the words it uttered, said that she was a sleeping beauty imprisoned in a tract house with a temperamental professor who had failed to be promoted.

The three-year-old butted at her, pressing her cotton dress tight between her round thighs.

"You're a pretty girl," I said, with Peter standing there as a chaperon.

"I used to be prettier—twelve years ago when I married him." She gestured with her hip. Then she picked up the child and carried him into the kitchen like a penitential burden.

A married woman with young children wasn't exactly my dish, but she interested me. I looked around her living room. It was shabby, with a worn rug and beat-up maple furniture. The walls were virtually papered with Post-Impressionist reproductions, visions of an ideally brilliant world.

The sunset at the window competed in brilliance with the Van Goghs and the Gauguins. The sun burned like a fire ship on the water, sinking slowly till only a red smoke was left trailing up the sky. A fishing boat was headed into the harbor, black and small against the enormous west. Above its glittering wake a few gulls whirled like sparks which had gone out.

"I'm worried about Ginny," Peter said at my shoulder.

I was worried, too, though I didn't say so. The sudden moment when Martel pulled a gun on Harry Hendricks, which hadn't seemed quite real at the time, was real in my memory now. Beside it the idea of testing Martel in French seemed faintly preposterous.

A redheaded boy about eleven came in the front door. He tramped importantly into the kitchen and announced to his mother that he was going next door to watch some television.

"No you're not." Her sharp maternal tone was quite different from the one she had used on her husband and me. "You're staying right here. It's nearly dinnertime."

"I'm starved," Peter said to me.

The boy asked his mother why they didn't have a television set.

"Two reasons. We've been into them before. One, your father doesn't approve of television. Two, we can't afford it."

"You're always buying books and records," the boy said. "Television is better than books and records."

"Is it?"

"Much better. When I have my own house I'm going to have color television in every room. And you can come and watch it," he concluded grandly.

"Maybe I will at that."

The door to the garage study opened, ending the interchange. Professor Tappinger came into the living room waving a sheet of paper in each hand.

"The questions and the answers," he said. "I've devised five questions which a well-educated Frenchman should be able to answer. I don't think anyone else could, except possibly a graduate student of French. The answers are simple enough so that you can check them without having to know too much French."

"That's good. Let's hear them, Professor."

He read aloud from his sheets: "One. Who wrote the original *Les Liaisons dangereuses* and who made the modernized film version? Choderlos de Laclos wrote the original, and Roger Vadim made the movie.

"Two. Complete the phrase: '*Hypocrite lecteur* . . .'

Answer: *Hypocrite lecteur, mon semblable, mon frère*—from the opening poem of Baudelaire's *Fleurs du mal*.

"Three. Name a great French painter who believed Dreyfus was guilty. Answer: Degas.

"Four. What gland did Descartes designate as the residence of the human soul? Answer: the pineal gland.

"Five. Who was mainly responsible for getting Jean Genet released from prison? Answer: Jean-Paul Sartre. Is this the sort of thing you had in mind?"

"Yes, but the emphasis seems to be a little one-sided. Shouldn't there be something about politics or history?"

"I disagree. If this man is an impostor passing himself off as a political refugee, the first thing he'd bone up on would be history and politics. My questions are subtler, and they cover a range that it would take years to bone up on." His eye brightened. "I wish I could put them to him myself."

"I wish you could, too. But it might be dangerous."

"Really?"

"Martel pulled a gun on another man today. I think you'd better let me go up against him."

"And me," Peter said. "I insist on going along."

Tappinger followed us out to our cars, as if to make up for his earlier impatience. I thought of offering him money for his work, five or ten dollars, but decided not to risk it. It might only remind him that he needed money and make him angry again.

VIII

I FOLLOWED PETER'S CORVETTE inland into the foothills. Their masses had been half-absorbed by the blue darkness of the mountains. A few lights, bright as evening stars, were scattered up their slopes. One of them shone from Martel's house.

Peter stopped just short of the mailbox. The name stenciled on it stood out black in his headlights: Major General Hiram Bagshaw, U.S.A. (ret.) He cut the lights and started to get out.

The quiet of the evening shivered like a crystal. A high thin quavering cry came from the direction of the house. It might have been a peacock, or a girl screaming.

Peter ran toward me. "It's Ginny! Did you hear her?"

"I heard something."

I tried to persuade him to wait in his car. But he insisted on riding up to the house with me.

It was a massive stone-and-glass building set on a pad which had been excavated above the floor of the canyon. A floodlight above the door illuminated the flagstone courtyard where the Bentley was parked. The door itself was standing open.

Peter started in. I held him back. "Take it easy. You'll get yourself shot."

"She's my girl," he said, in the teeth of all the evidence so far.

The girl appeared in the doorway. She had on a gray suit, the kind women use for traveling. Her movements seemed shaky and her eyes a little dull, as if she had already traveled too far and too fast.

Perhaps it was the brilliant light shining down on her face, but its skin appeared grayish and grainy. She had the sort of beauty—shape of head, slant of cheekbone and chin, curve of mouth—that made these other things irrelevant.

She held herself on the concrete stoop with a kind of forlorn elegance. Peter went to her and tried to put his arm around her. She disengaged herself.

"I told you not to come here."

"That was you screaming, wasn't it? Did he hurt you?"

"Don't be silly. I saw a rat." She turned her lusterless eyes on me. "Who are you?"

"My name is Archer. Is Mr. Martel home?"

"Not to you, I'm afraid."

"Tell him I'm here, anyway. All I want is a chance to talk to him."

She said to Peter: "Please go. Take your friend with you. You have no right to interfere with us." She managed to produce a little spurt of anger: "Go away now or I'll never speak to you again."

His large face contorted itself in the light, as if it could transform its homeliness by sheer expression. "I wouldn't care, Ginny, as long as you were safe."

"I'm perfectly safe with my husband," she said, and waited demurely for his surprise.

"You married him?"

"We were married on Saturday and I've never been happier in my life," she said without any visible sign of happiness.

"You can get it annulled."

"You don't seem to understand, I love my husband." Her voice was soft but there was a sting in the words which made him wince. "Francis is everything I've ever dreamed of in a man. You can't change that, and please stop trying."

"Thank you, *ma chérie*."

It was Martel, with his full accent on. No doubt he had been listening for an entrance cue. He appeared in the hallway behind Ginny and took hold of her upper arm. His hand against her light gray sleeve looked almost as dark as a mourning band.

Peter began to bite his mouth. I moved closer to him. Whether he was a French aristocrat or a cheap crook or a muddy mixture of the two, Ginny's husband would be a dangerous man to hit.

"Congratulations on your marriage," I said without much irony.

He bowed, touching his chest. "*Merci beaucoup*."

"Where were you married?"

"In the chambers of a judge, by the judge himself. That makes it legal, I believe."

"I meant what place."

"The place doesn't matter. Life has its private occasions, you know, and I confess to a passion for privacy. Which my dear wife shares.'' He smiled down into her face. His smile had changed when he looked up at me. It was wide and mocking. "Didn't we meet at the swimming pool today?"

"We did."

"This man was here before," Ginny said, "when the fellow tried to take your picture. I saw him in the fellow's car."

Martel stepped around his wife and came toward me. I wondered if his little gun was going to come into play. I also wondered what dark liquid had left a partial heelprint on the concrete stoop. More of it glistened on the heel of Martel's right shoe.

"Just who are you, *m'sieur*? And what gives you the right to ask questions?"

I told him my name. "I'm a detective, and I'm hired to ask them."

"Hired by this one here?" He gave Peter a black look of contempt.

"That's right," Peter said. "And we're going to keep after you until we know what you want."

"But I have what I want." He turned to Ginny with his arm stretched out. It was just a little like a scene from opera, more light than grand. Next minute the merry villagers would troop in for the nuptial dance.

I said to fend them off: "One question that interests me at the moment—is that blood on your heel?"

He looked down at his feet, then quickly back to me. "I expect it is blood."

Ginny's curled fingers had gone to her mouth, both hands, as if another peacock cry was surging up in her throat. Martel said quietly and smoothly:

"My wife was alarmed by a rat, as she told you." He had been listening. "I killed it."

"With your heel?"

"Yes." He stamped on the asphalt. "I'm a fencer, very fast on my feet."

"I bet you are. May I see the corpse?"

"It would be hard to find, perhaps impossible. I threw it into the undergrowth for the bobcats. We have wild animals up here in the hills, don't we, *ma chérie*?"

Ginny dropped her hands and said yes. She was looking at Martel with a combination of respect and fear. Perhaps it was a form of love, I thought, but not one of the usual forms. His voice filled the vacuum again:

"My wife and I are very fond of the wild animals."

"But not the rats."

"No. Not the rats." He offered me his wide cold grin. Above it his eyes and forceful nose seemed to be probing at me. "Can I persuade you to leave now, Mr. Archer? I've been quite patient with you and your questions. And please take this one with you." He jerked his head toward Peter as if the fat young man didn't quite belong to the human race.

Peter said: "Ask him the five questions, why don't you?"

Martel raised his eyebrows. "Five questions? About myself?"

"Not directly." Now that the time had come to ask the questions, they seemed childish, even ludicrous. The light-operatic note on which the scene had balanced was giving way to *opéra bouffe*. The courtyard under the light, surrounded by the amphitheater of the canyon, was like a stage where nothing real could happen.

I said reluctantly: "The questions are about French culture. I've been told that an educated Frenchman ought to be able to answer them."

"And you doubt that I am an educated Frenchman?"

"You have a chance to prove it once and for all. Will you take a stab at the questions?"

He shrugged. "*Pourquoi pas?* Why not?"

I got out the two sheets of paper. "One. Who wrote the original *Les Liaisons dangereuses* and who made the modernized film version?"

"*Les Liaisons dangereuses*," he said slowly, correcting my pronunciation. "Choderlos de Laclos wrote the novel. Roger Vadim made the cinema version. I believe that Vadim collaborated with Roger Vailland on the screen play. Is that enough, or do you want me to outline the plot for you? It's quite complex, having to do with diabolical sexual intrigue and the corruption of innocence." His voice was sardonic.

"We won't bother with that just now. Question two. Complete the phrase: '*Hypocrite lecteur*—' "

" '*Hypocrite lecteur, mon semblable, mon frère*.' Hypocritical reader, my brother, my—*comment-à-dire?*—duplicate?" He appealed to Ginny.

"Mirror image," she said with a small half-smile. "It's from the front of *Les Fleurs du mal*."

"I can recite many of those poems if you like," Martel said.

"That won't be necessary. Three. Name the great French painter who believed Dr.eyfus was guilty."

"Degas was the most prominent."

"Four. What gland did Descartes designate as the residence of the human soul?"

"The pineal gland." Martel smiled. "That's a rather obscure point, but it happens I read Descartes nearly every day of my life."

"Five. Who was mainly responsible for getting Jean Genet released from prison?"

"Jean-Paul Sartre, I suppose you mean. Cocteau and others also had a hand in the deliverance. Is that all?"

"That's all. You scored a hundred."

"Will you reward me now by disappearing?"

"Answer one more question, since you're so good at answering them. Who are you and what are you doing here?"

He stiffened. "I'm under no obligation to tell you."

"I thought you might want to lay the rumors to rest."

"Rumors don't bother me."

"But you're not the only person involved, now that you've married a local girl."

He saw my point. "Very well. I will tell you why I am here, in return for a *quid pro quo*. Tell me who is the man who tried to take my picture."

"His name is Harry Hendricks. He's a used-car salesman from the San Fernando Valley."

Martel's eyes were puzzled. "I never heard of him. Why did he try to photograph me?"

"Apparently someone paid him. He didn't say who."

"I can guess," Martel said darkly. "He was undoubtedly paid by the agents of *le grand Charles*."

"Who?"

"President de Gaulle, my enemy. He drove me out of my *patrie*—my native land. But my exile is not enough to satisfy him. He wants my life."

His voice was low and thrilling. Ginny shuddered. Even Peter looked impressed.

I said: "What has de Gaulle got against you?"

"I am a threat to his power."

"Are you one of the *Algérie-Française* gang?"

"We are not a gang," he retorted hotly. "We are a—how shall I say it?—a band of patriots. It is *le grand Charles* who is the enemy of his country. But I have said enough. Too much. If his agents have followed me here, as I believe, I must move on again."

He shrugged fatalistically, and looked around at the dark slopes and up at the star-pierced sky. It was a farewell look, consciously dramatic, as if the stars were part of his audience.

Ginny moved into the circle of his arm. "I'm going with you."

"Of course. I knew I would not be permitted to stay in Montevista. It is too beautiful. But I shall be taking a part of its beauty with me."

He kissed her hair. It hung sleek on her skull like a pale silk headcloth. She leaned against him. His hands went to her waist. Peter groaned and turned away toward the car.

"If you will excuse us now," Martel said to me, "we have plans to make. I've answered all your questions, have I not?"

"Just to nail it down, you could show me your passport."

He spread out his hands one either side of Ginny. "I wish I could, but I can't. I left France unofficially, shall we say?"

"How did you get your money out?"

"I had to leave much of it behind. But my family has holdings in other parts of the world."

"Is Martel your family name?"

He raised his hands, palms outward, like a man being held up. "My wife and I have been very patient with you. You don't want me to become impatient. Goodnight." He spoke quietly, with all his force poised behind the words.

They went into the house, closing the heavy front door. On my way to my car I glanced into the front of the Bentley. There was no registration card visible. The things which Martel had taken from his cabana were piled helter-skelter on the back seat. This suggested that he was planning to leave very soon.

There was nothing I could do about it. I got in beside Peter, and turned down the driveway. He rode with his head down, saying nothing. When I stopped at the mailbox, he turned to me in a sort of violent lunge:

"Do you believe him?"

"I don't know. Do you?"

"Ginny does," he said thoughtfully. "She knows him better than we do. He's very convincing."

"Too convincing. He has an answer for everything."

"Does that mean he's telling the truth?"

"He tells too much of it. A man in his position, wanted by the French government for plotting against de Gaulle, wouldn't spill his secrets to us. He wouldn't even tell his wife if he was smart. And Martel is smart."

"I can see that, the way he answered the professor's questions. What's the explanation, if he's lying? Who is he trying to fool?"

"Ginny, maybe. She married him."

Peter sighed. "I'm starved. I haven't really eaten since breakfast."

He climbed out of my car and started across the road to his Corvette. His foot kicked something which made a muted metallic noise. I peered out into the dark. It was the camera that Martel had smashed. I got out and picked it up and put it in my jacket pocket.

"What are you doing?" Peter said.

"Nothing. Poking around."

"I was just thinking, they're serving dinner at the club tonight. If you'll have dinner with me, we can discuss what to do."

I was getting a little tired of his mournful company. But I was hungry, too. "I'll meet you there."

IX

I WAS DELAYED on the way. A quarter of a mile down the road from Martel's driveway, a car was parked in the darkness under a live oak. Its lines resembled Harry Hendricks's Cadillac, and when I got out for a closer look with my flashlight, I saw that it was.

There was nobody in the decayed Cadillac, no registration on the steering post, and nothing in the dash compartment but a Los Angeles freeway map which was several years old and as obsolete as the Cadillac. Harry had probably borrowed the car from the used-car lot where he worked.

I lifted the hood and felt the engine. It was warm. I could imagine Harry skulking around in the bush near Martel's house. I thought of waiting for him, but my stomach decided against it. I could check on him later at the Breakwater Hotel.

I did call on Mrs. Bagshaw before dinner. I parked beside the deserted tennis court and made my way through the dense gloom under the eucalyptus trees to her cottage. She appeared at the door in a stiff, rustling gown, with a rope of pearls lying coiled on her crepe bosom.

"I was just about to go out. But I did make the call you suggested." It seemed to have upset her. Under her rouge, or because of it, she looked years older. She said without quite meeting my eyes: "My friends in Georgetown don't know Francis Martel, at least under that name. I can't understand it. He spoke of them with such zest and familiarity. He knew all about their house."

"He could have got that information from a servant."

"But he knows Washington," she said. "I couldn't be

mistaken about that. And I'm still personally convinced he knows or knew the Plimsolls—my friends in Georgetown. Perhaps he knew them under another name than Francis Martel."

"That's possible, too. Did you describe him to them?"

"It was Colonel Plimsoll I talked to, and I did make some attempt to describe him, yes. But it's difficult to describe someone, particularly these Latin types—they all look alike to me. The Colonel said if I could send him a picture of Martel—?"

"I'm sorry, I have no picture."

"Then I don't know what I can do." Her voice was apologetic, but there was an undertone of unwanted guilt which made it almost accusing. "I can't assume the responsibility for him, or for Miss Fablon. People have to look out for themselves in this world."

"The older ones try to look out for the younger ones, though."

"I brought up my own family," she said sharply, "sometimes under conditions which I would hesitate to describe. If Virginia made an unfortunate choice in men, it's hardly surprising. Her father did what he did when she was at a most vulnerable age. And even in life Roy Fablon was no great bargain." She shook her curls. "I'm expected for dinner now. You really must excuse me." The word had a double meaning. Excuse. Forgive.

I walked around the pool enclosure to the main club-house. A bevy of expensive-looking people went in ahead of me. From behind the front desk Ella Strome greeted each of them by name. But she seemed a little remote, consciously out of things.

"You look like a vestal virgin."

"I've been married twice," she said dryly. "Mr. Jamieson is expecting you in the dining room."

"Let him wait. I've only been married once."

"You're not doing your duty to American womanhood," she said with a smile which failed to touch her eyes.

"You sound as if you didn't enjoy being married."

"Being married was all right, it was the men I was married to. Do I project a maternal image or something?"

"No."

"I must. I seem to attract very peculiar types. Both of my husbands were peculiar types. It couldn't be pure chance. There aren't that many peculiar types."

"Yes, there are. Speaking of peculiar types, what's your opinion of Mr. Martel?"

"I have no particular opinion. He always treated me politely." Her hands came together on the polished black desk and pushed against each other, fingertip to fingertip. "Why don't you ask Mr. Stoll about him? He had a run-in with him, I believe."

"Who's Mr. Stoll?"

"The manager of the club."

I found him in the office behind the reception desk. The walnut-paneled walls were hung with photographs of parties and tennis matches and other sporting events. Stoll looked like a non-participant. He was a handsome cold-eyed man of forty, overdressed, with the little graces of a pleaser and a pleaser's lack of resonance. The nameplate on the desk said: "Reto Stoll, Manager."

He became quite cordial when I told him I was working for the Jamiesons. "Sit down, Mr. Archer." He had a faint German accent. "What can I do for you?"

I sat facing him across his desk. "Mrs. Strome said you had some trouble with Martel."

"A little, yes. But it's in the past. Let bygones be bygones, particularly since Mr. Martel is leaving us."

"Is he leaving because of the trouble with you?"

"Partly, I suppose. I didn't ask him to leave on account of it. On the other hand I didn't urge him to stay when he finally announced his intention of leaving. I breathed a sigh of relief when he turned in his keys today and paid his bill." Stoll spread his manicured hand on the front of his double-breasted waistcoat.

"Why?"

"The man was a volcano. He could erupt at any moment. We like a quiet friendly atmosphere in our club."

"Tell me about the trouble you had with him. It may be important. What did he do?"

"He offered to kill me. Do you want the whole story from the beginning?"

"Please."

"It happened several weeks ago. Mr. Martel ordered a drink brought up to his cabana. Absinthe. The bar-boy was busy so I took it up myself. I sometimes do that as a special courtesy. Miss Fablon was with him. They were talking in French. Since French is one of my native languages I hesitated behind the screen and listened. I wasn't consciously eavesdropping." Stoll raised his eyes to the ceiling, virtuously. "But he appeared to think that I was spying on him. He jumped up and attacked me."

"With his fists?"

"With a sword." His hand went down his body to his stomach. "He had a sword concealed in a bamboo cane."

"I've seen the cane. Did he actually stick you?"

"He held the point of it to my body." Stoll fondled the precious curve of his belly through his striped pants. "Fortunately Miss Fablon got him calmed down, and he apologized. But I was never at ease with him in the club again."

"What were they talking about when you overheard them?"

"He was doing all the talking. It sounded to me like some kind of mysticism. He was saying how this philosopher believed that thinking was the basis of everything—*la source de tout*." His mind moved back and forth between the two languages. "But Mr. Martel said the *philosophe* was wrong. *Realité* didn't come into being until two people thought together. So the basis of everything was *l'amour*." The corners of Stoll's mouth turned down. "It didn't make much sense to me."

"Did it to her?"

"Naturally. He was making love to her. That was the point. He was angry because I interrupted him in the middle of his pitch. When I think back over the episode, I'm convinced the man is psychopathological. Ordinary men don't get so excited over such a little thing." He clenched his fist, not very tight. "I should have asked him to give up his guest privileges then and there."

"I'm surprised you didn't."

He colored faintly. "Well, you know, he is—or was—Mrs. Bagshaw's protégé. She's one of our oldest members, and now she's moved into the cottage next to mine—I hated to upset her. I feel my essential role is that of a—buffer." He raised his eyes to the ceiling again, as if the god of innkeepers resided just over his head. "I try to stand between our members and the unpleasantness of life."

"You're very good at it, I'm sure."

He accepted the compliment formally with a bow. "Thank you, Mr. Archer. The Tennis Club is known in the trade as one of the better-run clubs. I've given it ten years of my life, and I was trained in the hotel schools of Zurich and Lausanne."

"What did you mean when you said that French was one of your native languages?"

He smiled. "I have four native languages. French and German and Italian and Romansch. I was born in the Romansch section of Switzerland, in Silvaplana." His tongue caressed the name.

"Where was Martel born, Mr. Stoll?"

"I have asked myself that question. He claims to be Parisian, Mrs. Bagshaw tells me. But from what little I heard of it, his French is not Paris French. It is too provincial, too formal. Perhaps it is Canadian, or South American. I don't know. I am not a linguistic scientist."

"You're the next thing to it," I said encouragingly. "So you think he might be Canadian or South American?"

"That's just a guess. I'm not really familiar with Canadian or South American French. But I'm quite sure Martel is not Parisian."

I thanked Stoll. He bowed me out.

I had noticed a bulletin board on the wall outside his office. Pinned to its cord surface were some blownup candid pictures of people dancing at a party. Below them, like a reminder of purgatory at the gates of paradise, was a typed list of seven members who were behind with their dues. Mrs. Roy Fablon was one of them.

I mentioned this to Ella.

"Yes, Mrs. Fablon's been having a hard time recently. She told me some of her investments went sour. I hated to post her name, but those are the rules."

"It raises an interesting question. Do you think Virginia Fablon is after Martel's money."

She shook her head. "It wouldn't make sense. She was going to marry Peter Jamieson. The Jamiesons have ten times as much money as Mr. Martel ever dreamed of."

"Do you know that?"

"I can tell people with money from people without, and people who have had it for a while from people who haven't. If you want my opinion, Mr. Martel is *nouveau riche*, and more *nouveau* than *riche*. He's felt out of place here, and he's been spending his money like a drunken sailor, and it hasn't helped much."

"Except that it's got him Ginny. They were married over the weekend."

"Poor girl."

"Why do you say that?"

"On general principles. Mr. Jamieson is having a long wait. Is he the one you're working for?"

"Yes."

"And you're a private detective, aren't you?"

"I am. What do you think of my client?"

"He reminds me of something I read once, that inside every fat man is a thin man crying to get out. Only Peter's just a boy, and that makes it worse." She added meditatively: "I suppose he has the makings of a man."

"We'll see." I jerked a thumb toward the bulletin board. "You have some pictures on the board. Does this club have a regular photographer?"

"A part time one. Why?"

"I was wondering if he took a picture of Martel."

"I doubt it. I could check with the photographer. Eric isn't on tonight though."

"Get him on. Tell him I'll pay him for his time."

"I'll try."

"You can do better than try," I said. "There's a question about Martel's identity, and we need a picture if there is one."

"I said I'd try."

She directed me to the dining room. It was actually two adjoining rooms, one of which had a polished dance floor. A small orchestra was on the stand, momentarily silent. The other room contained about thirty tables, brilliant with flowers and silver. Peter was sitting at a table by the windows, staring out gloomily at the dark beach.

He got up eagerly when he saw me, but his eagerness had more to do with dinner than with me. It was served buffet style by men in white hats. At the sight of food Peter underwent a transformation, as if his melancholy passion for Ginny had been switched to another channel. He loaded two plates for himself, one with five kinds of salad, cold ham, shrimp, crabmeat: the other with roast beef and potatoes and gravy and small green peas.

He gobbled the food with such eager straining gluttony that he made me feel like a voyeur. His eyes were fixed and mindless as he chewed. Sweat stood out on his forehead.

He wiped his plate with a piece of bread, which he ate. Then he went into contemplation, leaning his chin on his hand. "I can't decide what to have for dessert."

"You don't need dessert."

He looked at me as if I'd threatened to put him on bread and water for a month. I felt like telling him to go to hell. Watching him eat, I'd asked myself if I'd be doing Ginny a favor by bringing her back to my client. Martel at least was a man. Maybe Peter had the makings of a man, as Ella said, but when he sat down at the table he turned into something less, an appetite that only walked like a man.

"I don't know whether to have a chocolate eclair or a hot fudge sundae," he said seriously.

"Have both."

"That isn't funny. My body needs fuel."

"You've already stoked it with enough fuel to run a Matson liner to Honolulu."

He flushed. "You seem to forget that I'm your employer, and you're my guest here."

"I do, don't I? But let's get off the subject of personalities and food, and talk about something real. Tell me about Ginny."

"After I get my dessert."

"Before. Before you eat yourself stupid."

"You can't talk like that to me."

"Somebody should. But we won't argue about it. I want to know if Ginny is the kind of girl who goes off half-cocked about men."

"She never did before."

"Has she had much to do with men?"

"Very little," he said. "Mainly me, in fact." He flushed again, avoiding my eyes. "I wasn't always so fat, if you want to know. Ginny and I sort of went steady in high school. But after that for a long time she wasn't interested in—well, sex, necking and stuff. We were still friends, and I used to take her places sometimes, but we weren't going steady in the true sense anymore."

"What changed her?"

"She was hitting the books, for one thing. She did well at college. I didn't." The fact seemed to nag him. "But it was mainly what happened to her father."

"His suicide?"

Peter nodded. "Ginny was very much attached to her father. Actually it took her until just about now to get over his death."

"How long ago did it happen?"

"Nearly seven years. Seven years this fall. He came down to the beach one night and walked into the water with all his clothes on."

"This beach?" I gestured towards the window. The tide was out: the surf was far down the beach and visible only as a recurring whiteness.

"Not right here, no. He went in about half a mile from here." Peter pointed towards a headland which loomed dark against the more distant harbor light. "But there's a current in this direction and when his body came up it was right offshore here. I didn't go in the ocean for quite a while. I don't think Ginny ever went in again. She uses—she used the pool."

He sat hunched over in silence for a moment. "Mr. Archer, can't we do something about Martel? Find out if they're married legally or something?"

"I'm sure they are. Ginny would have no reason to lie, would she?"

"No. But she's very much under his spell. You could see for yourself that it isn't a natural situation."

"She seems to be in love with him."

"She can't be! We've got to prevent him from taking her away."

"With what? It's still a free country."

Peter leaned across the table. "Have you considered the possibility that he's in this country illegally? He admitted he had no passport."

"It might be worth looking into. But the worst they'd do is deport him. And Ginny would probably go along."

"I see what you mean. It would only make matters worse."

He lowered his cushioned chin onto his fist and became thoughtful. Our side of the dining room was filling up as people came in from outside or from the bar. A few of them wore dress clothes, and occasional diamonds and rubies sparkled on hands and throats like drippings from the past. The low sound of the ocean was lost in the rise and fall of conversation and music.

The people seemed to be talking against the darkness that pressed at the window. Fablon and his death were still on my mind. "You say that Ginny was very fond of her father?"

Peter came out of his thoughts with a start. "Yes. She was."

"What sort of man was he?"

"He was what they call a sportsman, I guess. He went in for big-game hunting and fishing and yachting and polo and sports cars and planes."

"All those?"

"At various times. He'd lose interest in one sport and try another. He couldn't seem to find the one thing that would absorb his mind. For a while, when I was a kid in high school, he let me follow him around. He even used to take me up in his plane." Peter's eyes blurred reminiscently. "He was in the Air Force at one time, until they invalided him out."

"What was the matter with him?"

"I don't know exactly. He crashed his plane in a training flight and so he never got into the war. That was a big disappointment to him. He walked with a bit of a limp. Which is one reason I think he went in for all those sports."

"What did he look like?"

"I suppose you'd say that he was good-looking. He was dark-haired and dark-eyed, and he always had a deep tan. Ginny got her coloring from her mother. But I don't know why you're so interested in her family. What's the point?"

"I'm trying to understand her, and understand why she fell so hard and suddenly for Martel. Does he resemble her father?"

"Some," he admitted reluctantly. "But Mr. Fablon was better-looking."

"You said he was partly French. Did he speak French?"

"I guess he could when he wanted to. He lived in France at one time, he told me."

"Where?"

"Paris. That was when he was studying painting."

I was beginning to get some idea of Fablon. In these circles he was a fairly common type: the man who tried everything and succeeded at nothing.

"Where did he get the money for all his hobbies? Was he in business?"

"He tried various businesses. Right after the war he started an air-freight business. The trouble was, he was in competition with airlines like the Flying Tiger. He told me once he lost fifty thousand dollars in six months. But he had a lot of fun with it, he said." Peter's tone was elegiac, nostalgic. At another time, in another body, he might have liked to live as the dead man had.

"Who paid for the fun?"

"Mrs. Fablon did, I guess. She was a Proctor." He paused, frowning slightly. "I just remembered something. It's nothing to do with anything, but it's interesting." He turned to the window, indicating the dark headland again. "That beach where Mr. Fablon walked into the water used to belong to the Proctors. It was part of their estate. Ginny's mother had to sell the estate about ten years ago."

"Three years before Fablon died."

"That's right. If she could have waited until now, she'd have got at least a million. But I heard it went for peanuts to pay Mr. Fablon's debts."

"Who bought it?"

"A cemetery company. They haven't put in the cemetery yet."

"I can hardly wait," I said.

Peter frowned at my levity. A minute later he left the table and ducked out of the room. I saw him a few minutes after that talking at the entrance with a tall man in a tuxedo. The tall man moved his head, and I noticed the hard line of his jaw. It was Dr. Sylvester, whose lunch with Mrs. Fablon I had interrupted.

He went into the bar. Peter trudged to the end of the line that had formed at the dessert table. He stood like an earnest communicant, his eyes dreaming over the pies and cakes and pastries.

X

I FOLLOWED DR. SYLVESTER into the bar. A bartender whose eyes moved like black quicksilver poured him a double scotch without being asked to. Sylvester called the bartender Marco. Marco wore a red waistcoat, a white shirt with long collarpoints, and a flowing black silk tie.

I waited until the doctor had knocked back about half of his drink. Then I sat on the bar stool beside him and watched Marco making a daiquiri.

Sylvester's square hairy-backed hands fiddled with his lowball glass. The hairs were slightly grizzled, like the hair on his head. The bones of his face were prominent, and accentuated by harsh lines running from the base of his nose to his mouth. He didn't look like an easy man to strike up a conversation with.

To have something to do with my hands, I ordered a bar bourbon. The bartender wouldn't accept my dollar.

"Sorry, no cash. Are you a member, sir?"

"I'm Peter Jamieson's guest."

"I'll put it on his bill, sir."

Dr. Sylvester turned and raised his black eyebrows at me. He used them so conspicuously that they seemed to be his main sense organs, distracting attention from his hard bright eyes.

"Jamieson senior or junior?"

"I know them both. I noticed you were talking to the young one."

"Yes?"

I told him my name and trade. "Peter hired me to look into this business of his ex-fiancée."

"I was wondering how you got in here." He wasn't trying to insult me, exactly, just letting me know my place in his scheme of things. "Didn't I see you at the Fablons' house this noon?"

"Yes. I understand you were Virginia Fablon's employer at one time."

"That's true."

"What do you think about her marriage?"

I had succeeded in interesting him. "Good Lord, did she marry the fellow?"

"So she told me. They were married on Saturday."

"You've talked to her?"

"An hour or so ago. I couldn't figure out what was going

on in her mind. Of course the circumstances weren't normal, either. But she seemed to be living out some kind of romantic dream."

"Most women are," he said dryly. "Did you see him?"

"I talked to them together at his house."

"I've never met him myself," Sylvester said. "I've seen him around here, of course, at a distance. What did you make of him?"

"He's a very intelligent man, highly educated, with a good deal of force. He seems to have Virginia pretty well dominated."

"It won't last," Sylvester said. "You don't know the young lady. She has a lot of personal force of her own." He added wryly: "I've served *in loco parentis* to her since her father died, and it hasn't always been easy. Virginia likes to make up her own mind."

"About men?"

"There haven't been any men in her life, not lately. That's one of the problems she's had. Ever since her father's death she's done nothing but work and study French. You'd think her life was nothing but a memorial to Roy. Then a few weeks ago, as you might expect, the whole thing broke down. She dropped her studies, when she was within easy shooting distance of her degree, and went hog-wild for this Martel." He sipped his drink. "It's a disturbing picture."

"Are you her doctor?"

"I was until quite recently. Frankly, we had a disagreement about the—the wisdom of her course. I thought it best to refer her to another doctor. Why do you ask?"

"I don't like the emotional risk she's taking. She's managed to convince herself that she's crazy about Martel, and she's perched way out on a limb. It could be brutal for her if the limb gets sawed off."

"I tried to tell her that," Sylvester said. "You think he's a phoney, eh?"

"He has to be at least partly phoney. I've had one Washington reference checked, and it didn't pan out. There were other things I won't go into." The rat, the blood on his heel, the gun peering out of his hand at Harry Hendricks.

"What can I do about it? She's got the bit in her teeth, and she running with it." Sylvester paused, and finished his drink.

"You want another, doctor?" the bartender asked.

"No thanks, Marco. One thing I've learned in twenty years of practicing medicine," he said to me: "you have to let people make their own mistakes. Sooner or later they come around to reason. The men with emphysema will eventually give up smoking. The women with chronic alcoholism will go on the wagon. And the girls with bad cases of romanticism turn into realists. Like my dear wife here."

A big woman in a kind of mantilla had come up behind us. Her chest gleamed like mother-of-pearl through black lace. She had bouffant yellow hair which made her as tall as I was when I stood up. Her mouth was discontented.

"What *about* me?" she said. "I love to be talked about by men."

"I was saying that you were a realist, Audrey. That women start out being romantic and end up realistic every time."

"Men force us into it," she said. "Is this my daiquiri?"

"Yes, and this is Mr. Archer. He's a detective."

"How fascinating," she said. "You must tell me the story of your life."

"I started out as a romantic and ended up as a realist."

She laughed and drank her drink, and they went in to dinner. Some other people followed them.

For a moment I was the only one at the bar. Marco asked me if I wanted another drink. He was staring at me intensely as if he had something on his mind. His mouth was sort of wreathed with unspoken language. I said that I would like another drink.

"On me," he said as he rapped it down, and poured himself a Cola to take with me. "I couldn't help hearing, you said you were a detective. And some of the things you said about Miss Fablon."

"You know her?"

"Seen her around. She don't drink. I've been here for over twelve years, I knew her father. He drank, and he could carry it. Mr. Fablon was a man. He had *machismo*." Marco's red lips protruded, savoring the word.

"I heard he committed suicide," I said without emphasis.

"Maybe. I never believed it." He shook his bushy black head.

"You think he drowned accidentally?"

"I didn't say that."

"The other alternative is murder."

"I didn't say that, either." Without moving from his position behind the bar, he seemed to back away from me. Then he crossed himself. "Murder is a big ugly word."

"It's an uglier fact. Was Mr. Fablon murdered?"

"Some people thought so."

"Who?"

"His wife, for instance. After he disappeared she was yelling bloody murder around the club here. Then suddenly she quit, and all you could hear from her was a loud silence."

"Did she accuse anyone?"

"Not that I heard. She didn't name any names."

"Why would she change her story?"

"Your guess is as good as mine, mister. Probably better." The subject seemed to make him nervous. He changed it: "But it wasn't that I wanted to talk about. This other guy—calls himself Martel—the big-shot Frenchman?"

"What about him?"

"I got a funny feeling I've seen him before someplace." He spread his fingers. "Anyway I'm sure he ain't no Frenchie."

"What is he?"

"Same like me, maybe." He made a stupid face, deliberately humbling himself in order to make what he said more insulting to Martel. "Just another *paisano*. He never came in here only the once, and then he took one look at me and never came back."

The orchestra had started up. Some people drifted in from

the dining room and ordered brandy. Dodging a few dancing couples, I went back to Peter's table. The dessert plate in front of him was empty except for a few faint smears of chocolate. He looked smug and guilty.

"I thought you'd left," he said.

"I was in the bar talking to some friends of the Fablons."

"Dr. Sylvester."

"He was one of them," I said.

"I had a word with him, too. He puts on that hard front of his, but he's worried about Ginny, I can tell."

"We all are."

"Do you think we better go back to Martel's house?" Peter made a move to get up.

"Not until we have something substantial to hit him with."

"Like what?"

"Some actual proof that he isn't what he claims to be. I'm trying to develop something now."

"And what am I supposed to do?"

Go and take another run on the beach, I almost said. I said: "You have to wait. And I think you better get used to the idea that this may not turn out the way you want it to."

"You've found out something?"

"Nothing definite, but I have a feeling. This one didn't start out happily and it may not end happily. I think it goes back at least as far as Roy Fablon's alleged suicide."

"Alleged?"

"At least one man who knew him doesn't believe he killed himself. Which implies that somebody else did."

"Whoever told you that is making it up."

"Perhaps. He's a Roman Catholic, and he admired Roy Fablon, and he wouldn't want to think that he was a suicide. Your father told me an interesting thing though."

"I didn't know you ever talked to my father." Peter's tone was formal and suspicious, as if I had gone over to the enemy.

"I went to your house to find you this afternoon. Your father told me among other things that Roy Fablon's body was so chewed up by sharks it could hardly be identified. Just what was the condition of his face?"

"I didn't see it myself. My father did. All they showed me was his overcoat."

"He went into the water wearing an overcoat?"

"It was more of a waterproof." He heard the word, and grimaced at the irony.

It caught in my own mind like a fishhook. It was hard to imagine a sportsman and athlete walking into the ocean in a waterproof coat, from a beach estate which his ways with money had forced his wife to sell, unless he meant to leave her and her daughter a legacy of malice.

"How do you know exactly where he went into the water?"

"He left his wallet and wristwatch on the beach. There wasn't anything in the wallet, except identification, but his watch was a very good one that Mrs. Fablon had given him. It had their initials on the back, and something engraved in Latin on the case."

"No suicide note?"

"If there was one, I never heard of it. That doesn't necessarily prove anything. The local police don't always release notes."

"Do you have a lot of suicides in Montevista?"

"We have our share. You know, when you have money to live on, and a nice house, and good weather most of the time, and *still* your life goes wrong—well, who can you blame?" Peter seemed to be talking about himself.

"Is that how it was with Roy Fablon?"

"Not exactly. He had his troubles. I was a guest in their house, and I shouldn't talk about them, but I suppose it doesn't matter now." He breathed in. "I heard him tell Mrs. Fablon he would kill himself."

"That same night?"

"A night or two before. I was there for dinner, and they were arguing about money. She said she couldn't give him any more money because there wasn't any more money."

"What did he want the money for?"

"Gambling losses. He called it a debt of honor. He said if he couldn't pay it he'd have to kill himself."

"Was Ginny there?"

"Yes. She heard everything. We both did. Mr. and Mrs. Fablon had reached the point where they weren't trying to hide anything. Each of them was trying to win us over."

"Who won?"

"Nobody won," he said. "Everybody lost."

The orchestra was playing again, and through the archway I could see people dancing in the adjoining room. Most of the tunes, and most of the dancers, had been new in the twenties and thirties. Together they gave the impression of a party that had been going on too long, till the music and the dancers were worn as thin as the husks of insects after spiders had eaten them.

XI

ELLA STROME crossed the corner of the dance floor and came to our table. "I've got hold of the photographer for you, Mr. Archer. He's waiting in the office."

He was a thin man in a rumpled dark business suit. He had a lot of brown hair, a lumpy Slavic jaw, and sensitive-looking eyes protected by horn-rimmed glasses. Ella introduced him as Eric Malkovsky.

"I'm glad to meet you," he said, but he wasn't. He glanced restlessly past me towards the door of the office. "I promised my wife to take her to the Film Society tonight. We have season tickets."

"I'll reimburse you."

"That's not the point. I hate to disappoint her."

"This may be more important."

"Not to me it isn't." He was speaking to me, but his real

complaint was directed towards Ella. I gathered she had used pressure to get him here. "Anyway, as I told Mrs. Strome, I have no pictures of Mr. Martel. I offered to take some the way I do with any other guest, but he said no. He was pretty emphatic about it."

"Unpleasant?"

"I wouldn't say that. But he certainly didn't want his picture taken. What is he, a celebrity or something?"

"Something."

My reticence irritated him, and he colored slightly. "The only reason I asked, another person was after me for a picture of him."

Ella said: "You didn't tell me that."

"I didn't have a chance to. The woman came to my studio in the Village just before I went home for dinner. When I told her I didn't have a picture of him, she offered me money to go to his house and take one. I told her I couldn't do that without Mr. Martel's permission. At which she got mad and stomped out."

"I don't suppose she gave you her name?"

"No, but I can describe her. She's a redhead, tall, with a gorgeous figure. Aged about thirty. As a matter of fact, I had a feeling that I've seen her before."

"Where?"

"Right here in the club."

"I don't remember any such woman," Ella said.

"It was before your time, at least five years ago." Malkovsky screwed up one side of his face as he was squinting through a view finder. "I think I took a picture or two of the woman. In fact I'm pretty sure I did."

"Would you still have those pictures?" I said.

"Maybe, but it would be a terrible job to find them. I don't keep files except for the current year and the year before." He looked at his wristwatch, dramatically. "I really have to go now. The wife would kill me if she misses the Buñuel. And the club doesn't pay me overtime for this kind of a deal." He tossed a sour look in the direction of Ella, who had gone back to the reception desk.

"I'll pay you double time for as long as it takes."

"That would be seven dollars an hour. It could take all night."

"I know."

"And there's no guarantee that I'll come up with anything. It may be an entirely different woman. If it's the same woman, she's changed the color of her hair. The woman I remember was a blonde."

"Blondes turn into redheads all the time. Tell me about the woman you remember."

"She was younger, then, of course, with the dew still on her. A lovely thing. I remember now. I did take some pictures of her. Her husband wasn't too crazy about the idea but she wanted it done."

"Who was her husband?"

"An older guy," he said. "They stayed in one of the cottages for a couple of weeks."

"What year were they here?"

"I couldn't nail it down—maybe six or seven years ago. But if I find those pictures I can tell you. I generally make a note of the date on the back."

By this time Malkovsky was eager to get to work. Before leaving for the Village, he gave me the address and telephone number of his studio. I said I would check with him there in an hour or so.

I thanked Ella, and went to the parking lot to get my car. An unsteady wind carrying a gritty taste of desert was blowing down from the direction of the mountains. The eucalyptus trees swayed and bowed and waved in the gusts like long-haired madwomen racked by impulse. The night which loomed above the trees and dwarfed them seemed threatening.

I had been concerned about Harry Hendricks ever since I found his car at the roadside near Martel's house. Harry had no more earned my concern than the alleged rat which Martel said he had killed. Still I had a foolish yen to see Harry alive.

The road to the harbor cut across the base of the headland where Fablon had taken his final swim, and back to the ocean. As I drove along the windswept boulevard, my mind was so fixed on Harry that when I saw the Cadillac parked at the curb I thought I was dreaming. I braked and backed and parked directly behind it, and got out. It was Harry's old Caddie, all right, standing there with a cold engine, empty and innocent, as if it had driven itself down from the foothills. The key was in the ignition. It hadn't been before.

I looked around me. It was a lonely place, especially at this time, with a wind blowing. There was no other car in sight, and nothing across the street but rattling palms and the sighing sea.

On the inland side a tall cypress hedge shielded the boulevard from a view of the railroad tracks and the hobo jungles. Through a hole in the hedge I could see the dark shapes of men crouched around a bonfire which flared and veered.

I went through the hole and approached them. There were three of them drinking dark red wine out of a half-gallon jug which was nearly empty. Their faces all turned toward me in the firelight: the seamed and gap-toothed face of an aging white man; the flat stubborn planes of a young Negro's head; a boy with Indian features and an Indian's stolid apathetic eyes. He wore nothing above the waist but an open black vest.

The Negro got up with five or six feet of two-by-four in his hands. He staggered toward me on the uneven ground.

"Amscray, 'bo. This is a private party."

"You can answer a civil question. I'm looking for a friend of mine."

"I don't know nothin' about no friends of yours." Big and drunk, he leaned on his two-by-four like a warrior on his spear. His tripod shadow wavered on the hedge.

"That's his car there," I said quickly. "The Cadillac. He's a medium-sized man in a checkered jacket. Have you seen him?"

"Naw."

"Just a minute." The white man rose unsteadily. "Maybe I seen him, maybe not. What's it worth to you?"

He came up close to me so that I could smell his fiery breath and look deep into the glaring hollows of his eyes.

They had a feverish brainwashed wino emptiness. He was so far gone that he would never come back.

"It isn't worth anything to me, old-timer. You're trying to promote the price of another jug."

"I seen him, honest I seen him. Little man in a checkered jacket. He gave me four bits, I thanked him very kindly. You don't forget a citizen like that." The breath whistled through the gaps in his teeth.

"Let's see the four bits."

He searched elaborately through his jeans. "I must have lost it."

I turned away. He followed me all the way to the car. His gnarled fists drummed on the window.

"Have a heart, for Christ's sake. Gimme four bits. I told you about your friend."

"No money for wine," I said.,

"It's for food. I'm starving. I came down here to pick oranges and they fired me, and I couldn't do the work."

"They'll feed you at the Salvation Army."

He puckered up his mouth and spat on the window. His saliva ran down the glass between him and me. I started the motor.

"Get away, you might get hurt."

"I'm hurt already,' he said with his life in his voice.

He staggered back to the hedge, disappearing suddenly through the hole like a man swallowed up by darkness.

XII

THE BREAKWATER HOTEL was only a few blocks from the place where Harry's Cadillac was parked. It was possible, though hardly likely, that he'd left it there, for reasons of his own, and gone the rest of the way on foot.

The lobby of the hotel was the mouth of a tourist trap which had lost its bite. There were scuff-marks on the furniture, dust on the philodendrons. The bellhop wore an old blue uniform which looked as if he had fought through the Civil War in it.

There was no one at the desk, but the register was lying open on it. I found Harry Hendricks's name on the previous page. He had room 27. I looked at the half-wall of pigeon-holes behind the desk, and couldn't see the key in 27.

"Is Mr. Hendricks in?" I asked the bellhop.

He stroked the growth of beard on his chin. It looked like moth-eaten gray plush, but it rasped like sandpaper. "I wouldn't know about that. They come and go. I'm not paid to keep track."

"Where's the manager?"

"In there."

He jerked a thumb toward a curtained doorway with an electric sign above it: Samoa Room. The name meant that it would have bamboo furniture and a fishnet ceiling: it had: and would serve rum drinks containing canned pineapple juice and floating fruit.

Three rather wilted-looking sharpies were rolling dice on the bar. The fat bartender watched them over his belly. A tired-looking hostess offered me the temporary use of her smile. I told her that I wanted to ask the manager a question.

"Mr. Smythe is the assistant manager. Mr. Smythe!"

Mr. Smythe was the sharpest-looking of the sharpies. He tore himself away from the dice for a moment. If they were his dice, they were probably gaffed. His true-blue All-American look was warped like peeling veneer around the edges.

"You wish accommodations, sir?"

"Later, perhaps. I wanted to ask you if Mr. Hendricks is in."

"Not unless he came in in the last few minutes. His wife is waiting in his room for him."

"I didn't know he was married."

"He's married all right. Very married. I'd give up the

joys of bachelorhood myself if I could latch onto a dish like that." His hands made an hourglass figure in the smoky air.

"Maybe she can tell me where he is."

"She doesn't know. She asked me. I haven't seen him since this afternoon. Is he in some kind of a jam?"

"Could be."

"You a cop?"

"An investigator," I answered vaguely. "What makes you think that Hendricks is in trouble?"

"He asked me where he could buy a cheap hand gun."

"Today?"

"This aft, like I said. I told him to try the pawnshops. Did I do wrong? He didn't shoot somebody?"

"Not that I know of."

"That's good." But he was subtly disappointed. "If you want to talk to Mrs. Hendricks, there's a room phone beside the desk."

I thanked him and he returned to the joys of bachelorhood. I didn't bother with the phone, or with the elevator. I found the fire stairs at the back of the lobby and went up the red-lit stairwell to the second floor.

Room 27 was at the end of the hall. I listened at the door. There was faint music behind it, a country blues. I knocked. The music was shut off abruptly.

"Who is it?" a woman said.

"Harry."

"It's about time!"

She unlatched the door and pulled it open. I walked in on her and took the doorknob out of her hand and swung the door shut behind me, in case the screaming expression on her face changed into sudden noise.

It didn't. The fixed lopsided rigor of her face didn't change. Her right fist rose of its own accord to the level of her eyes. She looked at me around it.

"Take it easy, Mrs. Hendricks. I won't hurt you."

"I hear you telling me." But she relaxed enough to unclench her fist and use it to smooth her red hair. Her lopsided mouth straightened itself. "Who are you?"

"A friend of Harry's. I said I'd look him up here."

She didn't believe me. She looked like a woman who had stopped believing almost everything except the number on bills, the price tag on clothes and people. She was dressed in style, in a brown loose kind of half-sleeved something which showed her figure without overemphasizing it. Her forearms and legs were beautifully made and deeply tanned.

But her face was made up as if she had begun to doubt her looks, or wished to hide them. From under eyelids greener than her eyes, through eyelashes that groped like furred antennae in the air, she peered at me distrustfully.

"What's your name?" she said.

"It doesn't matter."

"Then get out of my room." But she didn't really expect me to. If she had any expectations left, they had to do with possible disasters.

"It isn't your room. It's Harry's. He said he'd meet me."

She looked around the room, at the worn carpet, the faded flowers in the wallpaper, the beside lamp with its scorched paper shade, as if she was considering her relationship to it. Externally she didn't belong here at all. She had the kind of style that could be bought, but not suddenly, at Bullocks and I. Magnin's; the brown pouch on the bed with its gold tassels looked like Paris. But she belonged internally to the room, the way a prisoner belongs to his cell. She had done time in rooms like this, and it was setting in again.

"It's my room too," she said. To prove it, and to cheer things up a little, she went to the bedside table and turned up her portable radio. The country blues hadn't ended yet. It had been a long two minutes.

"What—?"' Her voice screeked on the word. She was still so full of tension that she was hardly breathing. She tried to swallow the tension; I watched the marvelous mechanism of her throat. "What kind of business do you have with Harry?" she finally managed to say.

"We were going to compare notes on Francis Martel."

She flapped her eyelashes. "Who?"

"Martel. The man you want a picture of."

"You must be thinking of two other people."

"Come on now, Mrs. Hendricks. I've just been talking to

the photographer Malkovsky. You wanted him to take a picture of Martel. Your husband risked his neck trying to get one this morning."

"Are you a cop?"

"Not exactly."

"How do you know so much about me?"

"That's all I know about you, unfortunately. Tell me more."

Laboriously, with hands that jerked a little, she got a gold cigarette case out of her brown pouch, opened it, took out a cigarette and put it between her lips. I lit it for her. She sat on the bed and leaned back on her arm, blowing smoke hard at the ceiling as if to conceal its dinginess.

"Don't stand over me like that. You look as though you're going to jump down my throat."

"I was admiring your throat." I pulled up the only chair in the room and sat on it.

"Swingin'." Her voice was sardonic. She covered her neck with the collar of her fingers, and studied me. "I can't figure you out, unless you're trying to soften me up with the sweet-and-sour treatment. Which will get you nowhere."

"Are you really Harry's wife?"

"Yes. I am." She sounded a little surprised herself. "I'd show you my marriage license but I don't seem to have it with me at the moment."

"How can he afford you?"

"He can't. We haven't been working at it lately. But we're still friends." She added with a kind of rough nostalgia: "Harry wasn't always on the skids. He used to be more fun than a barrel of monkeys."

"And you weren't always in the chips."

"Who told you that?"

"Nobody had to tell me." Your voice told me, doll, and the way you have to keep using your body in little conspicuous ways as if you were treading water. The way you looked at the room told me, and the way the room looked back.

"Are you from Vegas?" she said.

"People are supposed to smile when they say that."

"Are you?"

"I'm from Hollywood."

"What do you do for a living, Hollywood? If anything."

"Private investigations."

"And you're doing a job on me?"

Her look was fearful again. At the same time she signaled for the ashtray from the bedside table and butted her cigarette in it while I held it. She shifted her position, leaning heavily sideways with half-deliberate clumsiness to show how helpless her fine big body was. It needed no help from, me, though: it was perfectly at home on a hotel bed.

"You've got things twisted around," I said. "I was hired to do a job on Martel."

"Who by?" She corrected herself: "By whom?"

"A local man. His identity doesn't matter. Martel stole his girl."

"It figures. He's a thief."

"What did he steal from you, Mrs. Hendricks?"

"That's a good question. The real question, though, is whether he's the guy I think he is. Have you seen him?"

"Several times."

"Describe him for me, will you? We may be able to get together on this."

"He a medium-sized man, about five foot nine, not heavy, but compactly built, and quick in his movements. Age about thirty. He has black hair, jet black, growing fairly low on his forehead. He wears it combed straight back. His complexion is dark, almost Indian dark. He has a long nose with noticeably flaring nostrils. He speaks with a French accent, uses a lot of French, and claims to be a French political refugee."

She had been listening and nodding in confirmation, but my last sentence confused her. "What was that?"

"He says he's a Frenchman who can't live in France because he doesn't get along with de Gaulle."

"Oh." But she still didn't understand.

"De Gaulle is the President of France."

"I know that, stupid. You think I don't listen to the news?" She glanced at the radio, which was playing rock.

"Do you mind if I turn that thing off?" I said.

"You can turn it down a little, but leave it on. I hate the sound of the wind."

I turned the music not too far down. Based on such minor cooperations an intimacy was growing between us, as if the room had provided us with built-in roles. But it was a chancy intimacy, whose rhythm was an alternating current of fear and doubt. She asked me sensible questions and seemed to believe my answers. But her eyes weren't certain that I wouldn't kill her.

"Do you know who he is?" I said.

"I think so, and he isn't any Frenchman."

"What is he?"

"I'll tell you," she said crisply, as if she had decided on her story. "I happened to be the confidential secretary to a very important businessman in the Southland. This man who calls himself Martel wormed his way into my employer's good graces and wound up as his executive assistant."

"Where does he come from?"

"I wouldn't know that," she said. "He's some kind of South American, I think. My employer made the mistake of giving him the combination to the safe. I warned him not to. So what happens? Mr. so-called Martel takes off with a fortune in bearer bonds, which Harry and me—and I are trying to get back."

"Why not the police?"

She was ready with an answer. "My employer has a soft spot in his head for Mr.. Martel. Also our business is highly confidential."

"What is your business?"

"I'm not in a position to reveal that," she said carefully. She shifted the position of her body, as if its substantiality and symmetry might divert my attention from the jerry-built flimsiness of her story. "My employer has sworn me to secrecy."

"What's his name?"

"You'd know his name if I could tell it to you. He's a very important and well-heeled man in certain circles."

"The lower circles of hell?"

"What?" But I think she heard me.

She pouted, and frowned a little with her thin painted-on eyebrows. She didn't frown very hard because that gave girls wrinkles and besides I might kill her and she didn't want to die with a frown on her lovely face.

"If you'd take me seriously and help to get the money back, etcetera, I'm sure my employer would reward you handsomely. I'd be grateful, too."

"I'd have to know more about it," such as what she meant by "etcetera."

"Sure," she said. "Naturally. Are you going to help me?"

"We'll see. Have you given up on Harry?"

"I didn't say that."

But her green eyes were surprised. I think in her concentration on me and on her story—her late late movie story—she had forgotten Harry. The room provided roles for only two people. I guessed what mine would be if we stayed in it much longer. Her body was purring at me like a tiger, the proverbial kind of tiger which is dangerous to mount and even more dangerous to dismount.

"I'm worried about Harry," I said. "Have you seen him today?"

She shook her head. Her hair flared out like fire. The wind, momentarily louder than the music, was whining at the window.

"He was talking about buying a gun this afternoon."

"What for?" Gun talk seemed to frighten her basically.

"To use on Martel, I think. Martel gave him a bad time today. He ran him off with a gun and smashed his camera." I produced the flattened camera from my pocket.

She brooded over it. "That camera cost me a hundred and fifty bucks. I ought to've known better than to trust Harry."

"Maybe the picture bit wasn't a good idea. Martel is allergic to cameras. What's his real name, by the way?"

"I don't know. He keeps using different names." She changed the subject back to Harry: "You think Harry got hurt or something?"

"It's possible. His car is parked on the boulevard about half a mile from here, with the key in it."

She jerked herself upright. "Why didn't you say so?"

"I just did."

"Show it to me."

She picked up her radio and bag, got her coat out of the closet,and put it on while we were waiting for the elevator. It may have been the noise of the elevator, or the radio, or some perpetual sign which her body sent out, but when she crossed the lobby with me all three of the sharpies were watching from the curtained doorway of the Samoa Room.

We drove along the boulevard. The rising wind buffeted the car. Out to sea I could make out occasional whitecaps. Faintly phosphorescent, they rose up like ghosts which were quickly swept backward into darkness. The woman peered out along the empty beaches. She turned up the window on the ocean side.

"Are you okay, Mrs. Hendricks?"

"I'm okay, but please don't call me that." She sounded younger and less sure of herself. "It makes me feel like a phoney. Call me Kitty if you like."

"You're not Mrs. Hendricks?"

"Legally I am, but we haven't been living together. Harry would have divorced me long ago, only he's a practicing Catholic. And he has this crazy hope that I'll come back to him." She leaned forward to peer out of my side. "We've gone a half a mile. Where is his car?"

I couldn't find it. She began to get nervous. I turned my car and found the hole in the hedge and the fire behind it, which had burned down rapidly to a few breathing coals among the ashes. The three wine-drinkers had blown, leaving their empty jug and the smell of spilled wine.

Kitty Hendricks called to me: "What are you dong? Is Harry there?"

"No."

She came through the hedge. She still had her bag and radio looped over the wrist, and the radio was singing like a semidetached personality. She looked around her, hugging her coat to her body. There was nothing to see but the dying fire, the railroad tracks gleaming dully in the starlight, the trampled unlovely earth.

"Holy Mother," Kitty said, "It hasn't changed in twenty years."

"You know this place?"

"I ought to. I was born about two blocks from here. On the other side of the tracks." She added wryly: "*Both* sides of the tracks are the wrong side if you live close enough to them. The trains used to rattle the dishes in my mother's kitchen." She peered across the dark railroad yard. "For all I know my mother is still living there."

"We could go and see."

"No! I don't have enough left to put up a front for her, too. I mean, let bygones be bygones."

She made an unsettled movement toward the cypress hedge, as if the place might betray her into further candor. She could handle the dangers of a hotel room, but not the demands of the wild outer night.

Her feeling turned against me. "Why did you bring me here?"

"It was your idea."

"But you said that Harry's car—"

"Apparently it's been stolen."

She backed away from me, stumbling on her heels, into the ragged black branches of the cypress. All I could see was the pale shape of her face and glints of her eyes and mouth.

"There never was any car. What kind of a car was it?"

"A Cadillac."

"Now I know you're lying. Where would Harry get a Cadillac?"

"He probably took it off the lot. It's an old one."

She didn't seem to be following me. I heard her breath coming more rapidly.

"There never was any car," she whispered. "You're from Vegas, aren't you? And you brought me here to kill me."

"That's silly talk, Kitty."

"Don't you call me Kitty." Her voice was taking on more childish cadences. Perhaps her mind was tracking on something that had happened years ago, between the trains rattling her mother's dishes. "You conned me into coming to this place, and now you won't let me go."

"Go ahead. Go. Go-go."

She only backed deeper into the cypress, like a nocturnal animal. Her radio was trilling from the darkness. A gust of her perfume reached me, mixed with the smells of diesel oil and wine and fire.

I saw in a red flash of insight how two people and a set of circumstances might collaborate in an unpredictable murder. Almost, I thought, she wanted to be murdered. She huddled among the shadows, whimpering:

"You stay away from me, I'll tell my old man."

"Get out of there, stupid."

The scream for which she'd been tuning up came out. I reached for her blindly and got her by the waist and pulled her towards me. She gasped, and swung the radio at my head. It struck me a glancing blow and fell silent, as if the musical side of Kitty's personality had died a violent death.

I let her go. She ran away gawkily on her high heels, across the multiple tracks, until she was no more than a scrambling shadow, a hurrying sound in the night.

XIII

ERIC MALKOVSKY'S STUDIO in the Village was on the direct route to Martel's house. I stopped to see how he was getting on with his search. He had dust on his hands and fingerprints on his forehead, like a human clue.

"I almost gave up on you," he said.

"I almost gave up on myself. Did you find any pictures of her?"

"Five. I may have more."

He took me in to the back of the shop and laid them out

on a table like a poker hand. Four of them were pictures of Kitty, in a plain white bathing suit, taken at the Tennis Club pool. She stood and gazed romantically out to sea. She reclined erotically on a chaise longue. She posed dry on the diving board. Kitty had been a beautiful girl, but all four pictures were spoiled by her awkward staginess.

The fifth picture was different. Unposed and fully clothed in a sleeveless summer dress and a wide hat, she sat at a table with a drink at her elbow. A man's hand with a square-cut diamond on it lay on the table beside her arm. The rest of him was cut off, but Kitty seemed to be smiling in his direction. Behind her I could see the patio wall of one of the Tennis Club cottages overgrown with bougainvillea.

"This is the one she liked." Malkovsky showed me the notation on the back: six 4 x 6 copies @ 5.00–30.00 Pd. September 27, 1959. "She bought six copies, or her husband did. He was in the picture, too, but he made me crop it."

"Why?"

"I remember he said something about beauty and the beast. He wasn't that bad-looking but he was older, like I told you. And he'd taken some punishment in his time."

"What was his name?"

"I don't remember. I suppose I could check it out in the club records."

"Tonight?"

"If Mrs. Strome lets me. But it's getting awful late."

"Don't forget you're on double time."

He scratched at his hairline, and colored slightly, "Could I see a little of the money please?"

I looked at my watch. I had hired him roughly two hours ago. "How about fourteen dollars?"

"Fine. Incidentally," he said with further scratching of his head, "if you want any of these pictures it's only fair that you should pay me for them. Five dollars apiece."

I gave him a twenty-dollar bill. "I'll take the one she liked. I don't suppose there's any chance you could find the rest of it, the part you cropped off?"

"I might be able to find the negative."

"For that I'll pay higher."

"How much higher?"

"It depends on what's on it. Twenty dollars anyway."

I left him rooting enthusiastically among the dusty cartons on his shelves, and drove back into the foothills. This was the direction the wind was coming from. It rushed down the canyons like a hot torrent, and roared in the brush around the Bagshaw house. I had to brace myself against it when I got out of the car.

The Bentley was gone from the courtyard. I tried the front door of the house. It was locked.

There was no light in the house, and no response of any kind to my repeated knocking. I went back to the studio in the Village. With a twenty-dollar glint in each eye Malkovsky showed me the negative of the picture of Kitty.

Beside her sat a man in a striped suit, which was wrinkled by his heavy shoulders and heavy thighs. He was almost bald, but compensating curly hair, white in the negative, sprouting up through his open shirt collar. His black smile had a loose, bland empty cheerfulness which his narrow white eyes annulled.

Behind him near the patio wall, and out of focus, was a mustached young man in a busboy's jacket, holding a tray in his hands. He looked vaguely familiar: perhaps he was one of the servants I'd seen around the club.

"I should have a name for these people," Eric said. "Actually, it's just good luck that I found the negative."

"We can check them out at the club, as you suggested. Do you remember anything more about the man? Were he and the woman married?"

"They certainly acted that way. She did, that is. He was in poor health, and she fussed over him quite a bit."

"What was the matter with him?"

"I don't know. He couldn't move around much. He spent most of his time in his cottage or in the patio, playing cards."

"Who did he play with?"

"Various people. Don't get the idea that I saw much of the guy. The fact is, I avoided him."

"Why?"

"He was a rough customer, sick or not. I didn't like the way he talked to me, as if I was some kind of a flunky. I'm a professional man," he asserted.

I knew how Eric felt. I was a semi-professional man myself. I gave him another twenty dollars, and we drove in separate cars to the club.

Ella opened up the records room behind the manager's office, and Eric plunged in among the filing cabinets. He had a date to work from: Kitty's pictures had been paid for on September 27, 1959.

I went back to the pavilion. The music was still going on, but the party had narrowed down to its hard core and shifted its main focus to the bar. It wasn't late, as parties go, but in my absence most of the people had deteriorated, as if a sudden illness had fallen on them: manic-depressive psychosis, or a mild cerebral hemorrhage.

Only the bartender hadn't changed at all. He made the drinks and served them and stood back from the party, watching it with his quicksilver eyes. I showed him the picture of Kitty, and the negative.

He held it up to the fluorescent light at the back of the bar. "Yeah, I remember the man and the girl. She came in here with him one night and tried to get tight on B and B—that's all she knew about drinking—and she had a coughing fit. She had about four or five recruits patting her on the back at once and her husband started pushing them around. Me and Mr. Fablon got him calmed down, though."

"How did Mr. Fablon get into the act?"

"He was with them."

"They were friends of his?"

"I wouldn't want to say that, exactly. He was just with them. They drifted in together. Maybe he liked the woman. She was a knockout, I'll give her that."

"Was Fablon a woman chaser?"

"You're putting words into my mouth. He liked women. He didn't chase 'em. Some of them chased him. But he'd have more sense than mess with that dame. Her husband was bad news."

"Who is he, Marco?"

He shrugged. "I never saw him before or since, and I haven't been sitting around waiting to hear from him. He was bad news, a blowtop, a muscle."

"How did he get in?"

"He was staying here. Some of our members can't say no when they get asked for a guest card. It would save me a lot of trouble if they could learn to say no." He looked around the room with a kind of contemptuous tolerance. "Make you a drink?"

"No thanks."

Marco leaned toward me across the bar. "Maybe I shouldn't tell you this, but Mrs. Fablon was in here a little while ago."

"So?"

"She asked the same question you did, whether I thought her husband committed suicide. She knew him and I were friends, like. I told her no, I didn't think so."

"What did she say?"

"She didn't have a chance to say anything. Dr. Sylvester came into the bar and took her over. She wasn't looking too good."

"What do you mean?"

He moved his head in a quick negative gesture.

A woman came up and asked for a double scotch. She was behind me, and I didn't recognize her changed voice until she spoke.

"My husband's been drinking double scotches and I say what's sauce for the goose is sauce for the gander and vice versa."

"Okay, Mrs. Sylvester, if you say so."

Marco laid down the photograph and the negative on the bartop and poured her a very meager double scotch. She reached past me with both hands and picked up both the drink and the picture of Kitty. "What's this? I love to look at pictures."

"That's mine," I said.

Her whisky-stunned eyes didn't seem to recognize me. "But you don't mind if I look at it?" she said argumentatively. "That's Mrs. Ketchel, isn't it?"

"Who?"

"Mrs. Ketchel," she said.

"A friend of yours?"

"Hardly." She drew herself erect. Her bouffant hair was slipping down her forehead like a wig. "Her husband was one of my husband's patients at one time. A doctor can't pick and choose his patients, you know."

"I share the problem."

"Of course," she said. "You're the detective, aren't you? What are you doing with a picture of Mrs. Ketchel?"

She waved it in my face. For a moment all the people at the bar were looking in our direction. I took the picture out of her hands and put it and the negative back in my pocket.

"You can trust me with your dark secrets," she said. "I am a doctor's wife."

I slid off my stool and drew her away from the bar to an empty table. "Where's Dr. Sylvester?"

"He drove Henrietta Fablon home. She's—she was not in a good way. But he'll be back."

"What's the matter with Mrs. Fablon?"

"What isn't?" she said lightly. "Marietta a friend of mine, one of the oldest friends I have in this town, but she's certainly let herself go to pieces lately, physically *and* morally. I have no objection to people getting plastered—I'm slightly plastered myself, as a matter of fact, Mr. Arch—"

"Archer."

She went right on: "But Marietta came here really looped tonight. She walked in, if walking is the word, literally rubber-legged. George had to gather up the pieces and take her home. She's getting to be more and more of a burden to George."

"In what respect?"

"Morally and financially. She hasn't paid her bill, of course, within living memory, and that's all right, I suppose. She's a friend, live and let live. But when it comes to scrounging more money from him, that's too much."

"Has she been doing that?"

"Has she? Today she invited him for lunch—I happened

to be at the hairdresser's—and made a sudden pitch for five thousand dollars. We don't have that kind of ready money in the bank, which is the only way I know about it—he tried to get my signature on the loan. But I said nix." She paused, and her alcohol-angered face grew suddenly quiet with anxiety. I think her mind was playing back what she had said. "I've been telling you my deep dark secrets, haven't I?"

"It's all right."

"It isn't all right if you tell George what I said. You won't tell George what I said?" She had unloaded her malice but she didn't want to take the responsibility for it.

"All right," I said.

"You're nice." She reached for my hand on the tabletop and pressed it rather hard. She was more worried now than she was drunk, trying to think of something to make herself feel better. "Do you like dancing, Mr. Arch?"

"Archer."

"I love to dance myself."

Still holding on to my hand she rose and towed me out onto the dance floor. Round and round we went, with her hair slipping down into both our eyes and her breasts bouncing against me like the special organs of her enthusiasm.

"My first name is Audrey," she confided. "What's your first name, Mr. Arch?"

"Fallen."

Her laughter blasted my right ear-drum. When the music stopped I took her back to the table, and went out to the front office. Ella was still at her post, looking rather wan.

"Are you tired?" I asked her.

She glanced at herself in the wall mirror facing her desk. "Not so very. It's the music. It gets on my nerves when I'm not allowed to dance to it." She passed her hand over her forehead. "I don't know how much longer I can hold this job."

"How long have you been at it?"

"Just two years."

"What did you do before that?"

"I was a housewife. Actually I didn't do much of

anything.'' She changed the subject: ''I saw you dancing with Mrs. Sylvester.''

''Legwork.''

''I don't mean that,'' she said, not explaining what 'that' was. ''Be careful of Audrey Sylvester. She isn't a drunk exactly, but when she drinks she gets drunk.''

''What does she do then?''

''Anything that enters her head. Midnight swim in the ocean. Midnight roll in the hay.''

''Same midnight?''

''I wouldn't be surprised.''

''Can she be believed?''

''Depends on who and what she's talking about.''

''Her.'' I got out my picture of Kitty. ''She says her name is Ketchel, and her husband was one of Dr. Sylvester's patients.''

''I presume she'd know.''

''Speaking of Dr. Sylvester's patients, I understand he took Mrs. Fablon home.''

Ella nodded soberly. ''I helped her out to his car. It took two of us.''

''Was she plastered?''

''I doubt it. She hardly drinks at all.''

''Mrs. Sylvester says she was.''

''Mrs. Sylvester isn't a reliable witness, especially when she's drunk herself. Marietta—Mrs. Fablon was more sick than anything else, and upset. She's much more upset about Ginny than she lets on.''

''Did she say so?''

''Not in so many words. But she came down here for reassurance. She wanted someone to tell her that she had done the right thing in encouraging Ginny's elopement.''

''She knows about it then?''

Ella nodded. ''Ginny came home tonight. She wanted to pick up a few things and say goodbye. She didn't stay more than about five minutes. Which is what upset her mother, basically, I think.''

''When was this?''

''In the last hour or so.''

"You're a good witness. How would you like to join my staff permanently?"

"It would depend on what I had to witness."

We smiled at each other, warily. We had both had unsuccessful marriages.

I retreated into the records room. Malkovsky was bent over the pulled-out drawer of a cabinet, riffling through file cards.

"I'm making some progress. I hope. As far as I can see there were seven outside guests, individuals and couples in September of 1959. I've ruled out four of them—people I remember personally, mostly repeaters. That leaves three: the Sandersons, and the de Houvenels, and the Berglunds. But none of the names rings a bell."

"Try Ketchel."

"Ketchel!" He blinked and smiled. "I believe that's the name. I couldn't find it among the guest cards, though."

"It could have been taken out."

"Or lost," he said. "These older files are in a pretty poor shape. But I'm morally certain Ketchel is the name. Where did you pick it up from?"

"From one of the members." I got out the negative. "Can you make me some copies of this?"

"I don't see why not."

"How long would it take you?"

"I guess I could have some by tomorrow."

"Tomorrow morning at eight?"

After a moment's hesitation, he said: "I can try."

I gave him the negative, with a lecture about not losing it, and said goodnight to him at the front door. When he was out of hearing, Ella said dryly:

"I hope you're paying him decently. All he makes out of his photography is a bare living. And he has a wife and children."

"I'm paying him decently. There's no record in the files of the Ketchels being guests here."

"Mrs. Sylvester could have given you the wrong name."

"I doubt it. Eric recognized it. More likely someone took the record out of the files. Are they easily accessible?"

"I'm afraid they are. People are in and out of the office, and the records room is open a good deal of the time. Is it very important?"

"It may be. I want to know who sponsored the Ketchels as guests."

"Mr. Stoll might remember. But he's gone off for the night."

She directed me to the manager's cottage. It was closed and dark. The wind whimpered like a lost dog in the shrubbery.

I went back to the main entrance of the club. Dr. Sylvester still hadn't returned. I looked in at the bar, saw Mrs. Sylvester slouched over a drink, and retreated before she saw me.

Ella told me more about her second marriage. Her husband Strome was an attorney in the city, an older man, a widower when she married him. She had been his secretary originally, but being his wife was much more demanding, in subtle ways. Her first husband had been too young; her second was too old. An older man was deeply set in his habits, including sexual habits.

I let the conversation go on. Such desultory continuing conversations were one of my best sources of information. Besides I liked the woman, and I was interested in her marriage.

The story of it blended with the long rough night we were having. She'd stayed with Strome for six years but in the end she couldn't stick it out. She hadn't even asked for alimony.

Some people left the party, and Ella said goodnight to them by name. Others were staying on. Our conversation, or Ella's monologue, was punctuated by gusts of music, laughter, wind.

Dr. Sylvester's arrival brought it to a full stop. He pushed through the door with angry force.

"Is my wife still here?" he asked Ella.

"I think so, doctor."

"What kind of shape is she in?"

"She's still upright," I said.

He turned a stony eye on me. "Nobody asked you." He started off toward the bar, hesitated, and turned back to Ella: "Would you get her for me, Mrs. Strome? I don't feel like facing that mob again tonight."

"I'll be glad to. How is Mrs. Fablon?"

"She'll be all right. I got her calmed down. She's upset about her daughter, and it was complicated by barbiturates."

"She didn't try to take too many?"

"Nothing like that. She took regular sleeping pills and then decided to come down here to see her friends. Add one drink and the result was predictable." He paused, and dropped his professional tone: "Go and get Audrey, will you?"

Ella hurried away down the lighted corridor. I leaned on the reception desk and watched Dr. Sylvester in the mirror. He lit a cigarette and pretended to forget me, but my presence seemed to make him uncomfortable. He coughed smoke and said:

"Look here, what gives you the right to stand there watching me? Are you the new doorman or something?"

"I'm bucking for the job. The wages are poor but think of the fringe benefits, like getting to know all the best people."

"You're bucking to get thrown out on your ear." His jaw had converted itself into a blunt instrument. His hands were shaking.

He was big enough to hit, and unpleasant enough, but everything else about the occasion was wrong. Besides, he was in transit from one troubled woman to another, and it gave him a certain license.

"Take it easy, doctor. We're on the same side."

"Are we?" He looked at me over his cigarette, smoke crawling on his face. Then, as if its burning tip had touched off his outburst, he threw it down on the marble floor and scotched it under his heel. "I don't even know what the game is," he said in a friendlier tone.

"It's a new kind of game." I didn't have the negative of Kitty and Ketchel, so I described it to him. "The man in the picture, the one with the diamond ring, do you know who he'd be?"

It was an honesty test, but I didn't know whose honesty was being tested, his or his wife's.

He hedged: "It's difficult to tell from a verbal description. Does he have a name?"

"It may be Ketchel. I heard he was your patient."

"Ketchel." He stroked his jaw as if to massage it back into human shape. "I believe I did have a patient of that name once."

"In 1959?"

"It might have been. It might well have been."

"Did he stay here?"

"I believe he did."

I showed him Kitty's picture.

He nodded. "That's Mrs. Ketchel. I couldn't be mistaken about her. She came to my office once, before they left, to get instructions about a salt-free diet. I treated her husband for hypertension. His blood pressure was way up, but I managed to bring it down within the normal range."

"Who is he?"

Sylvester's face went through the motions of remembering. "A retired man from New York. He told me he got in at the start of the bull market, lucky stiff. He owned a cattle spread somewhere in the Southwest."

"In California?"

"I don't remember, at this late date."

"Nevada?"

"I doubt it. I'm hardly famous enough to attract out-of-state patients." The remark seemed forced.

"Would Ketchel's address be in the clinic records?"

"It might, at that. But why are you so interested in Mr. Ketchel?"

"I don't know yet. I just am." I threw him a question from far left field. "Wasn't it just about then that Roy Fablon committed suicide?"

The question took him by surprise. For a moment his face was trying on attitudes. It settled on a kind of false boredom just behind which his intelligence sat and watched me.

"Just about when?"

"The picture of the Ketchels was taken in September 1959. When did Fablon die?"

"I'm afraid I don't remember exactly."

"Wasn't he your patient?"

"I have a number of patients and, frankly, my chronological memory isn't so good. I suppose it was around about that time but if you're suggesting any connection—"

"I'm asking, not suggesting."

"Just what are you asking, again?"

"Did Ketchel have anything to do with Fablon's suicide?"

"I have no reason to think so. Anyway, how would I know?"

"They were both friends of yours. In a sense you may have been the connection between them."

"I was?" But he didn't argue the point. He didn't want to go into it at all.

"I've heard it suggested that Fablon didn't commit suicide. His widow raised the question again tonight. Did she raise it with you?"

"She did not," he said, without looking at me. "You mean he was drowned by accident?"

"Or murdered."

"Don't believe everything you hear. This place is a hotbed of rumors. People don't have enough to do, so they make up rumors about their friends and neighbors."

"This wasn't exactly a rumor, Dr. Sylvester. It was an opinion. A friend of Fablon's told me he wasn't the sort of man to commit suicide. What's your opinion?"

"I have none."

"That's strange."

"I don't think so. Any man is capable of suicide, given sufficient pressure of circumstances."

"What were the special circumstances of Fablon's suicide?"

"He was at the end of his rope."

"Financially, you mean?"

"And every other way."

He didn't have to explain what he meant. Towed by Ella, his wife hove into view. She had slipped another mental disc and was in a further stage of drunkeness. Her mouth was set in grooves of dull belligerence. Her eyes were fixed.

"I know where you've been. You've been in bed with her, haven't you?"

"You're talking nonsense." He fended her off with his hands. "There's nothing between me and Marietta. There never has been, Aud."

"Except five thousand dollars' worth of something."

"It was supposed to be a loan. I still don't know why you wouldn't co-operate."

"Because we'd never get it back, any more than the other money you've thrown away. It's my money just as much as yours, remember. I worked for seven years so that you could get your degree. And what did I ever get out of it? The money comes in and the money goes out but I never see any of it."

"You get your share."

"Marietta gets *more* than her share."

"That's nonsense. Do you want her to go under?" He looked from me to Ella. Throughout the interchange with his wife, he had been talking to all three of us. Now that his wife was thoroughly discredited, he said: "Don't you think you better come home? You've made enough of a spectacle of yourself for one night."

He reached for her arm. She backed away from him grimacing, trying to recover the feel of her anger. But she was entering a fourth, lugubrious stage.

Still backing away, she bumped into the mirror. She turned around and looked at herself in it. From where I stood I could see her reflected face, swollen with drink and malice, surmounted by a loosened sheaf of hair, with a little trickle of terror in the eyes.

"I'm getting old and heavy," she said. "I can't even afford to take a week in residence at the health farm. But you can afford to gamble our money away."

"I haven't gambled in seven years, and you know it."

Roughly he put his arm around her, and walked her out. She was tangle-footed, like a heavyweight fighter at the end of a bad round.

XIV

THERE WERE LIGHTS in the Jamieson house as I passed, and a single light in Marietta Fablon's. It was after midnight, a poor time for visiting. I went to see Marietta anyway. Her husband's drowned body seemed to be floating just below the surface of the night.

She took a long time to answer my knock. When she did, she opened a Judas window set in the door, and peered at me through the grille. She said above the sound of the wind:

"What do you want?"

"My name is Archer—"

She cut in on me sharply: "I remember you. What do you want?"

"A chance to talk seriously with you."

"I couldn't possibly talk tonight. Come back in the morning."

"I think we should talk now. You're worried about Ginny. So am I."

"Who said I was worried?"

"Dr. Sylvester."

"What else did he say about me?"

"I could tell you better inside."

"Very well. This is rather Pyramus and Thisbe, isn't it?"

It was a gallant effort to recover her style. I saw when she let me in to the lighted hallway that she was having a bad night. The barbiturates were still playing tricks with her eyes. Her body, uncorseted under a pink quilted robe, seemed to have slumped down on its fine bones. She had a pink silk cap on her head, and under it her face seemed thinner and older.

"Don't look at me please, I'm not lookable tonight."

She took me into her sitting room. Though she only turned on one lamp I could see that everything in the room, the print-covered chairs and settee and the gay rug and the drapes, was faintly shabby. The only new thing in the room was the pink telephone.

I started to sit on one of the fragile chairs. She made me sit on another, and took a third herself, by the telephone.

"Why did you suddenly get concerned about Ginny?" I said.

"She came home tonight. He was with her. I'm close to my daughter—at least I used to be—and I could sense that she didn't want to go with him. But she was going anyway."

"Why?"

"I don't understand it." Her hands fluttered in her lap, like birds, and one of them pecked at the other. "She seems afraid to go, and afraid *not* to go with him."

"Go where?"

"They wouldn't say. Ginny promised to get in touch with me eventually."

"What was his attitude?"

"Martel? He was very formal and distant. Aggressively polite. He regretted disturbing me at the late hour, but they'd made a sudden decision to leave." She paused, and turned her narrow probing face toward me. "Do you really think the French government is after him?"

"Somebody is."

"But you don't know who."

"Not yet. I want to try a name on you, Mrs. Fablon. Ketchel."

I spelled it. Her queer eyes widened. Her hands clenched knuckle to knuckle.

"Who gave you that name?"

"No one person. The name came up. I take it it's familiar to you."

"My husband knew a man named Ketchel," she said. "He was a gambler." She leaned toward me. "Did Dr. Sylvester give you that name?"

"No, but I understand that Ketchel was one of Dr. Sylvester's patients."

"Yes. He was. He was more than that."

I waited for her to explain what she meant. Finally I said: "Was Ketchel the gambler who took your husband's money?"

"Yes, he was. He took everything we had left, and wanted more. When Roy couldn't pay him—" She paused, as if she sensed that melodrama didn't go with her style. "We won't discuss it any more, Mr. Archer. I'm not at my best tonight. I should never have agreed to talk to you, under these conditions."

"What was the date of your husband's suicide?"

She rose, swaying a little, and moved towards me. I could smell her fatigue.

"You've really been digging into our lives, haven't you? The date, if you must know, was September 29, 1959."

Two days after Malkovsky was paid for his pictures. The coincidence underlined my feeling that Fablon's death was part of the present case.

Mrs. Fablon peered up at me. "That date seems to mean a great deal to you."

"It suggests some possibilities. It must mean a great deal more to you."

"It was the end of my life." She took an unsteady step backwards and sat down again, as if she were falling back into the past, helplessly but not unwillingly. "Everything since has been going through the motions. It's a strange thing. Roy and I fought like animals throughout our marriage. But we loved each other. At least I was in love with him, no matter what he did."

"What did he do?"

"Everything a man can think of. Most of it cost money. My money." She hesitated. "I'm not a money-oriented person, really. That was one of the troubles. In every marriage there should be one partner who cares about money more than other things. Neither of us cared. In the eighteen years of our marriage we went through nearly a million dollars. Please notice the first person plural pronoun. I share the blame. I didn't learn to care about money until it was too late." She stirred, and jerked her shoulders as if the thought of money was a palpable weight on them.

"You said the date of my husband's death suggested possibilities. What do you mean?"

"I'm wondering if he really killed himself."

"Of course he did." The statement sounded perfunctory, empty of feeling.

"Did he leave a suicide note?"

"He didn't have to. He announced his intention to me and Ginny a day or two before. God knows what it's done to my daughter's emotional life. I encouraged this Martel business because he was the only real man she's shown any interest in. If I've made a dreadful mistake—"

She dropped the end of the sentence, and returned to her first subject. Her mind was running in swift repetitious circles like a squirrel in a cage. "Can you imagine a man saying such a thing to his wife and his seventeen-year-old daughter? And then doing it? He was angry with me, of course, for running out of money. He didn't believe it could happen. There had always been another bequest coming in from some relative, or another house or piece of land we could sell. But we were down to a rented house and there were no more relatives to die. Roy died instead, by his own hand."

She kept insisting on this, almost as if she was trying to convince me, or persuade herself. I suspected that she was a little out of control, and I had no desire to ask her any more questions. But she went on answering unspoken questions, painfully and obsessively, as if the past had stirred and was talking through her in its sleep:

"That doesn't cover the situation, of course. There are always secret motivations in life—urges and revenges and desires that people don't admit even to themselves. I discovered the real source of my husband's death, quite by accident, just the other day. I'm planning to give up this house and I've been going through my things, sorting and throwing away. I came across a batch of old papers in Roy's desk, and among them was a letter to Roy from—a woman. It absolutely astonished me. It had never occurred to me that, in addition to all his other failings as a husband and father,

Roy had been unfaithful. But the letter went into explicit detail on that point."

"May I see it?"

"No. You may not. It was humiliating enough for me to read it by myself."

"Who wrote it?"

"Audrey Sylvester. She didn't sign it but I happen to know her handwriting."

"Was it still in its envelope?"

"Yes, and the postmark was clean. It was postmarked June 30, 1959, three months before Roy died. After seven years I understood why George Sylvester introduced Ketchel to Roy and stood by smiling while Ketchel cheated Roy out of thirty thousand dollars which he didn't have." She struck herself with her fist on her quilted thigh: "He may even have planned it all. He was Roy's doctor. He may have sensed that Roy was close to suicide, and conspired with Ketchel to push him over the edge."

"Isn't that stretching it a bit, Mrs. Fablon?"

"You don't know George Sylvester. He's a ruthless man. And you don't know Mr. Ketchel. I met him once at the club."

"I'd like to meet him myself. You don't know where he is, do you?"

"No, I do not. Ketchel left Montevista a day or so after Roy disappeared—long before his body was found."

"Are you implying that he knew your husband was dead?"

She bit her mouth, as if to punish it for saying too much. From her eyes I got the swift impression that my guess was accurate, and she knew it, but for some obscure reason she was covering it up.

"Did Ketchel murder your husband?"

"No," she said, "I don't suggest that. But he and George Sylvester were responsible for Roy's death." In the midst of her old grief and rage, she looked at me cautiously. I had the strange feeling that she was sitting apart from herself, playing on her own emotions the way another woman might play on an organ, but leaving one end of the keyboard wholly untouched. "It's indiscreet of me to tell you all this. I'll ask you not to pass it on to anyone, including—*especially* including—Peter and his father."

I was weary of her elaborate reconstructions and evasions. I said bluntly: "I won't pass your story on, and I'll tell you why, Mrs. Fablon. I don't entirely believe it. I don't think you believe it yourself."

She rose shakily. "How dare you speak to me in that way?"

"Because I'm really concerned about your daughter's safety. Aren't you?"

"You know I am. I'm terribly concerned."

"Then why won't you tell me the truth as you see it? Was your husband murdered?"

"I don't know. I don't know anything anymore. I had a real earthquake shock tonight. The ground was jerked right out from under me. It still isn't holding still."

"What happened?"

"Nothing *happened*. Something was said."

"By your daughter?"

"If I told you any more," she said, "I'd be telling you too much. I'm going to have to get more information before I speak out."

"Getting information is my business."

"I appreciate the offer, but I have to handle this my own way."

Another of her silences began, she sat perfectly still with her opposing fists pressed fiercely against each other, her eyes absorbing light.

Under the sound of the wind I heard a noise like rats chewing in the wall. I didn't connect it right away with Marietta Fablon. Then I realized that she was grinding her teeth.

It was time I left her in peace. I got my car out from under her groaning oak tree and drove next door to the Jamieson house. The lights were still on there.

XV

PETER'S FATHER ANSWERED the door. He had on pajamas and a bathrobe, and he looked even more transparent and withdrawn than he had in the morning.

"Come in, Mr. Archer, won't you? My housekeeper has gone to bed but I can offer you a drink. I was rather hoping you'd drop by, I have some information for you."

Talking as if it was the middle of the day, he led me along the hall to his library. His movements were uncertain but he managed to steer himself through the door and into his chair. There was a drink beside it. Jamieson seemed to be one of those drinkers who held themselves at a certain level of sobriety all day and all night.

"I'll let you make your own drink. My hands are a little unsteady." He raised his hands and examined their tremor with clinical interest. "I should be in bed, I suppose, but I've almost lost the ability to sleep. These night watches are the hardest. The image of my poor dead wife comes back most vividly. I feel my loss like a vast yawning emptiness, in me as well as the external universe. I forgot whether I've shown you a picture of my dead wife?"

Reluctantly I admitted that he hadn't. I had no desire to sit up all night with Jamieson and his irrigated memories. The drink I poured for myself from his fresh bottle was a careful ounce.

Jamieson groped in a leather box and produced a silver-framed photograph of a young woman. She wasn't especially pretty. There had to be other reasons for her husband's extended mourning. Maybe, I thought, grief was the only feeling he was capable of; or maybe it was just an excuse for drinking. I handed the photograph back to him.

"How long ago did she die?"

"Twenty-four years. My poor son killed her in being born. I try not to blame poor Peter, but it's hard sometimes, when I think of all I lost."

"You still have a son."

Jamieson's free hand made a small gesture, nervous and irritable. It said a good deal about his feelings for Peter, or his lack of them.

"Where is Peter, by the way?"

"He went out to the kitchen for a snack. He was on his way to bed. If you'd like to see him?"

"Later, perhaps. You said you had some information for me."

He nodded. "I talked to one of my friends at the bank. Martel's hundred thousand—actually it was closer to a hundred and twenty thousand—was deposited in the form of a draft on the *Banco de Nueva Granada*—the Bank of New Granada."

"I never heard of it."

"Neither had I, though I've been to Panama City. The New Granada has its headquarters in Panama City."

"Did Martel leave his hundred grand in the local bank?"

"He did not. I was coming to that. He withdrew every cent of it. In cash. The bank offered him a guard but he couldn't be bothered. He packed the money into a briefcase and tossed it into the back of his car."

"When did this happen?"

"Today at five minutes to three, just before the bank closed. He'd phoned first thing in the morning to make sure that they'd have the cash on hand."

"So he was already planning to leave this morning. I wonder where he went."

"Panama, perhaps. That seems to be the source of his money."

"I should report to your son. How do I find the kitchen?"

"It's at the other end of the hallway. You'll see the light. Come back and have another short one with me, won't you, afterwards?"

"It's getting late."

"I'll be glad to give you a bed."

"Thanks, I work better out of a hotel."

I made my way along the passageway toward the kitchen light. Peter was sitting at a table under a hanging lamp. Most of a roast goose lay on a wooden platter in front of him, and he was eating it.

I hadn't tried to soften the sound of my footsteps, but he hadn't heard me coming. I stood in the doorway and watched him. He was eating as I had never seen anyone eat. With both hands he tore chunks of flesh from the goose's breast and forced them into his mouth, the way you pack meat into a grinder. His face was distorted, his eyes almost invisible.

He tore off a drumstick and bit into its thick end. I crossed the kitchen toward him. The room was large and white and bleak. It reminded me of a disused handball court.

Peter looked up and saw me. He dropped the bird's leg guiltily as if it was part of a human body. His face was swollen tight and mottled, like a sausage.

"I'm hungry." His voice was fogged with grease.

"Still hungry?"

He nodded, with his dull eyes on the half-demolished bird. It lay in front of him like the carcass of his hopes.

I felt like getting out of there and sending him back the balance of his money. But I've always had trouble walking out on bad luck. I pulled up a chair and sat down across the table from him and talked him out of his stupor.

I don't remember everything I said. Mostly I tried to persuade the boy that he was within the human range. I do remember that my broken monologue was punctuated by a banging noise which came from the general direction of Marietta Fablon's house.

The first time I heard the noise, I thought it might be gunfire. I discounted this when it was repeated over and over at irregular intervals. More likely it was a shutter or an outside door banging in the wind.

Eventually Peter said in a clogged voice: "I apologize."

"Apologize to yourself."

"I beg your pardon?"

"Apologize to yourself. You're the one you're doing it to."

His face was like kneaded dough in the harsh light. "I don't know what gets into me."

"You should take it up with a doctor. It's a disease."

"You think I need a psychiatrist?"

"Most people do at one time or another. You're lucky you can afford one."

"I can't, though. Not really. I won't come into my real money for another year."

"Use your credit. You can afford a psychiatrist if you can afford me."

"You really think there's something the matter with my head?"

"Your heart," I said. "You have a hungry heart. You better find something to feed it with besides food."

"I know. It's why I have to get Ginny back."

"You need to do more than that. If she ever saw you on an eating binge—" It was a cruel sentence. I didn't finish it.

"She has," he said. "That's the trouble. As soon as people find out they turn against me. I suppose you'll be quitting too."

"No. I'd like to see things get straightened out for you."

"They'll never get straightened out. I'm hopeless."

He was trying to lean his full moral weight on me. I didn't want any more of it than I had, and I tried to objectify the situation a little.

"My grandmother who lived in Martinez was a religious woman. She always said it was sinful to despair."

He shook his head slowly. His eyes seemed to swing with the movement. A minute later he dashed for the kitchen sink and vomited.

While I was trying to clean it and him up, his father appeared in the doorway. He spoke across Peter as if he was deaf or moronic:

"Has my poor boy been eating again?"

"Lay off, Mr. Jamieson."

"I don't know what you mean." He raised his pale hands

as if to show what a gentle father he had been. "I've been both father and mother to my son. I've had to be."

Peter stood at the sink with his back to his father, unwilling to show his face. After a while his father drifted away again.

Attached to the great main kitchen, with its tiled counters and sinks and ovens, was a smaller outer kitchen like a glassed-in porch. I became aware of this outer kitchen because there was a noise at the door, a scrabbling and a snuffling which was nearer and more insistent than the banging noise.

"Do you have a dog out there?"

Peter shook his head. "It may be a stray. Let it in. We'll give it a piece of goose."

I turned on the light in the outer kitchen and opened the door. Marietta Fablon crawled in over the threshold. She rose to her knees. Her hands groped up my legs to my waist. There was blood like a dyer's error on her pink quilted breast. Her eyes were as wide and blind as silver coins.

"Shot me."

I got down and held her. "Who, Marietta?"

Her mouth worked. "Lover-boy." The residue of her life came out with the words. I could feel it leave her body.

XVI

PETER APPEARED in the kitchen doorway. He didn't come into the outer kitchen. Death took up all the room.

"What did she say?"

"She said lover-boy shot her. Who would she mean by that?"

"Martel." It was an automatic response. "Is she dead?"

I looked down at her. Death had made her small and dim, like something seen through the wrong end of a telescope.

"I'm afraid she is. You better call the county sheriff's office. Then tell your father."

"Do I have to tell him? He'll find a way to blame me."

"I'll tell him if you like."

"No. I will." He crossed the kitchen purposefully.

I went out into the blowing dark and got the flashlight out of my car. A well-defined path led from the Jamieson garden to the Fablon house. I wondered if Peter's childish feet had worn it.

There were evidences that Marietta had crawled along the path all the way from her house: spots of blood and knee marks in the dirt. Her pink silk cap had fallen off where the path went through a gap in the boundary hedge. I left it.

Her front door was banging. I went in and found the study. It was dominated by an ornate nineteenth-century desk. I went through the drawers. There was no sign of Audrey Sylvester's love-letter to Fablon, but I found a letter that interested me just as much. It had been written to Mrs. Fablon by Ricardo Rosales, a Vice-President of the Bank of New Granada, Panama City, in March 18 of this year. It said in rather stilted English that the special account from which the Bank had paid her periodic sums of money had been exhausted, and no further instructions had been received concerning it. Under the rules and regulations of the bank it was regrettably not possible for them to name their principal.

In a bottom drawer I came across a framed photograph of a young Air Force second lieutenant who was almost certainly Roy Fablon. The glass was missing from the frame, and small half-moon-shaped pieces of the photograph had been clumsily punched out. It took me a minute to come to the conclusion that it had been pierced repeatedly by the sharp heel of a woman's shoe. I wondered if Marietta had stamped on her husband's picture recently.

In the same drawer I found a man's thin wristwatch with four Latin words engraved on the back: *Mutuis animis amant amantur*. I didn't know Latin, but 'amant' meant something about love.

I looked at Fablon's picture again. To my instructed eyes his head was a cruel hollow-looking bronze. He had been dark and dashing, the kind of man a daughter could fall in love with. Though he had been handsome and Martel wasn't, I imagined I could see some resemblance between them, enough perhaps to account for Ginny's infatuation with Martel. I put the picture and the watch back in the drawer.

A light was burning in the sitting room where I had talked to Marietta, and listened to the grinding of her teeth. The cord of the pink telephone had been ripped out of the wall. There were spots of blood on the worn carpet. This was where her crawl had started.

I could hear a wailing in the distance now, louder than the wind and drearier. It was the sound of a siren, which nearly always came too late. I went outside leaving the light burning and the door banging behind me.

The Sheriff's men were in the Jamieson house before I got back to it. I had to explain who I was, and show them my photostat and get Peter to vouch for me before they would let me into the house. They refused to let me go back into the kitchen.

Their failure to co-operate suited me reasonably well. I felt justified in holding back some of the results of my own investigation. But I turned them loose on Martel. By two o'clock the officer in charge, Inspector Harold Olsen, came into the drawing room where I was waiting and told me he'd put out an all-points alarm for Martel. He added:

"You can go home now, Mr. Archer."

"I thought I'd stick around and talk to the coroner."

"I'm the coroner," Olsen said. "I told my deputy, Dr. Wills, not to bother coming out here tonight. He needs his rest. Why don't you go and get some rest, Mr. Archer?" He moved ponderously towards me, a big slow stubborn Swede who liked his suggestions to be taken as orders. "Relax and take it easy. We won't be getting autopsy results for a couple of days at least."

"Why not?" I said without getting up from my chair.

"We never do, that's why." He was in charge here, and his slightly bulging eyes were watching me for any questioning of his power. He gave the impression that if he had to choose he would rather own a case than solve it. "There's no hurry. She was shot in the chest, we know that now, probably through the lung. She bled to death internally."

"I'm interested in how her husband died."

"He was a suicide. You don't need Dr. Wills to tell you that. I handled the case myself." Olsen was watching me more closely. He was sensitive to the possibility that I might question his findings, and already quivering in advance with a faint sense of outrage. "It's a closed case."

"Doesn't this kind of reopen it?"

"No. It don't." He was retreating angrily into bad grammar. "Fablon committed suicide. He told his wife he was gonna, and he did it. There was no evidence of foul play."

"I thought he was badly bunged up."

"By sharks, and by the rocks. There's a lot of wave motion off of there, and it rolled him around on the bottom for ten days." Olsen made it sound a little like a threat. "But all the damage was done after he drowned. He died of drowning in salt water. Dr. Wills will tell you the same thing."

"Where can I find Wills tomorrow?"

"He's got an office in the basement of Mercy Hospital. But he can't tell you any more than I can."

Olsen left the room, wrapped in the brooding pride of a master craftsman, whose handiwork has been criticized by a journeyman. I waited until I couldn't hear his footsteps, then made my way to the library. The door was locked, but there was light under it.

"Who is it?" the housekeeper Vera said through the door.

"Archer."

She let me in. She had on a rayon sunburst kimono. When she sat down on the hassock at Jamieson's feet, I could see the two black braids hanging down her back like severed cables.

"It's a dreadful thing," he said weakly. "What do you make of it, Archer?"

"It's too soon to ask me that. Marietta said that lover-boy shot her. Does that have any special meaning to you?"

"No."

"Did she have a lover?"

"Certainly not to my knowledge."

"If she did have a lover, who would it be?"

"I have no idea. Frankly, I haven't had too much to do with the Fablons since Roy died, even before that. It's true we were close friends in college, and for a few years after, but our lives took different turnings. About Marietta's private life I'm completely ignorant. It does occur to me, though, that she may have meant somebody else's lover-boy."

"Martel, you mean?"

"It's the obvious thought, isn't it?"

"It's so obvious I'm afraid of it. But I did come across a peculiar connection between him and Marietta. She's been drawing some kind of an income from the Bank of New Granada."

"Marietta has?"

"That's right. It was cut off within the last couple of months."

"Who was the source of the income?"

"That isn't clear. It may have been Martel, and if it was it suggests a wild possibility. Marietta may have sold her daughter to him."

"She wouldn't do that!" Jamieson was as shocked as his anaesthetized condition would permit.

"Plenty of other mothers do. They don't call it selling, but that's what it boils down to. A debutante ball is the closest thing we have to the Sudanese slave markets."

Vera let out a ribald mirthless laugh. Her employer frowned severely at her, and said as if in rebuke:

"But Marietta is—was devoted to Ginny."

"She also knows how important money is. She told me so herself."

"Really? She used to throw her money around as if her resources were inexhaustible. I've had to bail her—"

Vera glanced up sharply, and Jamieson decided not to finish the sentence. I said:

"Maybe her daughter was the only resource she had left."

I was trying out the idea, and Jamieson sensed my purpose. "Possibly you could be right. Marietta's hardened in these last few years, since Roy died. But even assuming that you are right, why would she marry Virginia off to a dubious foreigner? She had my poor son Peter ready and willing."

"I don't know. The marriage may have been Ginny's idea after all. And the fact that Marietta and Martel got money from the same Panama bank may be pure coincidence."

"You don't believe it is, though?"

"No. I've lost my faith in pure coincidence. Everything in life tends to hang together in a pattern. Of course the clearest pattern so far in this case is death repeating itself. The fact that Mrs. Fablon was murdered brings up the question of her husband's death again."

"But wasn't it established that Roy killed himself?"

Vera frowned, as if he had said something obscene. Unobtrusively she crossed herself.

"That's the official story, anyway," I said. "It's open to question now. Everything is. I understand you identified his body."

"I was one of those who did."

"Are you certain it was Roy Fablon?"

He hesitated, and stirred in his chair uncomfortably. "I was certain at the time. That means I have to be certain now, doesn't it? It's not a memory I care to dwell on, frankly. His face was swollen, and terribly cut up."

Jamieson closed his eyes tight. Vera reached for his hand and held it.

"So you couldn't be certain it was him?"

"Not just by looking at him. He'd gone through quite a seachange. But I had no reason to doubt it was Roy, either. The doctor at the inquest, Dr. Wills, said he had irrefus—" He stumbled over the word—"irrefutable evidence that it was Roy."

"Do you recall what it was?"

"It had to do with X rays of the old fractures in his legs."

"That ought to take care of that, then."

"Of what?" he said rather irritably.

"The possibility that it was a faked suicide and that somebody else wore Fablon's overcoat into the ocean. It's a possibility worth considering when a man is deep in debt. But what you've just told me rules it out."

"I should think so."

"A minute ago," I said, "you started to tell me about bailing out Mrs. Fablon."

"That was in the distant past. I helped out both of them on occasion. In a way I felt responsible for Roy."

Vera stirred angrily. "You gave her the house."

"What house?"

Jamieson answered me: "The one she's living in—was living in. I didn't exactly give it to her. She had the use of it. After all she was kind to my poor son. And so was Roy in his time."

"Did he hit you for much?"

"A few thousand. It would have been more, but most of my capital was tied up in trust funds. Roy was desperate for money in his last days. He was gambling, with money that he didn't have."

"Gambling with a man named Ketchel?"

"Yes, that was his name."

"Did you know Ketchel?"

"I never met him, no. I heard about him."

"From whom?"

"From Marietta. During the ten or eleven days that Roy was missing, before his body came up, Marietta did quite a lot of talking about Ketchel. She seemed to suspect him of murdering Roy. But she had no evidence, and I dissuaded her from going to the police. After the fact of suicide was established, she dropped the idea."

Vera moved uneasily and tugged at Jamieson's hand, as if the dead woman was her subtle rival. "Come to bed, you're a crazy man sitting up all night."

The special proprieties of the house seemed to have broken down. I rose to go. Vera looked up with relief.

Jamieson said past her: "I assumed at the time that Marietta was fantasying about murder, simply because it was hard for her to face the fact of suicide. You don't suppose she had something after all?"

"Perhaps she did. Inspector Olsen tells me that Fablon definitely died by drowning in sea water. It could be a method of committing murder, though in this case it isn't a likely one. But I'd still like to talk to Ketchel. I don't suppose you know where I can find him?"

"I haven't the faintest idea. He's just a name to me."

Vera's eyes were on me, pushing me out.

The cops were still in the kitchen. Marietta wasn't. Neither was Peter. The big room had taken on an air of grimy official desolation which was familiar to me. I had once been a cop myself, on the Long Beach force, hardly more than a howitzer-throw from here.

XVII

I DROVE BACK toward the harbor by way of the ocean boulevard, to spend what was left of the night at the Breakwater Hotel. One or both of the Hendrickses might turn up there, though I didn't expect them to.

I found myself slowing down as I came near the hobo jungle. It was just as well I did, or I might not have noticed Harry's Cadillac. It was on a strip of grass on the ocean side, nosed into the trunk of a palm tree.

There had been a violent impact. The base of the tree was gashed. The Cadillac's heavy bumper had been forced back into the radiator. The shatterproof windshield was blurred in one place by a head mark. I found some spatterings of blood on the front seat.

Whoever had taken and wrecked the car had left the keys in the ignition. I did what I should have done before: used them to open the trunk.

Harry lay there with his back to me. I put my hand under his head and turned up his face. He had been badly beaten. Until he moaned I thought he might be dead.

I got my arms under his shoulders and legs and lifted him out. It was like delivering a big inert baby from an iron womb. I laid him out on the grass and looked around for help.

The wind hissed in the dry palm fronds overhead. There was nothing human in sight. But I didn't want to leave Harry. Somebody might steal him again.

I walked across the beach to wet my handkerchief in the water and got one of my feet wet, to no avail. Harry moaned when I wiped his face with the wet cloth, but he didn't come to. When I lifted one of his eyelids, all I could see was white.

I calculated that he had been unconscious in the trunk for six or seven hours: there wasn't much doubt in my mind that the blood on Martel's heel was Harry's blood: and I decided to get him to a hospital. I heaved him up in my arms again.

I was halfway to my car when a city patrol car with a red light on the roof drifted into sight. It stopped and an officer got out.

"What do you think you're doing?"

"This man was in an accident. I'm taking him to a hospital."

"We'll do that."

He was a young officer, with a keen edge on his voice. He lifted Harry out of my clutches and deposited him on the back seat of the patrol car. Then he turned back to me with his hand on his gun butt.

"Looks to me like he was beaten."

"Yeah."

"Let's see your hands. Come around in the headlights."

I showed him my hands under the white beam. A second officer got out of the driver's seat and came up behind me.

"I didn't beat him. You can see for yourself."

"Who did?"

"I wouldn't know." I didn't feel like going into the subject of Martel. "I saw the wrecked car and opened the trunk and he was in it. It's his car. I think it was stolen."

"You know him?"

"Slightly. His name is Harry Hendricks. We're both staying at the Breakwater Hotel. You can reach me there later if you want to." I told them who I was. "Right now you better get him to a hospital."

"Don't worry. We will."

"Which hospital?"

"It'll be County, unless you want to pay for him. Mercy asks for a one-day deposit."

"How much?"

"Twenty bucks, on the ward."

I gave him twenty of Peter's dollars. The officer said his name was Ward Rasmussen, and he would bring me a receipt from the hospital.

The lobby of the Breakwater Hotel was empty except for the ancient bellhop asleep on a settle. I touched him. He started and called out:

"Martha?"

"Who's Martha?"

He rubbed his bleared eyes. "I knew a girl Martha. Did I say Martha?"

"Yep."

"Must have been dreaming about her. I knew her in Red Bluff. Martha Truitt. I was born and raised in Red Bluff. That was a long time ago."

Eye-deep in time he trudged around behind the desk and let me register and gave me the key to room 28, which I asked for. The electric clock over his head said it was five minutes past three.

I asked the old man if the red-headed woman, Mrs. Hendricks, had come back to the hotel. He didn't remember. I left him shaking his head over Martha Truitt.

I fell into bed and dreamed about nothing at all. The wind died just before dawn. I heard the quiet and woke up wondering what was missing. Gray light fogged the window. I could hear the sea thumping like a beggar at the bottom of the town. I turned over and dropped back to sleep.

The telephone woke me. The desk said a policeman wanted to see me. It was full morning, a quarter to eight, by my watch.

While I thought of it, I phoned Eric Malkovsky's studio. He was there.

"Have you been up all night, Eric?"

"I get up early. I made some enlargements of that negative. Something came out on them that I want to show you."

"What is it?"

"I'd rather you saw them for yourself and drew your own conclusions."

"Can you bring them to the Breakwater Hotel?"

He said he could.

"I'll be either in room 28 or in the coffee shop."

I pulled on my clothes and went down to the lobby. The young officer, Rasmussen, was carrying Harry's pearl-gray hat. He handed me a receipt for twenty dollars.

"I hate to get you up so early," he said, "but I'm going off duty."

"It's time I was up. How's Harry?"

"He's coming out of it. They'll be shunting him off to County unless you deposit more money today."

"Does that make sense?"

"It's the way the hospital runs its business. I've seen people die on the way between Mercy and County. I don't mean that your friend is liable to die," he added carefully. "The doctor says he'll be okay."

"He isn't my friend, exactly."

"He must be twenty dollars' worth of a friend. Incidentally, if you're going out to the hospital you can give him his hat. I took it out of his car before the wreckers towed it away. It's a good hat, and he'll want it back."

He gave me the hat. I didn't bother pointing out that it had the wrong name in it. I was wondering who L. Spillman was, and how Harry got his hat.

"The car's totaled out," Rasmussen said. "It wasn't worth much, but auto theft is auto theft. We picked up three suspects, by the way. They made it easy for us. One of them got a cut head in the accident, and his buddies brought him to the emergency ward."

"The orange-pickers?"

"Pardon?"

"A white man and a couple of darker brothers?"

"You saw them, did you?" Rasmussen said.

"I saw them. What are you going to do with them?"

"It depends on what they did. I haven't figured it out yet. If they locked your friend in the trunk and drove him someplace, it's technically kidnapping."

"I don't think they knew he was in the trunk."

"Then who beat him up? The doctor said he took quite a clobbering, that he was beaten and kicked."

"I'm not surprised."

"Do you have any thoughts on who did it to him?"

"Yes, but it will take time."

He said he had plenty of time, all day in fact. I bought him breakfast, over his objections, and with his ham and eggs and coffee I made him the dubious gift of a piece of the Martel case.

Rasmussen listened intently. "You think Martel beat up Hendricks?"

"I'm morally certain he did—caught him spying on his house and let him have it. But there's not much point in speculating. Hendricks can tell us about it when he's able to talk."

Rasmussen sipped his coffee and made a bitter face. "How did Hendricks's car get down on the boulevard?"

"I think Martel drove it there, with Hendricks in the trunk, and left it where it would be liable to be stolen."

Ward Rasmussen looked at me sharply over his coffee cup. His eyes had the blue intensity of Bunsen flames. With his square jaw and disciplined young mouth it gave him a slightly fanatical look. "Who's this Martel? And why would Virginia Fablon marry him?"

"That's the question I'm working on. He claims to be a wealthy Frenchman who's in trouble with the French government. Hendricks says he's a cheap crook. Martel may be a crook, and I suspect he is, but he isn't a cheap one. He's traveling with a hundred grand in cash, in a Bentley, with the prettiest girl in town."

"I knew Virginia in high school," Rasmussen said. "She was a beautiful girl. And she had a lot on the ball. She made it to college when she was sixteen years old. She graduated from high school a whole semester ahead of the class."

"You seem to remember quite a lot about her."

"I used to follow her down the street," he said. "Just once I got up the nerve to ask her to go to a dance with me. That was when I was captain of the football team. But she was going with Peter Jamieson." A shadow of envy moved across his eyes. He lifted his crewcut head as if to shake it off. "It's funny she'd turn around and marry this Martel. You think he came to town to marry her?"

"That's what happened, anyway. I don't know what his original plans were."

"Where did he get the hundred thousand?"

"He deposited it in the form of a draft on a bank in Panama City, the Bank of New Granada. It fits in with his claim that his family has holdings in various foreign countries."

Rasmussen leaned across the table, elbowing his empty cup to one side. "It fits in equally well with the fact—the idea that he's a crook. A lot of criminal money gravitates to Panama, on account of their banking laws."

"I know. That's why I mentioned it. There's another thing. The woman who was shot last night, Virginia Fablon's mother, had an income from the same bank."

"How much of an income?"

"I don't know. You may be able to get the details from her local bank, the National."

"I'll give it a whirl." He took out a new-looking notebook.

While he was making some shorthand notes, Eric Malkovsky

arrived, carrying a manila envelope. I introduced the two men. Then Eric got his enlargements out of the envelope and spread them on the table.

They were about six-by-eight inches, fresh and clear as though they had been taken the day before. I could see every line on Ketchel's face. Though he was smiling, sickness lurked behind his smile. The lines around his mouth might just as well have meant dismay. He had the look of a man who had fought his way to the top, or what he considered the top, but took no pleasure in that or anything else.

In the enlargement, the meaning of Kitty's face had changed a little. Her eyes seemed to hold a faint suspicion that she was a woman who could do something better than just wear clothes. But in the Kitty I had met last night, here in the Breakwater Hotel, the suspicion seemed to have died and left no trace.

"You did a good job, Eric. These pictures will be a big help."

"Thanks." But he was impatient with me. He reached across me and stabbed at the top picture with his forefinger. "Take a good look at the man in the background, the one holding the tray."

Almost immediately I saw what he meant. Behind the busboy's wide black mustache I recognized a younger version of Martel.

"He was nothing but a waiter at the club," Malkovsky said. "Not even a waiter. A busboy. And I let him walk all over me."

Rasmussen said politely: "May I see one of those?"

I handed him the top picture, and he studied it. The waitress came to the table with a pot of coffee and a breakfast menu spotted with samples of past breakfasts. The waitress herself wore visible clues to her history, in her generous mouth and disappointed eyes, her never-say-die blonde hair, her bunion limp.

"You want to order?" she said to Eric.

"I've already eaten breakfast. I'll have some coffee."

I said that I would, too. The waitress noticed the picture in front of me when she was pouring it.

"I know that girl," she said. "She was in here last night. She changed the color of her hair, didn't she?"

"What time last night?"

"It must have been before seven. I went off at seven. She ordered a chicken sandwich, all white meat." She leaned above me confidentially. "Is she a movie star or something?"

"What makes you think she's a movie star?"

"I dunno. The way she was dressed, the way she looked. She's a very lovely girl." She heard her own voice, raised in enthusiasm, and lowered it. "Excuse me, I didn't mean to be nosey."

"That's all right."

She limped away, looking slightly more disappointed than she had. Rasmussen said when she was out of hearing:

"It's a funny thing, but I think I know her, too."

"You may at that. She says she was raised here in town, somewhere in the neighborhood of the railroad tracks."

Ward Rasmussen scratched his crewcut. "I'm pretty sure I've seen her. What's her name?"

"Kitty Hendricks. She is, or was, Harry Hendricks's wife. According to her, she's still married to Hendricks, but they haven't been living together. Seven years ago she was living with the man in the picture there—his name is Ketchel—and she probably still is. She fed me an elaborate story about being private secretary to a tycoon that Martel stole some securities from. But I don't put much stock in that."

Ward took some notes. "Where do we go from here?"

"You're in this, are you?"

He smiled. "It beats citing people for jaywalking. My ambition is to do detective work. Incidentally, may I keep a copy of this picture?"

"I want you too. Remember she's seven years older now, and redheaded. See if you can track down her family and get a line on her whereabouts. She probably knows a lot more than she told me. Also, she'll lead us to Ketchel, I hope."

He folded the picture into his notebook. "I'll get right on it."

Before he left, Ward wrote his address and telephone number on a page of his notebook. He was still living with his father, he said, though he hoped to get married soon. He handed me the torn out page, and strode out of the coffee shop, eager even on his own time.

My heart went out to the boy. More than twenty years ago, when I was a rookie on the Long Beach force, I had felt very much as he did. He was new to the harness, and I hoped it wouldn't cut too deep into his willing spirit.

XVIII

THE TENNIS CLUB didn't open till ten o'clock, Eric told me. I found Reto Stoll, the manager, in his cottage next door to Mrs. Bagshaw's. He was wearing a blue blazer with gilt buttons which went strangely with the heavy somber furniture in his living room. There was nothing personal in the room except the faint stale odor of burnt incense.

Stoll greeted me with anxious courtesy. He made me sit down in the armchair where he had obviously been reading the morning paper. He fidgeted and wrung his hands.

"This is terrible about Mrs. Fablon."

"It couldn't be in the paper yet."

"No. Mrs. Bagshaw told me. The old ladies in Montevista have a grapevine," he added parenthetically. "This news comes as a terrible shock to all of us. Mrs. Fablon was one of our most delightful members. Who would want to kill such a charming woman?" No doubt he was sincere, but he didn't have the knack of sounding that way about women.

"You may be able to help me answer that question, Mr.

Stoll." I showed him one of the enlargements. "Do you recognize these people?"

He carried the picture to the sliding glass door which opened onto his patio. His gray eyes narrowed. His mouth pursed in distaste.

"They stayed here as guests a number of years ago. Frankly, I didn't want to admit them. They weren't our type. But Dr. Sylvester made an issue of it."

"Why?"

"The man was his patient, apparently a very important patient."

"Did he tell you anything else about him?"

"He didn't have to. I recognized the type. It belongs in Palm Springs or Las Vegas, not here." He screwed up his face painfully, and slapped his forehead. "I should be able to remember his name."

"Ketchel."

"That's it. Ketchel. I put him and the woman in the cottage next to me"—he gestured towards Mrs. Bagshaw's cottage—"where I could keep an eye on them."

"What did you see?"

"They behaved better than I expected. There were no wild drinking parties, nothing like that."

"I understand they played a lot of cards."

"Oh?"

"And that Roy Fablon took part."

Stoll looked past me. He could see the threat of scandal a long way off. "Where did you hear that?"

"From Mrs. Fablon."

"Then I suppose it must be true. I don't remember, myself."

"Come off it, Reto. You're plugged into the Montevista grapevine, you must have heard that Fablon lost a lot of money to Ketchel. Mrs. Fablon blamed him for her husband's death."

The threat of scandal darkened on his face. "The Tennis Club is not responsible."

"Were you here the night Fablon disappeared?"

"No. I was not. I can't stay on duty twenty-four hours a

day.'' He looked at his watch. It was nearly ten o'clock. He was getting ready to terminate the interview.

''I want you to take another look at the picture. Do you recognize the young man in the white jacket?''

He held the picture up to the light. ''Vaguely I remember him. I think he only lasted a few weeks.'' He sucked in his breath abruptly. ''This looks like Martel. Is it?''

''I'm pretty sure it is. What was he doing working for you as a bus-boy?''

His hands made a helpless outward gesture encompassing the past and the present and a fairly dubious future. He sat down. ''I have no idea. As I recall he was only part-time help, doing mostly cleanup work. At the height of the season I sometimes use the cleanup boys to serve the cottages.''

''Where do you recruit the boys?''

''At the State Employment office. They're unskilled labor, we train them. Some we get from the placement bureau at the state college. I don't remember where we recruited this one.'' He looked at the picture again, then fanned himself with it. ''I could look it up in the records.''

''Please do. It could be the most important thing you do this year.''

He locked the door of his cottage and took me through the gate into the pool enclosure. Undisturbed by swimmers, the water lay like a slab of green glass in the sun. We walked around it to Stoll's office. He left me sitting at his desk, and disappeared into the records room.

He emerged in about five minutes with a filing card. ''I'm pretty sure this is the one we want, if I can trust my memory. But the name is not Martel.''

The name was Feliz Cervantes. He had been recruited through the state college and employed on a part-time basis, afternoons and evenings, at $1.25 an hour. His period of employment had been brief, extending from September 14 to September 30, 1959.

''Was he fired?''

''He quit,'' Stoll said. ''According to the record he left on September 30, without collecting his last two days' pay.''

"That's interesting. Roy Fablon disappeared on September 29. Feliz Cervantes quit September 30. Ketchel left October 1."

"And you connect those three happenings?" he said.

"It's hard not to."

I used Stoll's telephone to make an eleven o'clock appointment with the head of the placement bureau at the college, a man named Martin. I gave him the name Feliz Cervantes to check out.

While I was still at the club I paid a visit to Mrs. Bagshaw. Reluctantly she gave me the address of her friends in Georgetown, the Plimsolls, whom Martel had claimed to know.

I sent the address Airmail Special, along with Martel's picture, to a man named Ralph Christman who ran a detective agency in Washington. I asked Christman to interview the Plimsolls personally, and to phone the results to my answering service in Hollywood. I should get them some time tomorrow, if everything clicked.

XIX

THE COLLEGE WAS IN what had recently been the country. On the scalped hills around it were a few remnants of the orange groves which had once furred them with green. The trees on the campus itself were mostly palms, and looked as if they had been brought in and planted full grown. The students gave a similar impression.

One of them, a youth with a beard which made him look like a tall Toulouse-Lautrec, told me how to find Mr. Martin's office. Its entrance was behind a pierced concrete screen at the side of the administration building, which was one of a Stonehenge oval of buildings surrounding the open center of the campus.

I stepped out of the sunlight into the cold glare of fluorescent lights. A young woman came up to the counter and informed me that Mr. Martin was expecting me.

He was bald in shirtsleeves with a salesman's forceful stare. The paneled walls of his office were cool and impersonal, and made him look out of place.

"Nice office," I said when we had shaken hands.

"I can't get used to it. It's a funny thing. I'll be here five years in August, but I'm still nostalgic for the Quonset hut we started in. But you're not interested in past history."

"I am in Feliz Cervantes's past history."

"Right. That's quite a name. Feliz means 'happy,' you know. Happy Cervantes. Well, let's hope he is. I don't remember him personally—he didn't stay with us long—but I had his records pulled." He opened a manila folder on his desk. "What do you want to know about Happy Cervantes?"

"Everything you have."

"That isn't much, I'm afraid. Just why is Mr. Stoll interested in him?"

"He came back to town a couple of months ago, under an assumed name."

"Has he done something wrong?"

"He's wanted on suspicion of assault," I said, toning it down. "We're trying to establish his identity."

"I'm glad to co-operate with Mr. Stoll—he uses a lot of our boys—but I may not be too much help. Cervantes could be an assumed name, too."

"But don't your students have to present records, of birth and education and so on, before you let them in?"

"They're supposed to. But Cervantes didn't." Martin peered down at the contents of the folder. "There's a note here to the effect that he claimed to be a transfer student from L.A. State. We admitted him provisionally on the understanding that his transcripts would reach us by the first of October. By that time he'd already left us, and if the transcripts ever arrived we sent them back."

"Where did he go?"

He shrugged, retracting his bald head tortoiselike between his shoulders. "We don't keep track of our dropouts. Actually he never was our student." He had no transcript, Martin seemed to be saying, therefore he didn't exist. "You might try his old address here, in case he left a forwarding address. It's care of Mrs. Grantham, on Shore Drive, number 148. She has quite a few apartments which she rents to students."

I made a note of the address. "What courses was Cervantes taking?"

"I don't have a record of that. He didn't stay long enough to have his grades posted, and that's all we're interested in. I suppose you could try the Dean's office, if it's important. He's in this building."

I walked around the outside of the building to the Dean's office. His secretary was a large-busted brunette of uncertain age who handled herself with a kind of stylized precision. She typed Cervantes's name on a piece of paper and took it into a filing room, emerging with the written information that he had registered in French Language and Literature, on the senior level, and upper-division Modern European History.

I was certain for the first time that Feliz Cervantes and Francis Martel were the same man. I felt a certain humiliation for him. He had taken a big leap and found a toehold. Now he was falling.

"Who taught him French Language and Literature?"

"Professor Tappinger. He's still teaching the course."

"I was hoping it would be Professor Tappinger."

"Oh? Do you know him?"

"Slightly. Is he on campus now?"

"He is, yes, but I'm afraid he's in class." The woman glanced at the electric clock on the wall. "It's twenty minutes to twelve. He'll finish his lecture at twelve exactly. He always does." She seemed to take a certain pride in this.

"Do you know where everybody on campus is all the time?"

"Just some of them," she said. "Professor Tappinger is one of our institutions."

"He doesn't look much like an institution."

"He is, though. He's one of our most brilliant scholars." As if she was an institution herself, she added: "We consider ourselves very fortunate to have attracted him and kept him. I was worried he'd leave when he didn't get his promotion."

"Why didn't he?"

"You want the truth?"

"I couldn't live without it."

She leaned toward me and lowered her voice, as if the Dean might have the place bugged. "Professor Tappinger is too dedicated to his work. He can't be bothered with departmental politics. And frankly his wife is no help."

"I thought she was cute."

"I suppose she's cute enough. But she's a flibbertigibbet. If Professor Tappinger had a mature partner—" The sentence faded out. For a moment her efficient eyes were fixed on dreamland. It wasn't hard to guess the identity of the mature partner she had in mind for Tappinger.

She directed me in a rather proprietary way to his office in the Arts Building and assured me he always returned there with his lecture notes before he went home for lunch. She wasn't wrong. At one minute after twelve, the professor came marching down the corridor, flushed and bright-eyed, as if he had had a good class.

He did a double take when he saw me. "Why, it's Mr. Archer. I'm always surprised when I see somebody from the real world in these purlieus."

"This isn't real?"

"Not really real. It hasn't been here long enough, for one thing."

"I have."

Tappinger laughed. Away from his wife and family, he seemed to be much more cheerful. "We've both been around long enough to know who we are. But don't let me keep you standing out here." He unlocked the door of his office and urged me inside. Two walls of shelves were filled with books, many of them unbound French volumes and sets. "I suppose you've come to report the results of the test?"

"Partly. It was a success, from Martel's point of view. He answered every question correctly."

"Even the pineal gland?"

"Even that."

"I'm amazed, frankly amazed."

"It may be a sort of compliment to you. Martel seems to be a former student of yours. You had him for a week or two, anyway, seven years ago."

He gave me a startled look. "How can that be?"

"I don't know. But it can't be pure coincidence."

I got out Martel's picture and handed it to him. He nodded his head over it. "I remember the boy. He was a brilliant student, one of the most brilliant I've ever had. Unaccountably he dropped out, without a word to me." His cheerfulness had evaporated. Now he was shaking his head from side to side. "What happened to him?"

"I don't know. Except that he turned up here seven years later with a wad of money and a new identity. Do you recall the name he used in your class?"

"You don't forget a student like that. He called himself Feliz Cervantes." He looked down at the picture again. "Who are these other people?"

"Guests at the Tennis Club. Cervantes held a job there for a couple of weeks in September of '59. He was a part-time cleanup help."

Tappinger made a clucking sound. "I remember he seemed to be in need of money. The one time I entertained him in my house, he ate up virtually everything in sight. But you say he has money now?"

"At least a hundred thousand dollars. In cash."

He whistled. "That's just about ten years salary for me. Where did he get it?"

"He says it's family money, but I'm pretty sure he's lying."

He studied the picture some more, as if he was still a little confused by Martel's double identity. "I'm sure he had no family background to speak of."

"Do you have any idea where he came from?"

"I assumed he was a Spanish-American, probably a first

generation Mexican. He spoke with quite an accent. As a matter of fact, his French was better than his English."

"Perhaps he is a Frenchman after all."

"With a name like Feliz Cervantes?"

"We don't know that that's his real name, either."

"His transcripts would show his real name," Tappinger said.

"But they're not on file here. He was supposed to have gone to L.A. State College before he came here. Maybe they can help us."

"I'll query L.A. State. A former student of mine is teaching in the French department there."

"I can get in touch with him. What's his name?"

"Allan Bosch." He spelled the surname for me. "But I think it would be better if I made the contact. We university teachers have certain—ah—inhibitions about talking about our students."

"When can I check back with you?"

"Tomorrow morning, I should think. Right at the moment I'm on a very tight schedule. My wife is expecting me for lunch and I have to get back here in time to look over my notes for a two o'clock class." I must have showed my disappointment because he added, "Look here, old chap, come home with me for lunch."

"I can't do that."

"But I insist. Bess would insist, too. She took quite a liking to you. Besides, she may recall something about Cervantes that I don't. I remember she was impressed with him when he came to our party. And people, frankly, are not my *métier*."

I said I would meet him at his house. On the way there I bought a bottle of pink champagne. My case was starting to break.

Bess Tappinger had on a good-looking blue dress, fresh lipstick, and too much perfume. I didn't like the purposeful look in her eye, and I began to regret the pink champagne. She took it from my hands, as if she planned to break it over the prow of an affair.

She had covered the dinette table with a fresh linen cloth

cross-hatched with fold marks. "I hope you like ham, Mr. Archer. All I have is cold ham and potato salad." She turned to her husband. "Daddy, what do the wine books says about ham and pink champagne?"

"I'm sure they go together very well," he said remotely.

Tappinger had lost his effervescence. A glass of champagne failed to restore it. He chewed fitfully at a ham sandwich and asked me questions about Cervantes-Martel. I had to admit his former student was wanted on suspicion of murder. Tappinger shook his head over the young man's broken promise.

Bess Tappinger was excited by the champagne. She wanted our attention. "Who are we talking about?"

"Feliz Cervantes. You remember him, Bess."

"Am I supposed to?"

"I'm sure you remember him—the Spanish young man. He came to our *Cercle Français* icebreaker seven years ago. Show her the picture of him, will you, Archer?"

I put it down on the linen cloth beside her plate. She recognized the busboy right away. "Of course I remember him."

"I thought you would," her husband said meaningfully. "You talked about him afterwards."

"What impressed you, Mrs. Tappinger?"

"I thought he was good-looking, in a strong masculine way." There was bright malice in her eyes. "We faculty wives get tired of pale scholarly types."

Tappinger countered obliquely: "He was an excellent student. He had a passion for French civilization, which is the greatest since the Athenian, and a wonderfully good ear for French poetry, considering his lack of background."

His wife was working on another glass of champagne. "You're a genius, Daddy. You can make a sentence sound like a fifty-minute lecture."

Perhaps she meant it lightly, as her consciously pretty smile seemed to insist, but it fell with a dull thud.

"Please don't keep calling me Daddy."

"But you don't like me to call you Taps anymore. And you are the father of my children."

"The children are not here and I'm most definitely not your father. I'm only forty-one."

"I'm only twenty-nine," she said to both of us.

"Twelve years is no great difference." He closed the subject abruptly as if it was a kind of Pandora's box. "Where is Teddy, by the way, since he's not here?"

"At the co-operative nursery. They'll keep him till after his nap."

"Good."

"I'm going to the Plaza and do a little shopping after lunch."

The conflict between them, which had been submerged for a moment, flared up again. "You can't." He had turned quite pale.

"Why can't I?"

"I'm using the Fiat. I have a two o'clock class." He looked at his watch. "As a matter of fact I should be starting back now. I have some preparation to do."

"I haven't had much of a chance to talk to your wife—"

"I realize that. I'm sorry, Mr. Archer. The fact is I have to punch a time clock, almost literally, just like any assembly worker. And the students are more and more like assembly-line products, acquiring a thin veneer of education as they glide by us. They learn their irregular verbs. But they don't know how to use them in a sentence. In fact very few of them are capable of composing a decent sentence in English, let alone in French, which is the language of the sentence *par excellence*."

He seemed to be converting his anger with his wife into anger with his job, and the whole thing into a lecture. She looked at me with a faint smile, as if she had turned him out:

"Why don't you drive me to the Plaza, Mr. Archer? It will give us a chance to finish our talk."

"I'll be glad to."

Tappinger made no objection. He completed another paragraph about the occupational sorrows of teaching in a second-rate college, then retreated from the shambles of the lunch. I heard his Fiat put-put away. His wife and I sat in the dinette and finished the champagne.

"Well," she said, "here we are."

"Just as you planned."

"I didn't plan it. You did. You bought the champagne, and I can't handle champagne." She gave me a dizzy look.

"I can."

"What are you," she said, "another cold fish?"

She was rough. They get that way, sometimes, when they marry too young and trap themselves in a kitchen and wake up ten years later wondering where the world is. As if she could read my thought, she said:

"I know, I'm a bee-eye-tee-see-aitch. But I have some reason. He sits out in his study every night till past midnight. Is my life supposed to be over because all he cares about is Flaubert and Baudelaire and those awful students of his? They make me sick, the way they crowd around and tell him how wonderful he is. All they really want is a passing grade."

She took a deep breath and continued: "He isn't so wonderful, I ought to know. I've lived with him for twelve years and put up with his temperament and tantrums. You'd think he was Baudelaire himself, or Van Gogh, the way he carries on sometimes. And I kept hoping it would lead to something, but it never has. It never will. We're stuck in a lousy state college and he hasn't even got the manhood to engineer a promotion for himself."

The shabby little cubicle, or maybe the champagne that had been drunk in it, seemed to generate lectures. I made an observation of my own:

"You're being pretty hard on your husband. He has to go out and cut it. For that he needs support."

She hung her head. Her hair swung forward like a flexible ball. "I know. I try to give it to him, honestly."

She had reverted to her little-girl voice. It didn't suit her mood though, and she dropped it. She said in a clear sharp voice she had used with her son the day before:

"We never should have married, Taps and I. He shouldn't have married at all. Sometimes he reminds me of a medieval priest. The two best years of his life came before our marriage. He often tells me this. He spent them in the *Bibliothèque Nationale* in Paris, not long after the war. I knew nothing of this, of course, but I was just a kid and he was the white hope of the French department at Illinois and all the other sophomores said how wonderful it would be to be married to him, with his Scott Fitzgerald good looks, and I thought I could finish my education at home.'' She looked over the partition at the kitchen sink. ''That, I certainly have.''

''You married very young.''

''Seventeen,'' she said. ''The terrible thing is, I still feel seventeen inside.'' She touched herself between her breasts. ''With everything ahead, you know? But nothing is.'' For the first time the woman was coming through to me.

''You have your children.''

''Sure, I have my children. And don't think I don't do my best for them and always will. Is that all there is, though?''

''It's more than some people have.''

''I want more.'' Her pretty red mouth looked pathetically greedy. ''I've wanted more for a long time, but I've never had the nerve to take it.''

''You have to wait for it to be given,'' I said.

''You're full of sententious remarks, aren't you? You're fuller than La Rochefoucauld, or my husband. But you can't solve actual problems with words, as Taps thinks you can. He doesn't understand life. He's nothing but a talking machine, with a computer instead of a heart and a central nervous system.''

The thought of her husband seemed to nag her continually. It was almost making her eloquent, but I was growing weary of her boxed-in tension. Perhaps I had brought it on, but basically it had nothing to do with me. I said:

''This is all very interesting, but you were going to talk about Feliz Cervantes.''

''I was, wasn't I.'' Her look became meditative. ''He was a very interesting young man. A hot-blooded type, aggressive, the kind of man you imagine a bullfighter might be.

He was only twenty-two or three—so was I for that matter—but he was a man. You know?''

''Did you talk to him?''

''A little.''

''What about?''

''Our pictures, mostly. He was very keen on French art. He said he was determined to visit Paris some day.''

''He said that?''

''Yes. It's not surprising. Every student of French wants to go to Paris. I used to want to go myself.''

''What else did he say?''

''That was about all. Some of the other students turned up, and he shied away from me. Taps said afterward—we had a quarrel after the party—he said that I had been obvious with the young man. I think Taps brought you here to have me confess. My husband is a very subtle punisher.''

''You're both too subtle for me. Confess what?''

''That I was—interested in Feliz Cervantes. But he wasn't interested in me. I wasn't even in the room as far as he was concerned.''

''That's hard to believe.''

''Is it? There was a young blonde girl from one of Taps's freshman courses at the party. He followed her with his eyes the way I imagine Dante followed Beatrice.'' Her voice was cold with envy.

''What was her name?''

''Virginia Fablon. I think she's still at the college.''

''She quit to get married.''

''Really? Who was the lucky man?''

''Feliz Cervantes.'' I told her how this could be. She listened raptly.

While Bess got ready to go shopping I moved around the living room looking at the reproductions of a world that had never quite dared to exist. The house had taken on an intense interest for me, like a historical monument or the birth-place of a famous man. Cervantes-Martel and Ginny had met in this house; which made it the birthplace of my case.

Bess came out of her room. She had changed into a dress

which had to be hooked up the back and I was elected to hook it up. Though she had a strokeable-looking back, my hand were careful not to wander. The easy ones were nearly always trouble: frigid or nympho, schizy or commercial or alcoholic, sometimes all five at once. Their nicely wrapped gifts of themselves often turned out to be homemade bombs, or fudge with arsenic in it.

We drove to the Plaza in ticking silence. It was a large new shopping center, like a campus with asphalt instead of lawns where nothing could be learned. I gave her money, which she accepted, to take a taxi home. It was a friendly gesture, too friendly under the circumstances. But she looked at me as if I was abandoning her to a fate worse than life.

XX

SHORE DRIVE RAN along the sea below the college in an area of explosive growth and feeble zoning. It was a jumble of apartment buildings, private houses, and fraternity houses with Greek letters over the door.

Behind the stucco house numbered 148 a half-dozen semi-detached cottages were huddled on a small lot. A stout woman opened the door of the house before I reached it.

"I'm full up till June."

"I don't need lodging, thanks. Are you Mrs. Grantham?"

"I never buy door-to-door, if that's what's on your mind."

"All I want is a little information." I told her my name and occupation. "Mr. Martin at the college gave me your name."

"Why didn't you say so? Come in."

The door opened into a small, densely furnished living

room. We sat down facing each other, knees almost touching. "I hope it isn't a complaint about one of my boys. They're like sons to me," she said with a professionally maternal smile.

She made an expansive gesture toward the fireplace. The mantel and the wall above it were completely taken up with graduation pictures of young men.

"Not one of your recent boys, anyway. This one goes back seven years. Do you remember Feliz Cervantes?" I showed her the picture with Martel-Cervantes in the background, Ketchel and Kitty in the foreground. She put on glasses to study it.

"I remember all three of them. The big man and the blondie, they came by and picked up his stuff when he left. The three of them rode away together."

"Are you sure of that, Mrs. Grantham?"

"I'm sure. My late husband always said I've got a memory like an elephant. Even if I hadn't, I wouldn't forget that trio. They rode away in a Rolls Royce car, and I wondered what a Mexican boy was doing in that kind of company."

"Cervantes was Mexican?"

"Sure he was, in spite of all his stories. I didn't want to take him in at first. I never had a Mexican roomer before. But the college says you have to or lose your listing, so I rented him a room. He didn't last long, though."

"What stories did he tell?"

"He was full of stories," she said. "When I asked him if he was a Mex, he said he wasn't. I've lived in California all my life, and I can tell a Mex when I see one. He even had an accent, which he claimed was a Spanish accent. He said he was a pure-blooded Spaniard, from Spain.

"So I said, show me your passport. He didn't have one. He said he was a fugitive from his country, that General Franco was after him for fighting the government. He didn't take me in though. I know a Mex when I see one. If you ask me he was probably a wetback, and that's why he lied. He didn't want the Immigration to put him on a bus and send him home."

"Did he tell any other lies?"

"You bet he did, right up to the day he left. He said when he left he was on his way to Paris, that he was going to the University there. He said the Spanish government had released some of his family money, and he could afford to go to a better school than ours. Good riddance of bad rubbish is what I said."

"You didn't like Cervantes, did you?"

"He was all right, in his place. But he was too uppity. Besides, here he was leaving me on the first of October, leaving me stuck with an empty room for the rest of the semester. It made me sorry I took him in the first place."

"How was he uppity, Mrs. Grantham?"

"Lots of ways. Do you have a cigarette by any chance?" I gave her one and lit it for her. She blew smoke in my face. "Why are you so interested in him? Is he back in town?"

"He has been."

"What do you know. He told me he was going to come back. Come back in a Rolls Royce with a million dollars and marry a girl from Montevista. *That* was uppity. I told him he should stick to his own kind. But he said she was the only girl for him."

"Did he name her?"

"Virginia Fablon. I knew who she was. My own daughter went to high school with her. She was a beautiful girl, I imagine she still is."

"Cervantes thinks so. He just married her."

"You're kidding."

"I wish I were. He came back a couple of months ago. In a Bentley, not a Rolls, with a hundred and twenty thousand instead of a million. But he married her."

"Well, I'll be." Mrs. Grantham drew deep on her cigarette as if she were sucking the juice from the situation. "Wait until I tell my daughter."

"I wouldn't tell anyone for a day or two. Cervantes and Virginia have dropped out of sight. She may be in danger."

"From him?" she said with avidity.

"Could be." I didn't know what he wanted from Virginia: it was probably something that didn't exist and I didn't know what he'd do when he found out that it didn't exist.

Mrs. Grantham put out her cigarette in a Breakwater Hotel ashtray and dropped the butt into a handleless teacup which contained other butts. She leaned toward me confidentially, heartily:

"Anything else you want to know?"

"Yes. Did Cervantes give you any explanation about the people who took him away?"

"This pair?" She laid a finger on the picture in her lap. "I forget what he said exactly. I think he said they were friends of his, coming to pick him up."

"He didn't say who they were?"

"No, but they looked like they were loaded. I think he said that they were Hollywood people, and they were going to put him on the plane."

"What plane?"

"The plane to France. I thought at the time it was a lot of malarkey. But now I don't know. Did he ever make it to France?"

"I think he did."

"Where did he get the money? You think his family really has money in Spain?"

"Castles in Spain, anyway."

I thought as I drove away that Martel was one of those dangerous dreamers who acted out his dreams, a liar who forced his lies to become true. His world was highly colored and man-made, like the pictures on the Tappingers' walls which might have been his first vision of France.

XXI

THE CASHIER of Mercy Hospital had eyes like calculators. She peered at me through the bars of her cage as if she was estimating my income, subtracting my expenses, and coming up with a balance in the red.

"How much am I worth?" I said cheerfully.

"Dead or alive?"

That stopped me. "I want to pay for Mr. Harry Hendricks for another day."

"It isn't necessary," she said. "His wife took care of it."

"The redhead? Was she here?"

"She came in and visited him for a few minutes this morning."

"Can I see him?"

"You'll have to ask the head nurse on the third floor."

The head nurse was a starched, thin-mouthed woman who kept me waiting while she brought her records up to date. Eventually she let me tell her that I was a detective working with the police. She got quite friendly then.

"I don't see any reason why you shouldn't ask him some questions. But don't tire him, and don't say anything to upset him."

Harry was in a private room with windows which overlooked the city. With the bandages on his head and face he looked like an unfinished mummy.

I was carrying the pearl-gray hat, and his eyes focused on it. "Is that my hat?"

"It's the one you were wearing yesterday. The name inside is Spillman, though. Who's he?"

"I wouldn't know."

"You were wearing his hat."

"Was I?" He lay and thought about it. "I got it at a rummage sale."

I didn't believe him, but there was no point in saying so. I tossed the hat onto the chest of drawers. "Who clobbered you, Harry?"

"I don't know for sure. I didn't see him. It was dark, and he knocked me out from behind. Then he stomped on my face, the doctors says."

"Nice guy. Was it Martel?"

"Yeah. It happened up at his place. I was poking around

the back of his house. The wind was making so much noise I didn't hear him come up behind me." His fingers crawled over the sheet which covered his body. "He must of given me quite a going over. I'm sore all over."

"You were in an auto accident."

"I was?"

"Martel put you in the trunk of your car and parked it on the waterfront. Some winos stole and wrecked it."

He groaned. "It isn't mine. My own clunk died on me, and I borrowed the Caddie off the lot. No insurance, no nothing. Is she a total goner?"

"It wouldn't be worth the price of the body work."

"Wouldn't you know it. There goes another job." He lay silent for a minute, looking at the sky. "I've been thinking about myself this aft. I bet—no, I won't bet, I'll just say it: I'm the biggest failure west of the Mississippi. I don't even deserve to live."

"Everybody deserves that."

"It's nice of you to say so. Incidentally, they told me a Mr. Archer made the down payment on this pad. Was that you?"

"I chipped in twenty."

"Thanks muchly. You're a real pal."

"Forget it. I'm on an expense account."

But he was touched. "I guess I'm lucky—lucky to be alive, for one thing. Then my wife came to see me, which makes it old home week."

"Is Kitty still in town?"

"I doubt it. She said she was leaving." His head lay inert on the pillow for a moment. "I didn't know you knew her."

"We had a talk last night. She's a beautiful woman."

"Don't I know it. When I lost her it was like losing the moon and stars, boy."

"Did Ketchel take her away from you?"

Another silence. "You know *him,* too?"

"I know something about him. What I know I don't like."

"The more you learn the less you'll like it," he said.

"The one great foolish mistake of my life was getting caught in his meathooks. It lost me Kitty."

"How so?"

"I'm a gambler," he said. "I don't know why. I just am. I love to gamble. It makes me feel alive. I must be nuts." His eyes seemed to be looking down a hole. "So one hot morning about dawn I walked out of the Scorpion Club into Fremont Street with nothing, no wife, nothing. How do you like that? I lost my wife in a crap game. She was so disgusted with me she went with him and stayed."

"With Ketchel?"

Harry lay looking at the hat on the bureau. "His real name is Leo Spillman. Ketchel is just a name he uses. It's an old-time boxing name. Kayo Ketchel, he called himself. He was a pretty good light-heavy before he went into the rackets full-time."

"What rackets is he in, Harry?"

"Name it and he has a piece of it, or used to have. He started in slot machines in the Middle West and got fat off of army bases. You might say that he's still in slot machines. He's majority owner of the Scorpion Club in Vegas."

"Funny I never heard his name."

"He's a concealed owner, I think they call it. He learned to keep his name quiet, like traveling under the name of Ketchel. Leo Spillman is a name with a bad smell. Of course he's semiretired now, I haven't seen him for years."

"How did you get hold of his hat?"

"Kitty gave it to me when she came to see me last week. Leo's a much bigger man than I am but we have the same size head, seven-and-a-quarter. And I needed a hat to go up against the people in Montevista."

"Where can I find Leo?"

"I guess you could try the Scorpion Club. He used to have a suite there next to his office. I know him and Kitty have a hideout someplace in Southern Cal, but she never gave me a hint of where it is."

"What about his cattle ranch?"

"He sold that long ago. Kitty didn't like to see them branding the calves."

"You've kept in pretty close touch with her."

"Not really. But I've seen her over the years. When she gets in a real jam, or has a real need, she comes to old Harry." He raised his head a few inches from the pillow and looked at me. "I'm leveling with you, Archer, and you know why? I need a cohort, a partner."

"So you said yesterday."

"I need one worse today." With a slow sweep of his chin he called attention to his helplessness, and let his head fall back on the pillow. "And you've been a real pal. I'm going to offer you an equal share of a really big deal."

"Like a concussion?"

"I'm serious. There may be more than a hundred grand up for grabs. Is that laughable?"

"You mean the money Martel-Cervantes stole?"

"Martel-who-did-you-say?"

"Cervantes. That's another name Martel used."

"Then he's the man!" Harry sat up in his excitement. "We've got him."

"Unfortunately we haven't got him. He's on the run, with a hundred grand in cash. Even if we do get hold of it, won't Leo Spillman want it back?"

"Naw." His hand slid up in a steep gesture. "A hundred grand or two hundred is just peanuts to Leo. He'll let us keep it, Kitty said he would. The money they're really after, Kitty and him, is up in the millions." His hand went up to the full length of his arm and stayed there for a second in a kind of salute. He fell back onto the pillow.

"Martel stole millions from him?"

"So Kitty said."

"She must be stringing you. There's no way to steal a million dollars, unless you rob a Brink's truck."

"Yes, there is. And she isn't lying, she never has to me. You got to understand that this is the chance of a lifetime."

"The chance of a deathtime, Harry."

The thought sobered him. "Yeah. That, too."

"Why would Leo Spillman put it in your hands?"

"Kitty did. I'm the only one she trusts." He must have noticed my dubious look because he added: "That may sound funny to you, but it's a fact. I love Kitty, and she knows it. She says if I can pull this out she might even come back to me." His voice rose, trying to make it truer.

I could hear soft rapid nurse-footsteps approaching in the hall.

"Kitty told me she used to live here in town."

"That's right, Kitty was a local girl. Matter of fact, we had our first honeymoon in the Breakwater Hotel." His eyes rolled under his bandages.

"What was her maiden name?"

"Sekjar," he said. "Her old man was some kind of Polak. So's her mother. She hated my guts for robbing the cradle, she called it."

The head nurse opened the door and stuck her head in. "That's enough now. You said you'd keep it quiet."

"Harry got a little excited."

"We can't have that." She opened the door wide. "Out now."

"Are you with me, Archer?" Harry said from the bed. "You know what I mean."

I wasn't with him and I wasn't against him. I made a circle with my thumb and forefinger and showed it to him in a gesture of encouragement.

XXII

IN THE NEIGHBORHOOD of Mercy Hospital there were several satellite treatment centers and clinics, and Dr. Sylvester's clinic was one of them. It was smaller and less prosperous-looking than most of its neighbors. A visibly threadbare path crossed the rug in the lobby from the front door to the reception desk. Several doctors and their specialists, headed by George Sylvester, Internal Medicine, were listed on a board beside the door.

The girl behind the desk told me that Dr. Sylvester was still out to lunch. He had a free half-hour scheduled, if I cared to wait.

I gave her my name and sat down among the waiting patients. After a while I began to feel like one of them. The pink champagne, or the lady I had drunk it with, had left me with a dull headache. Other parts of my anatomy began to nag. By the time Dr. Sylvester appeared, I was just about ready to break down and tell him my symptoms.

He looked as though he had symptoms of his own, probably hangover symptoms. He was clearly not glad to see me. But he gave me his hand and a professional smile, and escorted me past his formidable-looking secretary into his consulting room.

He changed into the white coat. I glanced at the diplomas and certificates on the paneled walls. Sylvester had trained in good schools and hospitals, and passed his Boards. He had at least the background of a responsible doctor. It was the foreground that worried me.

"What can I do for you, Archer? You look tired, by the way."

"That's because I am tired."

"Then take the weight off your feet." He indicated a chair at the end of his desk, and sat down himself. "I only have a few minutes, so let's get with it, boy." The sudden camaraderie was forced. Behind it he was watching me like a poker player.

"I found out who your patient Ketchel is."

He raised his eyebrows but said nothing.

"He's a Vegas casino owner," I said, "with a very extensive background in the rackets. His actual name is Leo Spillman."

Sylvester was not surprised. He said smoothly. "It fits in with our records. I checked them this morning. He gave his address as the Scorpion Club in Las Vegas."

"It's too bad you couldn't remember that last night when I could have used it."

"I can't remember everything."

"Try your memory on this one. Did you introduce Leo Spillman to Roy Fablon?"

"I don't remember."

"You know whether you did or not, doctor."

"You can't talk to me like that."

"Answer my question," I said. "If you won't, I'll find somebody who will."

His face slanted forward in thought. It looked both precarious and threatening, like a piece of rock poised on the edge of a cliff.

"Why would Marietta Fablon apply to you for money?" I said.

"I'm an old friend. Who else should she go to?"

"Are you sure she wasn't trying to blackmail you, old friend?"

He looked around his office as though it was a kind of public cage. The lines bracketing his mouth were deep and cruel, like self-inflicted scars.

"What are you trying to cover up, doctor?"

After a thinking pause, he said: "The fact that I'm a god-damn fool." He glanced sharply into my eyes. "Can you keep a secret?"

"Not if it involves a crime."

"What crime?" He spread out his large hands palms up on the desk. "There hasn't *been* any crime."

"Then why are you so worried?"

"This town is a hotbed of rumors, as I told you last night. If the word gets out about Leo Spillman and me, I'm dead." His hands curled up very slowly, like two starfish. "I'm moribund now, if you want the truth. There are too damn many doctors in this town. And I've had financial losses."

"Gambling losses?"

He was startled. "Where did you dig that up?" He pounded the desk with his curled hands, not threateningly, more like someone trying to get out. He wasn't a subtle man, and his anxiety had blunted him even more. "What are you trying to do to me?"

"You know what I'm trying to do—get at the facts about

this man Martel, and incidentally clear up any doubts about what happened to Fablon. The two things are connected by way of Spillman, possibly in other ways. When Spillman left town, two days after Fablon's death, he took Martel with him. Did you know that?"

He looked at me in a confused way. "Are we talking about seven years ago?"

"That's right. You're involved in all this because you brought Spillman here."

"I didn't *bring* him. He invited himself. As a matter of fact it was his woman's—his wife's idea. Her idea of heaven was two weeks at the Tennis Club." His mouth lifted on one side showing the edges of his teeth.

"Did you owe Spillman money?"

"Did I not." His eyes were bleak, looking past me at his life. "If I give you straight answers to some of these questions, what use do you intend to make of them?"

"I'll keep the facts to myself, so far as I can. A client once told me he could drop a secret into me and never hear it hit bottom. You're not my client, but I'll do what I can to protect your *bella figura*."

"I'll take you at your word," he said. "Don't get the idea that I'm one of those compulsive gamblers. It's true I'm in the market, it's the only way to outwit these confiscatory taxes nowadays—but I'm not the Vegas type of gambler. I stay away from Vegas."

"And that's why you never met Leo Spillman."

"I admit I went there in the past. The last time I went to Vegas I was in a bad mood, a destructive mood. I didn't care what happened. My wife—" He compressed his lips.

"Go on."

He said haltingly: "I was just going to say my wife wasn't with me."

"I thought you were going to say she was having an affair with another man."

His face twisted in pain. "Good Lord, did *she* tell you that?"

"No. It doesn't matter how I found out."

"Do you know who the other man was?" he said.

"Roy Fablon. It gave you a reason for wanting him dead."

"Is that an accusation?"

"I just thought I'd mention it, Doctor."

"Thanks very much. You throw some wicked curves."

"Life does, anyway. What happened your last time in Vegas?"

"Plenty. First I lost a few hundred on the tables. Instead of cutting my losses, I got mad and plunged. Before I was through I'd exhausted my credit—it still hasn't recovered completely—and I owed Leo Spillman nearly twenty thousand.

"He called me into the office to talk about it. I told him I could raise ten at most, he'd have to wait for the rest. He blew a gasket and called me a cheat and a fourflusher, and a good many other names. He would have attacked me physically, I think, if the woman hadn't restrained him."

"Was Kitty there?"

"Yes. She was interested in me because she'd found out that I came from here. She reminded Spillman that it was a felony for him to use his fists. Apparently he was an ex-professional boxer. But he was in terrible shape, and I think I could have taken him." Sylvester caressed his fist. "I did some boxing in college."

"It's just as well you didn't try. Very few amateurs ever take a pro."

"But he was a sick man, physically and emotionally sick."

"What was the matter with him?"

"I could see that one of his optic nerves was jumping. After he calmed down a bit, I persuaded him to let me look into his eyes and take his blood pressure. I had the equipment in my car. That may seem like a strange thing to do, under the circumstances, but I was concerned about him as a doctor. With good reason. He had a bad case of hypertension, and his blood pressure was up in the danger zone. It turned out that he'd never been to a doctor, never had a checkup. He thought all that was for sissies.

"At first he thought I was trying to frighten him. But with the woman's help I got the fact across to him, that he was in danger of a stroke. So he suggested a deal. I was to rake up ten thousand in cash, treat his hypertension, and get the two of them a cottage at the Tennis Club. I imagine it was the weirdest deal in history."

"I don't know. Spillman once won a man's wife in a crap game."

"So he told me. He's full of little anecdotes. You can imagine how I felt injecting a man like that into my club. But I had no choice, and he was willing to pay nearly ten thousand dollars."

"It didn't cost him anything."

"It cost him ten thousand less the value of my services."

"Not if you paid him the other ten thousand in cash. He'd save more than enough in taxes to make up the difference."

"You think he was dodging taxes?"

"I'm sure of it. They're doing it all the time in Vegas. The money they hold back is known as 'black money,' and that's a good name for it. It runs into the millions, and it's used to finance about half of the illegal enterprises in the country, from Cosa Nostra on down."

Sylvester said in a chilly voice: "I couldn't be held responsible, could I?"

"Morally, you could. Legally, I don't know. If everybody who collaborated with organized crime was held responsible, half the boobs in the country would be in jail. Unfortunately that won't happen. We treat the crime capital of the United States as if it was a second Disneyland, smelling like roses, a great place to take the family or hold a convention."

I stopped myself. I was slightly hipped on the subject of Vegas, partly because the criminal cases I handled in California so often led there. As this one was doing, now, I said:

"Did you know that Martel left town with Spillman seven years ago?"

"I heard you tell me. I didn't understand what you meant."

"He was a student at the local college, working part-time as a flunky at the Tennis Club."

"Martel was?"

"In those days he called himself Feliz Cervantes. He met Ginny Fablon, or at least saw her, at a gathering of French students, and fell for her. He may have taken the job at the club so he could see her more often. He ran into Spillman there."

Sylvester was listening closely. He was quiet and subdued, as if the building might collapse in ruins around him if he moved. "How do you know all this?"

"Part of it's speculation. Most of it isn't. But I've got to talk to Leo Spillman, and I want your help in reaching him. Have you see him recently?"

"Not in seven years. He never came back here. I didn't urge him to, either. Apart from my professional contact with him, I did my best to avoid him. I never invited him to my house, for instance."

Sylvester was trying to rescue his pride. But I suspected it had been permanently lost, within the past half-hour, in this room.

XXIII

THROUGH THE DOOR behind me I heard the telephone ring in Sylvester's outer office. About twenty seconds later the telephone on his desk gave out a subdued echo of the ring. He picked it up and said impatiently:

"What is it, Mrs. Loftin?"

The secretary's voice came to me in stereo, partly through the telephone and partly through the door. It was just loud enough for me to hear what she said:

"Virginia Fablon wants to talk to you. She's in a state. Shall I put her on?"

"Hold it," Sylvester said. "I'll come out there."

He excused himself and went out, shutting the door

emphatically behind him. Refusing to take the hint, I followed him into the outer office. He was standing over the secretary's desk, pressing her telephone to the side of his head like a surgical device which held his face together.

"Where are you?" he was saying. He interrupted himself to bark at me: "Give me some privacy, can't you?"

"Please step out into the hall," Mrs. Loftin said. "The doctor is advising an emergency patient."

"What's the emergency?"

"I can't discuss it. Please step outside, won't you?"

Mrs. Loftin was a large woman with a square determined face. She advanced on me, ready to use physical force.

I retreated into the hallway. She closed the door. I leaned my ear against it and heard Sylvester say:

"What makes you think he's dying?" Then: "I see . . . Yes, I'll come right away. Don't panic."

A few seconds later Sylvester emerged from the office in such a blind rush that he almost knocked me over. He was carrying a medical bag and still wearing his white coat. The prosthetic telephone was no longer holding his face together.

I walked beside him toward the front door of the clinic. "Let me drive you."

"No."

"Has Martel been hurt?"

"I prefer not to discuss it. He insists on privacy."

"I'm private. Let me drive you."

Sylvester shook his head. But he paused on the terrace above the parking lot and stood blinking in the sun for a moment.

"What's the matter with him?" I said.

"He was shot."

"That puts him in the public domain, and you know it. My car's over here."

I took him by the elbow and propelled him toward the curb. He offered no resistance to me. His movements were slightly mechanical.

I said as I started the car: "Where are they, doctor?"

"In Los Angeles. If you can get onto the San Diego Freeway—they have a house in Brentwood."

"They have another house?"

"Apparently. I took down the address."

It was on Sabado Avenue, a tree-lined street of large Spanish houses built some time in the twenties. It was one of those disappearing enclaves where, in a different mood from mine, you could feel the sunlit peace of prewar Los Angeles. Sabado Avenue had a Not a Through Street sign at its entrance.

The house we were looking for was the largest and most elaborate on the long block. Its walled and fountained grounds reminded me a little of Forest Lawn. So did the girl who answered the front door. I would hardly have recognized Ginny, she was so drawn around the mouth and swollen around the eyes.

She started to cry again into the front of Sylvester's white coat. He patted her shuddering back with his free hand.

"Where is he, Virginia?"

"He went away. I had to go next door to phone you. Our phone isn't connected yet." Her sentences were broken up by hiccuping sobs. "He took the car and drove away."

"How long ago?"

"I don't know. I've lost track of time. It was right after I phoned you."

"That makes it less than an hour," I said. "Is your husband badly hurt?"

She nodded, still clinging to Sylvester. "I'm afraid he's bleeding internally. He was shot in the stomach."

"When?"

"An hour or so ago. I don't know exactly what time. The people who rented the house to us didn't leave any clocks. I was taking a siesta—we were up most of the night—and somebody rang the doorbell. My husband answered it. I heard the shot, and I ran down here and found him sitting on the floor."

She looked down at her feet. Around them on the parquetry were rusty spots that looked like drying blood.

"Did you see who fired the shot?"

"I didn't actually see him. I heard the car drive away. My

husband—" She kept repeating the phrase as if it might help him and her marriage to survive.

Sylvester broke in: "We can't keep her standing here while we cross-question her. One of us ought to call the police."

"You should have called them before you left your office."

Ginny seemed to think I was blaming her. "My husband wouldn't let me. He said it would mean the end of everything." Her heavy look swung from side to side, as if the end of everything was upon her.

Sylvester quieted her against his shoulder. Slowly and gently he walked her into the house. I went next door. A stout executive type in a black alpaca sweater was standing outside on his front lawn, looking helpless and resentful. He owned a house on Sabado Avenue, and this was supposed to guarantee a quiet life.

"What do you want?"

"The use of your phone. There's been a shooting."

"Is that what the noise was?"

"You heard the gun?"

"I thought it was a backfire at the time."

"Did you see the car?"

"I saw a black Rolls drive away. Or maybe it was a Bentley. But that was sometime later."

This wasn't much help. I asked him to show me a telephone. He took me in through the back door to the kitchen. It was one of those space age kitchens, all gleaming metal and control panels, ready to go into lunar orbit. The man handed me a telephone and left the room, as if to avoid finding out something that might disturb him.

Within a few minutes a squad car arrived, followed closely by a Homicide Captain named Perlberg. Not long after that we located Martel's Bentley. It hadn't gone far.

Its gleaming nose was jammed against the metal safety barrier at the dead end of Sabado Avenue. Beyond the barrier the loose ground sloped away to the edge of a bluff which overlooked the Pacific.

The Bentley's engine was still running. Martel's chin

rested on the steering wheel. The dead eyes in his yellow face were peering out into the blue ocean of air.

Perlberg and I knew each other, and I gave him a quick rundown on the case. He and his men made a search for Martel's hundred thousand, but found no trace of it in the car or at the house. The gunman who took Martel had taken the money too.

Ginny was in slightly better shape by this time, and Sylvester gave Perlberg permission to question her briefly. He and I sat in the living room with them, and monitored the interview. Ginny and Martel had been married by a judge in Beverly Hills the previous Saturday. The same day he had rented this house, completely furnished, through an agent. She didn't know who the legal owner was.

No, she didn't know who had shot her husband. She had been asleep when it happened. It was all over when she came downstairs.

"But your husband was still alive," Perlberg said. "What did he say?"

"Nothing."

"He must have said something."

"Just that I wasn't to call anyone," she said. "He said he wasn't badly hurt. I didn't realize he was until later."

"How much later?"

"I don't know. I was so upset, and we have no clocks. I sat and watched the life draining out of his face. He wouldn't speak to me. He seemed to be profoundly—humiliated. When I finally realized how badly off he was, I went next door and called Dr. Sylvester." She nodded toward the doctor who was sitting near her.

"Why didn't you call a local doctor?"

"I didn't know any."

"Why didn't you call us?"

"I was afraid to. My husband said it would be the end of him."

"What did he mean by that?"

"I don't know, but I was afraid. When I finally did make a call, he went away."

She covered her face with her hands. Sylvester persuaded

the Captain to cut the questioning short. Perlberg's men took pictures, and shavings of the blood-spotted parquetry, and left us alone with Ginny in the big echoing house.

She said she wanted to go home to her mother. Sylvester told her that her mother was dead. She didn't seem to take it in.

I volunteered to get some of her things together. While Sylvester stayed with her in the living room, I went up to the master bedroom on the second floor. The bed, which was its central feature, was circular, about nine feet in diameter. I was beginning to see a good many of these king-sized beds, like hopeful altars to old gods. The bed had been left unmade, and the tangled sheets suggested lovemaking.

The suitcases were on the floor of the closet under a row of empty hangers. They had been left unpacked except for a few overnight things: Ginny's nightgown and hairbrush and toothbrush and cosmetics, Martel's pajamas and safety razor. I went through his suitcases quickly. Most of his clothes were new and of fine quality, some with Bond Street labels. Apart from a book by Descartes, *Méditations*, in French, I could find nothing personal, and even this book had no name on the flyleaf.

Later, as we drove through the endless suburbs to Montevista, I asked Ginny if she knew who her husband was. Sylvester had given her a sedative, and she rode between us with her head on his extended arm. The shock of Martel's death had pushed her back toward childishness. Her voice sounded just a little like a sleep-talker's:

"He's Francis Martel, from Paris. You know that."

"I thought I did, Ginny. But just today another name came up. Feliz Cervantes."

"I never heard of any such person."

"You met him, or at least he met you, at a *Cercle Français* meeting at Professor Tappinger's house."

"When? I've been to dozens of *Cercle Français* meetings."

"This one was seven years ago, in September. Francis Martel was there under the name Cervantes. Mrs. Tappinger identified a photograph of him."

"Can I see the photograph?"

I moved over into the slow lane and worked the picture out of my jacket pocket. She took it from me. Then for some time she was silent. The afternoon traffic fled by us on the left. The drivers looked apprehensive, as if they had been kidnapped by their cars.

"Is this really Francis standing by the wall?"

"I'm almost certain that it is. Didn't you know him in those days?"

"No. Was I supposed to have?"

"He knew you. He told his landlady that he was going to get rich some day and come back and marry you."

"But that's ridiculous."

"Not so very. It happened."

Sylvester, who had been quiet until now, growled something at me about shutting up.

Ginny hung her head in thought over the picture. "If this is Francis, what's he doing with Mr. and Mrs. Ketchel?"

"You know the Ketchels?"

"I met them once."

"When?"

"September seven years ago. My father took me to lunch with them. It was just before he died."

Sylvester scowled across her at me. "This is enough of this, Archer. It's no time to poke around in explosive material."

"It's the only time I have." I said to the girl: "Do you mind talking to me about these things?"

"Not if it will help." She managed a wan smile.

"Okay. What happened at this lunch with the Ketchels?"

"Nothing, really. We had something to eat in the patio of his cottage. I tried to make conversation with Mrs. Ketchel. She was a local girl, she said, but that was the only thing we had in common. She hated me."

"Why?"

"Because Mr. Ketchel liked me. He wanted to do things for me, help me with my education and so on." Her voice was toneless.

"Did your father know about this?"

"Yes. It was the purpose of the lunch. Roy was very

naïve about exploiting people. He thought he could use a man like Mr. Ketchel without being used.''

''Use him for what?'' I said.

''Roy owed him money. Roy was a nice man, but by that time he owed everybody money. I couldn't help him. It wouldn't have done any good to go along with Mr. Ketchel's plan. Mr. Ketchel is the kind of man who takes everything and gives nothing. I told Roy that.''

''Just what was the plan?''

''It was rather vague, but Mr. Ketchel offered to send me to school in Europe.''

''And your father went for this?''

''Not really. He just wanted me to butter up Mr. Ketchel a little bit. But Mr. Ketchel wanted everything. Men get that way when they're afraid they're dying.''

The girl surprised me. I reminded myself that she wasn't a girl, but a woman with a brief tragic marriage already behind her. And what sounded like a long tragic childhood. Her voice had changed perceptibly, almost as though she had skipped from youth to middle age, when she began to call her father ''Roy.''

''How often did you see Ketchel?''

''I talked to him just the once. He had noticed me at the club.''

''You say the lunch with him occurred shortly before your father died. Do you mean the same week?''

''The same day,'' she said. ''It was the last day I ever saw Roy alive. Mother sent me to look for him that night.''

''Where?''

''Down at the beach, and at the club. Peter Jamieson was with me a part of the time. He went to the Ketchel's cottage—I didn't want to—but they weren't there. At least they didn't answer.''

''Do you think Ketchel and your father quarreled over you?''

''I don't know. It's possible.'' She went on in the same flat voice: ''I wish I had been born without a nose, or only one eye.''

I didn't have to ask Ginny what she meant. I had known a number of girls for whom men insisted on doing things.

"Did Ketchel murder your father, Ginny?"

"I don't know. Mother thought so, at the time."

Sylvester groaned. "I don't see the point in raking it over."

"The point is that it's connected with the present situation, doctor. You don't want to see the connection because you're part of the chain of cause and effect."

"Do we have to go into that again?"

"Please." Ginny screwed up her face and rolled her head from side to side. "Please don't argue across me. They always used to argue across me."

We both said we were sorry. After a while she asked me in a soft voice: "Do you think Mr. Ketchel killed my husband?"

"He's the leading suspect. I don't think he'd do it personally. He'd more likely use a hired gunman."

"But why?"

"I can't go into all the circumstances. Seven years ago your husband left Montevista with Ketchel. Apparently Ketchel sent him to school in France."

"As a substitute for me?"

"That hardly seems likely. But I'm sure Ketchel had his uses for your husband."

She was offended. "Francis wasn't like that at all."

"I don't mean sex. I believe he used Francis in his business."

"What business?"

"He's a big-time gambling operator. Didn't Francis ever mention Ketchel?"

"No. He never did."

"Or Leo Spillman, which was Ketchel's real name?"

"No."

"What did you and Francis talk about, Ginny?"

"Poetry and philosophy, mostly. I had so much to learn from Francis."

"Never real things?"

She said in her anguished voice: "Why do real things always have to be ugly and horrible?"

She was feeling the pain now, I thought, the cruel pain of coming home widowed after a three-day marriage.

It was time to leave the freeway. I could see Montevista in the distance: its trees were like a green forest on the horizon. The access road straightened out toward the sea.

My mind was on Francis Martel, or whoever he was. He had driven his Bentley down this road a couple of months ago, on the track of a seven-year dream. The energy that had conceived the dream, and forced it briefly into reality, had all run out now. Even the girl beside me was lax as a doll, as if a part of her had died with the dreamer. She didn't speak again until we reached her mother's house.

The front door was locked. Ginny turned from it with a rejected air. "It's her bridge day. I should have remembered." She found the key in her bag, and opened the door. "You don't mind bringing my suitcases in? I'm feeling a little weak."

"You have reason to," Sylvester said.

"Actually, I'm relieved that Mother isn't here. What could I say to her?"

Sylvester and I looked at each other. I got the suitcases out of the trunk of my car and carried them into the front hall. Ginny said from the sitting room:

"What happened to the phone?"

"There was trouble here last night."

She leaned in the doorway. "Trouble?"

Sylvester went to her and put his hands on her shoulders. "I'm sorry I have to tell you this, Ginny. Your mother was shot last night."

She slipped from his hands onto the floor. Her skin was gray and her eyes indigo, but she didn't faint. She sat with her back against the wall.

"Is Marietta dead?"

"I'm afraid she is, Ginny."

I squatted beside her. "Do you know who shot your mother?"

She shook her head so hard that her hair fell like a blonde screen across her face.

"Your mother was deeply upset last night. Was something said to her, by you or Martel?"

"We said goodbye." She gasped over the finality of the word. "That was about all, except that she didn't want me to go. She said she'd get money some other way."

"What did she mean?"

"That I had married Francis for his money, I suppose. She didn't understand."

I said: "She told me before she died that lover-boy shot her. Who would lover-boy be?"

"Francis, maybe. But he was with me all the time." Her head fell against the wall with a thud. "I don't know what she could have meant."

"Lay off her," Sylvester said. "I'm speaking as a friend and as a doctor."

He was right. I felt like a tormenting devil squatting beside her. I got to my feet and helped Ginny to hers. "She ought to have protection. Will you stay with her, doctor?"

"I can't possibly. I must have a dozen patients stacked up waiting for me." He glanced at his wristwatch. "Why don't you stay with her yourself? I can call a cab."

"I have things to do in town." I turned to Ginny: "Could you stand having Peter around?"

"I guess so," she said with her head down, "so long as I don't have to talk any more to anyone."

I found Peter at home and explained the circumstances. He said he knew how to use a gun—trapshooting was one of his sports—and he'd be glad to stand guard.

He loaded a shotgun and brought it along, carrying it with a slightly military air. The news of Martel's death seemed to have lifted his spirits.

Ginny greeted him quietly in the hall. "This is nice of you, Peter. But we won't talk about anything. Okay?"

"Okay. I'm sorry, though."

They shook hands like brother and sister. But I saw his eyes take possession of her injured beauty. It came to me with a jolt that for Peter the case had just ended. I left before he realized it himself.

XXIV

I DROVE SLOWLY up the pass road which was the shortest route between Montevista and the city, Sylvester kept looking back into the valley where we had left Ginny. The rooftops were half submerged among the trees like flotsam in a turbulent green flood. I said:

"Shouldn't she be in the hospital, or at least have a nurse?"

"I'll see about that later, when I've cleaned up my work at the clinic."

"Do you think she'll be all right?"

Sylvester was slow in answering. "She's a durable girl. Of course she's had lousy luck, compounded by bad judgment. She should have married Peter as she was supposed to. She would have been safe with him, at least. Maybe now she will."

"Maybe. You seem fond of the girl."

"As fond as I dare be."

"What does that mean, doctor?"

"Just what I said. She's a beautiful kid and she trusts me. You make everything sound like an accusation."

"I don't think so."

"Then listen to yourself. You'll see what I mean."

"You may be right." I wanted him to keep talking. After a moment, I said: "You knew Roy Fablon. Was he the kind of a man who would try to use his daughter to pay off gambling losses?"

"Why ask me?"

"Ginny seems to think he was."

"I didn't gather that from the conversation. At worst, Roy may have been using her, or trying to, to make Spillman more lenient. You don't know how desperate a man can get when a gorilla like Spillman has you by the—" He suppressed the end of the sentence. "I do."

"What you say adds up to an affirmative answer. Fablon was the kind of man who would try to use his daughter."

"He didn't, anyway. He didn't have a chance to. Say he made an offer to Spillman and then withdrew it. A blowtop like Spillman might very easily have killed him."

"It works just as well the other way," Sylvester said. "Better, if you know the background situation. Put a man like Roy in a moral vise like that, and he's liable to kill himself. Which is what happened. I checked back with Dr. Wills this morning, incidentally—he's the deputy coroner who performed the autopsy on Roy. He found definite evidence, *chemical* evidence that Roy drowned himself in the ocean."

"Or was drowned."

"There are cases of murder by drowning," Sylvester said. "But I never heard of one committed by a sick man in the sea at night."

"Spillman was and is in a position to have these things done for him."

"He had no motive."

"We've just been talking about one possible motive. A more obvious one was that Fablon owed him thirty thousand dollars and he couldn't pay. Spillman wouldn't take it lightly. You're a witness to that."

Sylvester moved restlessly in the seat. "Marietta really put a bee in your bonnet. She was cracked on the subject of Spillman."

"Did she talk to you about him recently?"

"Yesterday at lunch, when you barged in."

"You must take her seriously or you wouldn't have checked with Dr. Wills today."

"Check with Wills yourself. He'll tell you the same thing."

We had reached the low summit of the pass. In a sloping

field to my left an old palomino stallion wandered in the sunlight, white-maned, like a survivor.

I adjusted my windshield visor against the light as we started down the hill. The city below resembled a maze, put together by an inspired child: it looked both intricate and homemade. Beyond it lay the changing blue mystery of the sea.

I dropped Sylvester off in front of his clinic and crossed the street to Mercy Hospital. The deputy coroner had his office and laboratory in the basement, next to the hospital morgue.

Dr. Wills was a small thin man with a dedicated-scientist look, intensified by steel-rimmed glasses. He handled himself as if his hands, his fingers, even his eyes and mouth were technical instruments, useful but not alive; and the real Dr. Wills sat hidden in his skull directing their operations.

He didn't even blink when I told him that there had been another killing.

"It's getting a little thick," was all he said.

"Have you done your p.m. on Mrs. Fablon?"

"Not a complete one. It hardly seemed necessary. The bullet nicked her aorta, and that was it." He gestured toward an inner door.

"What kind of bullet?"

"It looks like a .38. It came through in fair condition, and should be good for comparison if we ever find the gun."

"May I see it?"

"I've already turned it over to Inspector Olsen."

"Tell him it should be compared with the slug that killed Martel."

Wills gave me a quizzical look. "Why don't you tell him yourself?"

"He'll like it better if he hears it from you. I also think he should reopen the Roy Fablon case."

"I disagree about that," Wills said crisply. "A murder, or two murders, in the present, don't change a suicide in the past."

"Are you quite certain it was a suicide?"

"Quite. I had occasion to look over my notes only this morning. There's no question that Fablon committed suicide by drowning. The external contusions were almost certainly inflicted after death. In any case they wouldn't have been sufficient to cause death."

"I gather he took quite a beating."

"Bodies do in these waters. But there's no doubt he was a suicide. In addition to the physical evidence, he threatened suicide in the presence of his wife and daughter."

"So I've been told."

The thought of it, coming on top of my talks with Sylvester and Ginny, was depressing. The present couldn't alter the past, as Wills had said, but it could make you painfully aware of its mysteries and meanings.

Wills misinterpreted my silence: "If you doubt my word, you can look up the record of the coroner's inquest."

"I don't doubt you're giving me an accurate report, doctor. Who gave the testimony about the suicide threat?"

"Fablon's wife. You can't question that."

"You can question anything human." The ambiguities of last night's conversation with Marietta still teetered in my mind. "I understand that before the inquest she claimed her husband was murdered."

"Perhaps she did. The physical evidence must have persuaded her otherwise. At the inquest she came out strongly for the idea of suicide."

"What was the physical evidence you referred to?"

"The chemical content of the blood taken from the heart. It proved conclusively that he was drowned."

"He could have been knocked out and drowned in a bathtub. It's been done."

"Not in this case." Dr. Wills answered smoothly and rapidly, like a well-programmed computer. "The chloride content of the blood in the left ventricle was over twenty-five percent above normal. The magnesium content was greatly increased, as compared with the right ventricle. Those two indicators taken together prove that Fablon drowned in ocean water."

"And there's no doubt that the body was Fablon's?"

"None whatever. His wife identified it, in my presence." Wills adjusted his glasses and looked at me through them diagnostically, as if he suspected that I had an obsession. "Frankly I think you're making a mistake in trying to connect what happened to him with—this." He gestured again toward the wall on the other side of which Marietta lay in her refrigerated drawer.

Perhaps I should have stayed and argued with Wills. He was an honest man. But the place and its basement chill were getting me down. The cement walls and high small windows made it resemble a cell in an old-fashioned jail.

I got out of there. Before I left the hospital I found a telephone booth and made a long-distance call to Professor Allan Bosch of Los Angeles State College. He was in his office and answered the phone himself.

"This is Lew Archer. You don't know my name—"

He cut in: "On the contrary, Mr. Archer, your name was mentioned to me within the past hour."

"You've heard from Tappinger then."

"He just left here. I gave him as full a report as I could on Pedro Domingo."

"Pedro Domingo?"

"That's the name Cervantes used when he was my student. I believe it's his true name, and I know for a fact that he's a native of Panama. Those are the points at issue, aren't they?"

"There are others. If I could talk to you in person—"

His rapid young voice cut in on me again. "I'm jammed at the moment—Professor Tappinger's visit did nothing for my schedule. Why don't you get the facts from him and if there's anything else you need to know you can get in touch with me later?"

"I'll do that. In the meantime there's something you ought to know, Professor. Your former student was shot dead in Brentwood this afternoon."

"Pedro was shot?"

"He was murdered. Which means that his identity is something more than an academic question. You better get in touch with Captain Perlberg of Homicide."

"Perhaps I had better," he said slowly, and hung up.

I checked with my answering service in Hollywood. Ralph Christman had phoned from Washington and dictated a message. The operator read it to me over the line:

"Colonel Plimsoll identifies mustached waiter in photograph as South or Central American diplomat named Domingo, he thinks. Do I query the embassies?"

I asked the operator to call Christman for me and tell him to try the embassies, especially the Panamanian one.

Past and present were coming together. I had a moment of claustrophobia in the phone booth, as if I was caught between converging walls.

XXV

SEKJAR, KITTY'S MAIDEN NAME, wasn't in the telephone book. I went to the public library and looked it up in a city directory. A Mrs. Maria Sekjar, hospital employee, was listed at 137 Juniper Street. I found the poor little street backed up against the railway yards. The first person I saw on Juniper Street was the young policeman, Ward Rasmussen, marching toward me along the dirty path which served as a sidewalk.

I got out of my car and hailed him. He looked a little disappointed to see me. You feel that way sometimes, when you're out bird-dogging and another man crosses your path.

"I found Kitty's mother," he said. "I went to high school and dug up the girls' counselor who remembered Kitty."

"That was resourceful."

"I wouldn't say that." But he was soberly pleased. "I didn't have much luck with the mother, though. Maybe she'll say more to you. She seems to think her daughter's in serious trouble. She's been in trouble since she was in her teens, the counselor told me."

"Boy trouble?"

"What else?"

I changed the subject. "Did you have a chance to get to the bank, Ward?"

"Yessir, I had better luck there." He got his notebook out of his pocket and flipped the pages. "Mrs. Fablon has been getting a regular income from that bank in Panama, the New Granada. They sent her a draft every month until last February, when it stopped."

"How much every month?"

"A thousand. This went on for six or seven years. It added up to around eighty thousand."

"Was there any indication of its source?"

"Not according to the local people. It came from a numbered account, apparently. The whole transaction was untouched by the human hand."

"And then it stopped."

"That's correct. What do you make of it, Mr. Archer?"

"I wouldn't want to jump to any conclusions."

"No, of course not. But it could be underworld money. You remember that thought came up at breakfast this morning."

"I'm pretty sure it is. But we're going to have a hell of a time proving it."

"I know that. I talked to the foreign-exchange man at the National. The Panama banks are like the Swiss banks. They don't have to reveal the source of their deposits, which makes them a natural for mobsters. What do you think we should do about it?"

I was anxious to talk to Mrs. Sekjar, and I said: "Get the law changed. Do you want to wait for me in my car?"

He got in. I approached the Sekjar on foot. It was a small frame dwelling which looked as if the passing trains had shaken off most of its paint.

I knocked on the rusty screen door. A woman with dyed black hair appeared behind it. She was large and heavy, aged about fifty, though the dyed hair made her look older.

Handsome, but not as handsome as her daughter. Her cheap dye job was iridescent in the late afternoon sun.

"What do you want?"

"I'd like to talk to you—"

"About Kitty again?"

"More or less."

"I don't know anything about her. That's what I told the other ones and that's what I'm telling you. I've worked hard all my life so I could hold my head up in this town." She lifted her chin. "It wasn't easy, and Kitty was no help. She has nothing to do with me now."

"She's your daughter, isn't she?"

"Yeah, I guess she is." Her voice was rough. "She don't act like a daughter. I'm not responsible for what she does. I used to beat her until she was bloody, it did no good. She was as wild as ever, making mock of the teachings of the Lord." She looked up through the rusty screen. Her own eyes were rebellious.

"May I come in, Mrs. Sekjar? My name is Archer, I'm a private detective." Her face was unyielding, and I went on rapidly: "I've got nothing against your daughter, but I'm trying to locate her. She may be able to give some information about a murder."

"Murder?" She was appalled. "The other one didn't say nothing about a murder. This is a decent home, mister," she said, with the tense precarious respectability of the poor.

"It's the first time since Kitty left me that a policeman came to this door." She glanced up and down the street, as if her neighbors were spying on us now. "I guess you better come on in."

She unhooked the screen door and opened it for me. Her living room was small and threadbare. It contained a daybed and two chairs, a faded rag rug, a television set tuned in on a daytime serial which said, in the snatch I heard of it, that things were tough all over.

Mrs. Sekjar switched it off. On top of the television were a large Bible and one of those glass balls that you shake to make a snowstorm. The pictures on the walls were all religious, and there were so many of them that they suggested a line of defense against the world.

I sat on the daybed. It smelled of Kitty, faintly but distinctly. The odor of her perfume seemed strange in these surroundings. It wasn't the odor of sanctity.

"Kitty was here last night, wasn't she?"

Mrs. Sekjar nodded, standing over me. "She came over the fence from the tracks. I couldn't turn her away. She was scared."

"Did she say what of?"

"It's her way of life. It's catching up with her. The kind of men she runs with, punks and hoodlums—" She spat dry. "We won't discuss it."

"I think we should, Mrs. Sekjar. Did Kitty do any talking to you last night?"

"Not much. She did some crying. I thought I had my own girl back for a while. She stayed all night. But in the morning she was as hard as ever."

"She isn't that hard."

"She didn't start out to be, maybe. She was a nice enough girl when her father was with us. But Sekjar got himself sick and spent his last two years in the County Hospital. After that Kitty got hard as nails. She blamed me and the other adults for putting him in the County Hospital. As if I had any choice.

"When she was a sixteen-year-old girl she went for my eyes with her thumb nails. I chopped them off for her. If I hadn't been stronger than her, she'd of blinded me. After that I couldn't do anything with her. She ran wild with the boys. I tried to stop her. I know what comes of running wild with the boys. So just to spite me she turned around and married the first man that asked her." She paused glaring among her angry memories. "Is Harry Hendricks the one that died?"

"No, but he was injured."

"So I heard at the hospital. I'm a nurse's aide," she explained with some pride. "Who got murdered?"

"A woman named Marietta Fablon, and a man who called himself Francis Martel."

"I never heard of either of them."

I showed her the picture of Martel, with Kitty and Leo Spillman in the foreground. She exploded:

"That's him! That's the man, the one who took her away from her lawful husband." She jabbed her forefinger at Spillman's head. "I'd like to kill that man for what he did to my daughter. He took her and rolled her in the mud. And there she sits with her legs crossed, smiling like a cat."

"Do you know Leo Spillman?"

"That wasn't his name."

"Ketchel?"

"Yeah. She brought him here to the house, it must have been six or seven years ago. She said he wanted to do something for me. That kind always wants to do something for you, and then before you know it they own you. Like he owns Kitty. He said he owned an apartment in L.A. and I could move in rent-free and retire from hospital work. I told him I would rather go on working than take his money. So they left. I didn't see her again until last night."

"Do you know where they live?"

"They used to live in Las Vegas. Kitty sent me a couple of Christmas cards from there. I don't know where they live now. She hasn't sent me any mail for years. And last night when I asked her she wouldn't tell me where she lived."

"So you don't have any idea where I can find her?"

"No, sir. If I did I wouldn't tell you. I'm not going to help you send my daughter to the pen."

"I'm not trying to put her in jail. I just want information—"

"You don't fool me, mister. They're wanted for income tax, ain't they?"

"Who told you that?"

"A man from the government told me. He was sitting where you are sitting, within the last two weeks. He said I'd be doing my daughter a favor if I could talk her into coming forth, that her and me could even get a percentage of the money because they're not lawful man and wife. I said it was Judas money. I said I'd be a fine mother, wouldn't I, if I spread my daughter's shame in all the papers. He said it was my duty as a citizen. I said there was duty and duty."

"Did you talk to Kitty about it?"

"I tried this morning. That's when she left. We never could get along. But that's a far cry from turning her in to the government. I said it to the other one and I'm saying it to you. You can go back and tell the government I don't know where she is and I wouldn't tell you if I did know."

She sat there breathing defiance. A train whistled from the direction of Los Angeles. It was a long freight train, moving slowly. Somehow it reminded me of the government.

Before it had finished rattling the dishes in the kitchen, I said goodbye to Mrs. Sekjar and left. I dropped Ward off at his father's house, which was just about one grade better than Mrs. Sekjar's, and advised him to get some sleep. Then I drove to International Airport and bought a return ticket to Las Vegas.

XXVI

It was still day, with a searchlight sun glinting along the sea, when the plane took off for Las Vegas. We flew away from the sun and came down into sudden purple dusk.

I took a cab to Fremont Street. The jostling neon colors of its signs made the few stars in the narrow sky look pale and embarrassed. The Scorpion Club was one of the larger casinos on the street, a two-story building with a three-story sign on which an electric scorpion twitched its tail.

The people at the slot machines inside seemed to work by similar mechanisms. They fed in their quarters and dollars with the left hands and pulled the levers with their right like assembly-line workers in a money factory. There were smudge-eyed boys so young that they hadn't begun to shave yet, and women with workmen's gloves on their lever hands, some of them so old and weary that they leaned on the machines to stay upright. The money factory was a hard place to work.

I worked my way through the early-evening crowd, past blackjack and roulette tables, and found a pit boss watching the crap tables at the rear of the big room. He was a quick eyed man in an undertaker's suit. I told him I wanted to see the boss.

"I'm the boss."

"Don't kid me."

His glance darted up to the ceiling. "If you want to see Mr. Davis, you got to have a good reason. What's your reason?"

"I'll tell him."

"Tell me."

"Mr. Davis might not want me to."

His gaze came to rest on my face. I could feel his dislike. "You want to see Mr. Davis, you got to tell me the nature of your business."

I told him my name and occupation, and the fact that I was investigating two murders.

He didn't change expression. "You think Mr. Davis can help you out?"

"I'd like to ask him."

"Wait here."

He disappeared behind a curtain. I heard him going upstairs. I stood by one of the green tables and watched a girl in a low-backed gown fling herself and the dice around. This was the creative end of the money factory, where you got a chance to finger the dice, and talk to them.

"They're getting hot for me," she said.

She was a nice looking-girl with a cultivated voice, and she reminded me of Ginny. The man who stood behind her and provided her with money wore furry black sideburns and dude clothes, including high-heeled boots. From time to time, when the girl won, he let out a synthetic vaquero whoop. His hand kept slipping lower on her back.

The pit boss came downstairs and jerked a thumb at me from the edge of the curtain. I followed him behind it. A second man loomed up behind the arras and went over me for iron. His head looked like a minor accident on top of his huge neck and shoulders.

"You can go on up." He followed me.

Mr. Davis was waiting at the end of the stairs. He was a smiling man with a politician's malleable face and a lot of wavy gray hair. He wore a pin-striped gray suit with slanting pockets and pleated shoulders, for action. Mr. Davis hadn't had much action lately. Even the careful tailoring of his suit couldn't harden or conceal the huge soft egg of his belly.

"Mr. Archer?"

"Mr. Davis."

He didn't offer me his hand, which was just as well. I don't like shaking hands with men wearing rings with stones in them.

"What can I do for you, Mr. Archer?"

"Give me a few minutes. We may be able to do something for each other."

He looked dubiously at my plain old California suit, and at my shoes which needed polishing. "That I doubt. You mentioned murder downstairs. Anyone I know?"

"I think so. Francis Martel."

He didn't react to the name. I showed him the picture. He reacted to it. He snatched it out of my hand and hustled me into his office and closed the door.

"Where did you get hold of this?"

"In Montevista."

"Was Leo there?"

"Not recently. This isn't a recent picture."

He took it to his desk to study it under the light. "No, I see it isn't recent. Leo will never be that young again. Neither will Kitty." He seemed to take pleasure in this fact, as if it made him younger by comparison. "Who's the character with the tray?"

"I was hoping you could tell me."

He looked up at me. "It wouldn't be Cervantes?"

"Feliz Cervantes, alias Francis Martel." Alias Pedro Domingo. "He was shot today, on Sabado Avenue in Brentwood."

Davis's eyes went dead. I noticed that this kept happening. They would show a flicker of interest or curiosity, or even malice, then sink back into lifelessness.

"You want to tell me about the shooting?" he said.

"Not keenly, but I will." I gave him a short account of Martel's death and what led up to it. "You can read the rest of it in the early-morning papers."

"And the killer got the money, is that right?"

"Evidently. Whose money is it?"

"I wouldn't know," he said with sudden vagueness.

He got up and walked away from me the length of the long office, surveying the desert photomurals on the walls. His footsteps were silent on the desert-colored rug. There was something a little female about his movements, and more than a little ominous, as if his huge belly was pregnant with death.

"It wouldn't be your money, would it, Mr. Davis?"

He turned and opened his mouth as if to yell, but produced no sound. Soundlessly he walked toward me, making a little sideways dance-step as he passed the horseshoe desk.

"No," he whispered into my face. "It wouldn't be my money and I had nothing to do with knocking him off." He smiled and nudged me as if he was going to tell me a joke, but there was no humor in his smile. "In fact I don't know why you come to me with this spiel of yours."

"You're Leo's partner, aren't you?"

"Am I?"

"And Cervantes was his boy."

"How do you mean, his boy?" David nudged me again. His pleated shoulders opened and closed with the gesture, making it obscene.

"I thought you'd be able to tell me, Mr. Davis."

"Think again. I only saw Cervantes once in my life, and that was last year when he came here with Leo. I don't know what the deal was. Whatever it was, I don't want any part of it. I'm a legitimate businessman conducting a legal business, and incidentally Leo is not my partner. There's nothing on the record that says he owns any part of this casino. As for me, I want no part of him."

It was a bold statement. David didn't quite strike me as a bold man. I was beginning to wonder if Leo Spillman was dead, too.

"Where can I find Leo?"

"I wouldn't know."

"You send him money, don't you?"

"He should send *me* money."

"How so?"

"You ask too many questions. Beat it now, before you make me nervous."

"I think I'll stick around. I need help with an income tax problem. Not mine, Leo's. And maybe yours."

Davis leaned on the wall, sighing. "Why didn't you tell me you were Internal Revenue?"

"I'm not."

"Then you misrepresented yourself just now."

"The hell I did. You can talk about income tax without working for the federal government."

"Not to me you can't. You can't con your way into my office masquerading as a federal agent."

He knew I hadn't, but he needed some point of focus for his anger. He seemed to have no focal point in himself. I'd known other front men like him in Vegas and Reno; bar-room gladhanders who had lost their gladness, smilers who gradually realized that they were fronting for death and belonged to it.

"The feds are looking for Leo. I guess you know that," I said.

"I guess I do."

"Why can't they find him? Is he dead?"

"I wish he was." He snickered.

"Did you have Cervantes shot?"

"Me? I'm a legitimate businessman."

"So you were telling me. It doesn't answer the question."

"It wasn't a good question."

"I'll see if I can frame a better one—the hypothetical kind they ask the experts in court."

"I'm no expert, and we're not in court."

"Just in case you ever are, it will be good practice for you."

He didn't feel the needle, which probably meant he was feeling deeper pains. "How much black money did Leo siphon out of your counting room?"

He answered blandly. "I don't know anything about it."

"Naturally you wouldn't know about it. You're too legitimate."

"Watch it," he said. "I've taken as much from you as I've ever taken from anybody."

"Did he make discount deals with the big losers and use Cervantes to collect and stash the money?"

Davis looked at me carefully. His eyes were dead but unquiet. "You ask the kind of questions that answer themselves. You don't need me."

"We need each other," I said. "I want Leo Spillman, and you want the money he milked out of the business."

"If you're talking about that money in L.A., it's gone. There's no way for me to get it back. Anyway, it's nickels and dimes. Our counting room handles more than that every day of the year."

"So you have no problem."

"None that you can help me with."

Davis took another of his walks to the end of the room and back. He moved warily, with a kind of female stealth, as if his desert-colored office was actual desert, with rattlesnakes under the rug.

"If you do catch up with Leo," he said, "you might let me know. I'm willing to pay you for the information. Say five grand, if it's exclusive."

"I wasn't planning to hire myself out as a finger."

"Weren't you?" He took another good look at my suit. "Anyway, the offer stands, bud."

He opened the door for me. The man with the wide shoulders and narrow head was waiting to accompany me downstairs. The girl who reminded me of Ginny was at one of the crap tables with a different escort. Everything that happened in Vegas seemed to be a repetition of something that had happened before.

I caught a plane back to Los Angeles and slept in my own bed.

XXVII

A JAY WHO LIVED in my neighborhood woke me up in the morning. He was perched on a high limb outside my second-story apartment window, and he was yelling his head off for salted peanuts.

I looked in the cupboard: no salted peanuts. I scattered some wilted cornflakes on the windowsill. The jay didn't even bother to come down from his perch. He cocked his head on one side and looked sardonically at the last of the big spenders. Then he dove off the limb and flew away.

The milk in the refrigerator was sour. I shaved and put on clean linen and my other suit and went out for breakfast. I read the morning paper over my bacon and eggs. The killing of Martel was on the second page, and it was handled as a gang killing. The killing of Marietta Fablon was buried back in the Southland News. No connection was drawn between the two crimes.

On the way to my office on Sunset Boulevard I took a long detour to the Hall of Justice. Captain Perlberg had a preliminary report from the Crime Laboratory. The slug which Dr. Wills had removed from Marietta Fablon's chest had almost certainly come from the same gun as the slug that killed Martel. The gun itself, which was probably an old .38-caliber revolver, had not been found, and neither had the person who fired it.

"Got any ideas on the subject?" Perlberg asked me.

"I know a fact. Martel worked for a Vegas casino owner named Leo Spillman."

"Doing what?"

"I think he was Spillman's courier. Recently he went into business for himself."

Perlberg gave me a melancholy look. He lit a cigarette and blew smoke at me across his cluttered desk. He wasn't hostile or aggressive, but he had a kind of enveloping Jewish force.

"Why didn't you mention this yesterday, Archer?"

"I went to Vegas last night and asked some questions. I didn't get very good answers, but I got enough to suggest that Martel was co-operating with Spillman in a tax-evasion dodge. Then he stopped co-operating. He wanted the cash for himself."

"And Spillman gunned him?"

"Or had him gunned."

Perlberg puffed on his cigarette, filling the small office with the fumes, as if smog was the native element in which his brain worked best.

"How does Mrs. Fablon fit into this hypothesis?"

"I don't know. I have a theory that Spillman killed her husband and she knew it."

"Her husband was a suicide, according to the Montevista people."

"So they keep telling me. But it isn't proven. Say he wasn't."

"Then we have three unsolved killings instead of two. I need an extra killing like an extra hole in my head." He stubbed out his cigarette violently. It was the only show of impatience he permitted himself. "Thanks for the information, though, and the ideas. They may be helpful."

"I was hoping for a little assistance myself."

"Anything, if it don't cost the taxpayers money."

"I'm trying to find Leo Spillman—"

"Don't worry. I'll be on it as soon as you leave this office."

It was an invitation to depart. I lingered in the doorway. "Will you let me know when you locate him? I'd give a lot for a chance to talk to him."

Perlberg said he would.

I drove across town to my own office. There was a sheaf

of mail in the letterbox, but nothing that looked interesting. I carried it into the inner office and filed it on top of my desk. A thin film of dust on the desk reminded me that I hadn't been there since Friday. I dusted it with a piece of Kleenex and called my answering service.

"A Dr. Sylvester has been trying to get you," the girl on the switchboard said.

"Did he leave a number?"

"No, he said he had to make some hospital calls. He'll be in his office after one o'clock."

"What did he want, do you know?"

"He didn't say. He sounded as if it was important, though. And last night you had a call from a Professor Tappinger. He did leave his number."

She recited it, and I dialed Tappinger's house direct. Bess Tappinger answered.

"This is Lew Archer."

"How lovely," she said in her little-girl voice, her statutory-rape voice. "And what a coincidence. I was just thinking about you."

I didn't ask her what she had been thinking. I didn't want to know.

"Is your husband there?"

"Taps is teaching all morning. Why don't you come over for a cup of coffee? I make a very good Italian coffee."

"Thanks, but I'm not in town."

"Oh, where are you?"

"In Hollywood."

"That's only fifty miles. You could still get here before Taps comes home for lunch. I want to speak to you, Lew."

"What about?"

"Us. Everything. I was up most of the night thinking about it—about the change in my life—and you're part of it, I mean it, Lew."

I cut her short: "I'm sorry, Mrs. Tappinger. I've got a job to do. Counseling discontented housewives isn't my line."

"Don't you like me at all?"

"Sure I like you." I was the last of the big spenders, I couldn't refuse her that.

"I knew you did. I could tell. When I was sixteen I went to a gypsy fortune-teller. She said there'd be a change in my life in a year, that I'd meet a handsome clever man and he would marry me. And that's the way it worked out. I married Taps. But the fortune-teller said there'd be another change when I was thirty. I can feel it coming. It's almost like being pregnant again. I mean it. I thought my life was over and done with—"

"Al this is very interesting," I said. "We'll go into it another time."

"But it won't wait."

"It will have to."

"You said you liked me."

"I like a lot of women."

It was an oafish remark.

"I don't like many men. You're the first since I—"

The sentence died unfinished. I didn't encourage her to resurrect it. I didn't say a word.

She burst into tears, and hung up on me.

Bess was probably schitzy, I told myself, or addled on bedroom novels, suffering from cabin fever or faculty-wife neurosis or the first untimely hint of middle age, like frost on the Fourth of July. Clearly she had troubles, and a wise man I knew in Chicago had said once and for all: "Never sleep with anyone whose troubles are worse than your own."

But Bess was hard to put out of my mind. When I got my car out of the parking lot and headed south on the San Diego Freeway, she was the one I felt I was driving toward, even though it was her husband I was going to see.

At noon I was waiting outside his office in the Arts Building. At one minute after twelve he came down the corridor.

"I could set my watch by you, professor."

He winced. "You make me feel like a mechanical man. Actually I hate being on this rigid schedule." He unlocked the door and flung it open. "Come in."

"I understand you found out something more about Cervantes."

He didn't answer me until we were sitting facing each other across his desk. "I did indeed. After I left you yesterday I decided to throw the schedule overboard for once. I canceled my afternoon class and drove up to Los Angeles State with that picture you gave me of him." He patted his breast pocket. "His name is Pedro Domingo. At least he was registered at L.A. State under the name. Professor Bosch thinks it's his true name."

"I know. I talked to Bosch yesterday."

Tappinger looked displeased, as if I'd gone over his head. "Allan didn't tell *me* that."

"I called him after you left. He was busy, and I got very little from him. He did say that Domingo was a native of Panama."

Tappinger nodded. "That was one of the things that got him into trouble. He'd jumped ship and was in this country illegally. It's why he changed his name when he came here to us. The Immigration officials were after him."

"When and where did he jump ship?"

"It was sometime in 1956, according to Allan, when Pedro was twenty. He came ashore at San Pedro. Perhaps he thought the place would be lucky for him. Anyway, he practically stepped off the boat into a classroom. He attended Long Beach State for a year—I don't know how he got the college to accept him—and then he shifted to Los Angeles State.

"He was there for two years, and Allan Bosch got to know him fairly well. He struck Allan in very much the same way he struck me—as a highly intelligent young man with problems."

"What kind of problems?"

"Social and cultural problems. Historical problems. Allan described him as a kind of tropical Hamlet trying to cope with contemporary reality. Actually that description applies to most of the Central and South American cultures. Domingo's problems weren't just personal, they belonged to his time and place. But he yearned for the luminous city."

Professor Tappinger seemed to be on the brink of a lecture. I said: "The what?"

"The luminous city. It's a phrase I use for the world of spirit and intellect, the distillation of the great minds of past and present." He tapped the side of his head, as though to claim membership in the group. "It takes in everything from Plato's Forms and Augustine's *Civitas Dei* to Joyce's epiphanies."

"Could you take it a little slower, professor?"

"Forgive me." He seemed confused by my interruption. "Was I talking academic jargon? Actually Pedro's dilemma can be stated quite simply: he was a poor Panamanian with all the hopes and troubles and frustrations of his country. He came out of the Santa Ana slums. His mother was a Blue Moon girl in the Panama City cabarets, and Pedro himself was probably illegitimate. But he has too much gumption to accept his condition or remain in it.

"I know something of what he must have felt. I wasn't a bastard, but I worked my way up out of a Chicago slum, and I knew what it was to go hungry in the Depression. I'd never have made it through university without the G.I. bill. So you see, I can sympathize with Pedro Domingo. I hope they won't punish him too severely when they catch him."

"They won't."

He noticed the finality of my tone. Slowly his eyes came up to mine. They were sensitive, rather feminine eyes, which had probably been fine-looking before strain reddened the whites. "Has something happened to him?"

"He's dead. A gunman shot him yesterday. Don't you read the papers?"

"I have to confess that I very seldom look at them. But this is dreadful news." He paused, his sensitive mouth pulled out of shape. "Do you have any notion who killed him?"

"The prime suspect is a gambler named Leo Spillman. He's the other man in the picture I gave you."

Tappinger got it out of his pocket and studied it. "He *looks* dangerous."

"Domingo was dangerous, too. It's fortunate for Ginny that she got out of this alive."

"Is Miss Fablon all right?"

"She's as well as can be expected, after losing her mother and her husband in the same week."

"Poor child. I'd like to see her, and comfort her if I could."

"You better check with Dr. Sylvester. He's looking after her. I'm on my way to see him now."

I rose to go. Tappinger came around the desk. "I'm sorry I can't invite you to lunch today," he said with a kind of aggressive fussiness. "There isn't time."

"I don't have time, either. Give my regards to your wife."

"I'm sure she'll be glad to have them. She's quite an admirer of yours."

"That's because she doesn't know me very well."

My attempt to treat it lightly didn't come off. The little man looked up at me with strained and anxious eyes.

"I'm concerned about Bess. She's such a dreamer, so addicted to *Bovarysme*. And I don't think you're good for her."

"Neither do I."

"You won't take it personally, Mr. Archer, if I suggest that perhaps you'd better not see her again?"

"I wasn't planning to."

Tappinger seemed relieved.

XXVIII

ON MY WAY into town I stopped at a gas station with an outside telephone booth and called Christman in Washington. He was still out to lunch. The operator transferred my call to the restaurant where he ate, and eventually I heard him say:

"Christman here. I've been trying to get you, Lew. You're never in your office."

"I haven't been in for the last few days. Do you have anything more on our friend?"

"A little. Until a few months ago he was a second secretary at the Panamanian Embassy. He was fairly young for the job, but apparently he's very highly qualified. He has an advanced degree from the University of Paris. Before they transferred him to Washington he held the post of third secretary in Paris."

"Why did he leave the diplomatic service?"

"I don't know. The man I talked to said he resigned for personal reasons. He didn't explain what he meant by personal reasons. But Domingo didn't leave under a cloud, so far as I could ascertain. Do you want me to dig some more?"

"There wouldn't be much point," I said. "You might tell whoever you talked to in the Embassy that their boy was shot in Los Angeles yesterday."

"Dead?"

"Very. They'll probably want to do something about the body, when the police release it. Captain Perlberg is in charge of the case."

I was a few minutes late for my appointment with Sylvester, but he was later. He arrived at the clinic about half-past one, looking harried, and took me into his consultation room.

"I'm sorry to keep you waiting, Archer. I thought I'd better drop in on Ginny Fablon."

"How is she?"

"I believe she'll be all right. Of course she's woozy from shock, and I have her under fairly heavy sedation. But she's accepted the fact of her mother's death, as well as her husband's, and she can see beyond them to some kind of future."

"I still don't think she should be left by herself."

"She isn't by herself. The Jamiesons have given her a guest cottage. They're providing her meals, and Peter is there to wait on her, of course, which is all he ever wanted. She may have a happy ending yet."

"With Peter?"

"I wouldn't be surprised." He added with a sidewise cheerless grin: "You understand my idea of a happy marriage is essentially anything that works."

"How's your own marriage working?"

"Audrey and I will muddle through. We've both had a lot to forgive. But I didn't ask you here as a marriage counselor. I have some information for you." He brought a manila folder out of a drawer of his desk. "You're still looking for Leo Spillman, aren't you?"

"I am. So are the police."

"What if I told you where and how to find him? Could I count on a certain amount of tolerance from you?"

"You'd better explain what you mean by that."

He bit his thumb and studied the dent his teeth made. "I let down my back hair yesterday. Frankly I was rattled. The fact is, you know more about me than anyone else in town. It's beginning to look as if everything connected with this mess is going to be spread out in the public prints. All I'm asking from you is a certain amount of decent reticence about my part in it. I have a great deal to lose."

"What do you want suppressed?"

"Well, I wouldn't want the details of my co-operation with Spillman—Couldn't we keep it a doctor-patient relationship? That's what it was essentially."

"That's what it became, anyway. I'll hold back the rest of it if I possibly can."

"Then the thing that Audrey and Fablon had—does it have to come out?"

"I don't see why it should have to. Anything else?"

"I won't try to press this too far," he said, with a wary eye on my face, "but that money Marietta tried to borrow from me Monday—could we keep it confidential?"

"I doubt it. Mrs. Strome at the club knows about it."

"I've already talked to her. She's safe."

"I'm not."

Sylvester's eyes became shallow and hard.

"Why are you balking at that? It's the least embarrassing thing, really."

"Not if Marietta was trying to blackmail you."

"For what? The Spillman-Fablon business? I thought that was settled."

"It isn't settled to my satisfaction."

"But you can't accuse Marietta of being a blackmailer. It was just a friendly loan she asked me for. Naturally I was hoping she'd keep quiet about the Spillman bit, and Audrey's mixup with her husband."

"Naturally. Was there anything else you wanted kept quiet?"

"By you?"

"By anybody. I've been wondering for instance, why and how Ginny came to work for you. I understand she was a receptionist here for a couple of years."

"That's right, until two years ago this summer. Then she went back to school."

"Why did she leave school to go to work?"

"She'd been overstudying."

"Was that your opinion?"

"I agreed with Marietta about it. The girl needed a change."

"She didn't come to work here for personal reasons, then?"

"I wasn't her lover," he said in a grating voice, "If that's what you're getting at. I've done some lousy things in my life but I don't mess around with young girls."

He glanced up at his framed diplomas on the wall. There was a puzzled expression in his eyes, as if he couldn't remember how he had acquired them. His expression turned faraway, further and further away, as if his mind was climbing back over the curve of time to the source of his life.

I brought him back to the present. "You were going to tell me how to find Spillman."

"So I was."

"If you'd given me the information yesterday, you'd have saved trouble, possibly a life."

"I didn't have the information yesterday. That is, I didn't know I had it. I stumbled across it early this morning when I was going over Spillman's medical records." He opened the folder in front of him. "About three months ago, on February 20, we had a request for a copy of the records from a Dr. Charles Park, in Santa Teresa. I didn't fill the request myself—Mrs. Loftin's initials are on the notation—and she neglected to mention it to me. Anyway, as I said, I came across it."

"What were you looking for?"

"I wanted to check how sick Spillman really was. He was sick, all right. Apparently he still is. I called Dr. Park's office as soon as I found the notation. He wasn't in yet himself, but his girl confirmed that Ketchel was still his patient. Apparently Spillman is using the name Ketchel in Santa Teresa."

"Did you get his address there?"

"Yes, I did. It's 1427 Padre Ridge Road."

I thanked him.

"Don't thank me. You and I have an agreement, for what it's worth. I want to add one other small item to it. You mustn't tell Leo Spillman I sicced you on to him."

He was afraid of Spillman. The fear hissed like escaping gas in his voice, and lingered like an odor in my mind. On my way north to Santa Teresa I stopped at my apartment to pick up a hand gun.

XXIX

THE CITY OF SANTA TERESA is built on a slope which begins at the edge of the sea and rises more and more steeply toward the coastal mountains in a series of ascending ridges. Padre Ridge is the first and lowest of these, and the only one inside the city limits.

It was a fairly expensive territory, an established neighborhood of well-maintained older houses, many of them with brilliant hanging gardens. The grounds of 1427 were the only ones in the block that looked unkempt. The privet hedge needed clipping. Crabgrass was running rampant in the steep lawn.

Even the house, pink stucco under red tile, had a disused air about it. The drapes were drawn across the front windows. The only sign of life was a house wren which contested my approach to the veranda.

I lifted the lion's-head knocker and let it drop, hardly expecting an answer. But after a while soft footsteps came from the back of the house. The door was opened, minimally, by a hefty middle-aged woman in a wet blue cotton bathing suit.

"My name is Archer. Is Mrs. Ketchel home?"

"I'll see."

The woman stepped out of the puddle that had formed on the tile around her bare feet, and disappeared into the back of the house. I pushed the front door wide open and walked in, conscious of the gun bulging like a benign tumor in my armpit.

There were several closed doors in the hallway, and an open door at the end. Through it I could see across a room, through sliding glass, to the dappled blue water of a swimming pool.

Kitty came out of the water dripping. She crossed the room, leaving wasp-waisted footprints on the rug, and faced me in the doorway. She had on a white elastic bathing suit and a white rubber cap shaped like a helmet which made her look like an Amazon sentinel.

"You get out of here. I'll call the cops."

"Sure you will. They're combing the state for Leo as it is."

"He hasn't done anything wrong." She hedged. "Not recently."

"I want to hear him tell me that himself."

"No. You can't talk to him."

She stepped forward, pulling the door shut behind her, moving so abruptly that she blundered into me. She put her hands on my shoulders to regain her balance, and recoiled as if I was very hot or cold.

She must have felt the holster under my jacket. Her fear came back. It made her face work as if she had swallowed poison.

"You came here to kill us, didn't you?"

"You and I have been through all this before. You seem to have killing on your mind."

"I've seen too many—" She caught herself.

"Seen too many people die?"

"Yeah. In traffic accidents and stuff like that." She tried to put on an innocent expression. With her paint removed, and her garish hair covered, she looked younger and realer. But not innocent. "What do you want from us? Money? We have no money."

"Don't try to snow me, Kitty. This is the head office of the money factory."

"It's true what I tell you. That cat who calls himself Martel eloped with our ready cash, and we can't realize on our investments."

"How did he get his hands on the cash?"

"He was supposed to be bringing it to Leo. Leo trusted him. I didn't, but Leo did."

"Martel was shot to death in Los Angeles yesterday. Another accident for your memory book. He had a hundred thousand dollars in cash with him."

"Where is it?"

"I thought it might be here. It was black money, wasn't it, Kitty?"

She flung up her arms in a jagged movement, bringing her fists to her shoulders, then flung them down again. "I'm not admitting anything."

"It's time you did some talking, don't you think? There's such a thing as buying immunity with information, especially on an income tax rap."

Though it wasn't cold in the hall, she had begun to shiver.

"On a murder rap," I said, "it isn't so easy. But you can't afford to hold back. Did Leo or one of his boys knock off Martel?"

"Leo had nothing to do with it."

"If he did, and you know he did, you better tell me. Unless you want to go on trial with him."

"I know he didn't. He hasn't left this house."

"You have."

She was shivering violently. "Listen, mister, I don't know what you're trying to do to us—"

"You've done it to yourselves. What you do to other people you do to yourself—that's the converse of the Golden Rule, Kitty."

"I don't know what you're talking about."

"Three murders. Martel yesterday. Marietta Fablon the night before, when incidentally you were in Montevista. And Roy Fablon seven years before that. Remember him?"

She nodded jerkily.

"Tell me what happened to Fablon. You were there."

"Let me get some clothes on first. I'm freezing. I've been in with Leo for about an hour."

"Is he out by the pool?"

"Yes, he's working with his physiotherapist. Don't say anything in front of her, will you? She's a square."

Kitty peeled off her rubber cap. Her red hair blossomed out. When she opened one of the closed doors, I caught a glimpse of a tousled pink female bedroom with a mirror in the ceiling over the king-sized bed, alas.

I went outside. A wheelchair stood among the poolside furniture. The woman in the blue bathing suit was standing breastdeep in the water with a man in her arms. His face was moon-shaped and flaccid, his body loose. Only his black eyes held some measure of controlled adult life.

"Hello, Mr. Ketchel."

"I'll say hello for him," the woman said. "Mr. Ketchel had a little cerebral accident about three months ago and he hasn't said a word since. Have you, honey?"

His sad black eyes answered her. Then they shifted apprehensively to me. He smiled placatingly. Saliva dripped from one corner of his mouth.

Kitty appeared at the sliding glass doors and beckoned me inside. She had put on sequined slacks which winked suggestively, a high-necked angora sweater, a hasty paint job which reduced her face to meaninglessness. It was hard to tell what she had in mind for me.

She took me into a small front room, out of sight of the swimming pool, and opened the drapes. She stood at the window competing with the view. Beside the bulbs and hollows of her body, the sails on the sea looked dinky and remote, like cocked white napkins on a faded blue tablecloth.

"You see what I've got on my hands?" she said with her hands out. "A poor little sick old man. He can't walk, he can't talk, he can't even write his name. He can't tell me where anything is. He can't protect me."

"Who do you need protection from?"

"Leo made a lifetime of enemies. If they knew he was helpless, his life wouldn't be worth that." She snapped her fingers. "Neither would mine. Why do you think we're hiding out in the tules here?"

To her, I thought, the tules meant any place that wasn't on the Chicago-Vegas-Hollywood axis. I said: "Is Leo's partner Davis one of the threats?"

"He's the main one. If Leo dies or gets knocked off, Davis has the most to gain."

"The Scorpion Club."

"He already owns it on paper: the Tax Commission made Leo give it up. And he has a beef against Leo."

"I talked to Davis last night. He offered me money to tell him where Leo is."

"So that's why you're here."

"Stop jumping to conclusions. I turned him down."

"Really?"

"Really. What's his beef against Leo?"

She shook her head. Her hair flared out in the sunlight. Oddly it reminded me of the orange-pickers' fire in the railroad yards. The queer forced intimacy of that night still hung as a possibility between me and Kitty.

"I can't tell you that," she said.

"Then I'll tell you. Internal Revenue is after Leo for the money he took off the top. If they can't find him and the money, maybe even if they can, they'll pin the rap on Davis. At the very least he'll lose his license for fronting for a concealed interest. At worst he'll go to the federal pen for the rest of his life."

"He isn't the only one."

"If you mean Leo, the rest of his life isn't worth much."

"What about the rest of my life?" She touched her furred angora breast. "I'm not even thirty yet. I don't want to go to prison."

"Then you better make a deal."

"And turn Leo in? I will not."

"They won't do anything to him, in his condition."

"They'll lock him up. He won't get his therapy. He'll never learn to talk or write or—" She stopped herself in mid-sentence.

"Or tell you where the money is?"

She hesitated. "What money? You said the money was gone."

"The hundred grand is. But my information is that Leo took millions off the top. Where is it?"

"I wish I knew, mister." Through her composed mask I could see the calculation going on behind her eyes. "What did you say your name was?"

"Archer. Does Leo know where the money is?"

"I think so. He still has some of his brain left. But it's hard to tell how much he understands. He always pretends to understand everything I say. So the other day I tried him on some gibberish. He smiled and nodded just the same."

"What did you say?"

"I wouldn't want to repeat it. It was just a lot of dirty words about what I'd do for him if he'd learn to talk. Or even write." Tensely, she clasped her arms across her chest. "It drives me crazy when I think of what I went through in the hopes of a little peace and security. The beatings he handed out, and the other stuff. Don't think I didn't have other chances. But I stuck with Leo. Stuck is the word. Now I'm stuck with a cripple and it's costing us two grand a month to live—six hundred a month just for doctors and therapy—and I don't know where next month's money is coming from." Her voice rose. "I'd be a millionaire if I had my rights."

"Or your wrongs."

She tossed her head. "I earned that money, I ground it out like coffee over the years. Don't tell me I've got no right to it. I've got a right to a decent living."

"Who told you that?"

"Nobody had to tell me. A woman with my looks—I can pick and choose." It was childish talk, self-hypnotic and pathetic. It gave me a hint of the self-enclosed fantasy that had paired her off with Leo Spillman and kept her with him, insulated from life by his larger fantasy.

"You mean you get picked and chosen. Why don't you go out and hustle? You're a big strong girl."

She as still on her adolescent high horse. "How dare you? I'm not a prostitute."

"I don't mean that kind of hustle. Get a job."

"I've never had to work for a living, thank you."

"It's time you did. If you keep dreaming about those vanished millions you'll dream yourself into Camarillo or Corona."

"Don't you dare make threats to me!"

"It isn't me threatening you. It's your dreams. If you won't lift a finger to help yourself, go back to Harry."

"That feeb? He couldn't even stay out of the hospital."

"He gave everything he had."

She was silent. Her face was like a colored picture straining in agony to come to life. Life glittered first in her eyes. A tear made a track down her cheek. I found myself standing beside her comforting her. Then her head was like an artificial dahlia on my shoulder, and I could feel the sorrowful little movements of her body becoming less sorrowful.

The therapist tapped on the door and opened it. She had

changed into street clothes. "I'm leaving, Mrs. Ketchel. Mr. Ketchel is safe and snug in his wheelchair." She looked at us severely: "But don't leave him out too long now."

"I won't," Kitty said. "Thank you."

The woman didn't move. "I was wondering if you can pay me something on last week, and for staying Monday night. I have bills to meet, too."

Kitty went to her bedroom and came back with a twenty-dollar bill. She thrust it at the woman. "Will this take care of it for now?"

"I guess it will have to. I don't begrudge my services, understand, but a woman has a right to honest pay for honest work."

"Don't worry, you'll get your money. Our dividend checks are slow in arriving this month."

The woman gave her disbelieving look, and left the house. Kitty was rigid with anger. She rapped her fists together in the air.

"The old bag! She humiliated me."

"Are there any dividends coming?"

"There's nothing coming. I'm having to sell my jewels. And I was saving them for a rainy day."

"It looks like a wet summer."

"What are you, a rainmaker?"

She moved toward me, humming an old song about what we'd do on a rain-rain-rainy day. Her breast nudged me gently. "I'd do a lot for any man who would help me find Leo's money."

She was being deliberately provocative now, but our moment had passed.

"Would you tell me the truth, for instance?"

"What about?"

"Roy Fablon. Did Leo kill him?"

After a long thinking pause, she said: "He didn't mean to. It was an accident. They had a fight about—something."

"Something?"

"If you have to know, it was Roy Fablon's daughter. The older Leo got, the more he went for the young chicks. It was embarrassing. Maybe I shouldn't have done what I did, but I passed the word to Mrs. Fablon about Leo making a deal for the girl with Fablon."

"You told Mrs. Fablon?"

"That's correct. I was acting in self-defense. Also I was doing the girl a favor. Mrs. Fablon straightened her husband out, and he said nix to Leo."

"I can't understand why he didn't say nix in the first place."

"He owed Leo a lot of money, and that was all the leverage Leo ever needed. Also Fablon pretended not to know what the deal meant. You know what I mean?"

"I know what you mean."

"Like Leo was a philanthropist or something. He'd sell his sick mother's blood for ten dollars a pint and take a deposit on the bottle, Leo would. But he was going to send the girl to school in Switzerland, to improve her mind. And Fablon thought that would be great, until his wife got wind of it. Frankly I think that Fablon hated the girl."

"I thought he was crazy about her."

"Sometimes there isn't much difference between the two. Ask me, I'm an expert. Fablon turned against her when she got pregnant by some fellow, apparently, and Fablon would go to any lengths to get her away from him."

"Who was he?"

"I don't know. Mrs. Fablon didn't know, either, or else she didn't want to tell me. Anyway, Fablon came to the cottage that night and called the whole deal off. Leo and him had a big fight, and Fablon took quite a beating. Leo used to be terrible with his fists, even when he was sick. Fablon stumbled out of the cottage in bad shape. He lost his way in the dark and fell in the pool and drowned."

"Did you see him?"

"Cervantes did."

"He must have been lying. According to the chemical evidence, Fablon drowned in salt water. The pool is fresh."

"Maybe it is now. It was salt in those days. I ought to know. I swam in it every day for two weeks."

Her voice lingered on the memory. Maybe she was

running into rainy days, and having to sell her jewelry. But she had spent two weeks in the Tennis Club sun.

"What did Cervantes have to say about it, Kitty?"

"He found Roy Fablon in the pool, and came and told Leo. It was a bad scene. Leo was committing a felony just by using his fists. When Fablon drowned it was technically murder. Cervantes suggested he could chuck the body in the sea and fake a suicide. He'd been sucking around Leo before, and this was his chance for an in. When we left town the next day or so, we took him along. Instead of sending the Fablon girl to school in Switzerland, Leo sent the Cervantes boy to college in Paris, France.

"I told Leo he was nuts. He said the reason he was a success was because he looked years ahead. He had a use for Cervantes, he said, and he knew he could trust him, after the Fablon business. That was one time he was wrong. As soon as Leo got sick this last time, Cervantes turned on him." Her voice deepened. "It's funny about Leo. Everybody was afraid of him, including me. He was the big shot. But as soon as he got really sick, he was just a nothing man. A flunky like Cervantes could take him for everything he had."

"At least it was a switch. How did Cervantes get hold of the money?"

"Leo turned it over to him, a piece at a time, over the last three-four years. Cervantes got some kind of a government job, and he could cross the border without being searched. He stashed the money someplace out of the country, maybe Switzerland, in one of those numbered bank accounts they have."

I didn't think the money was in Switzerland. There were numbered accounts in Panama, too.

"What are you thinking?"

"I was wondering," I said, "if Mrs. Fablon was blackmailing Leo for killing her husband."

"She was. She came to see him in Vegas after the body was found. She told him she protected him at the inquest, and the least he could do was help her out a little. He hated the hell to do it, but I think he sent her payments from then on." She paused, and looked at me sharply. "I've told you everything I know about the Fablons. Are you going to try to trace that money for me?"

"I'm not saying no. Right now I have another client, and two other murders to work on."

"There's no money in that, is there?"

"Money isn't the only thing in life."

"That's what I used to think, until this. What are you, a do-gooder or something?"

"I wouldn't say so. I'm working at not being a do-badder."

She gave me a puzzled look. "I don't get you, Archer. What's your angle?"

"I like people, and I try to be of some service."

"And that adds up to a life?"

"It makes life possible, anyway. Try it sometime."

"I did," she said, "with Harry. But he didn't have what it takes. I always get stuck with feebs and cripples." She shrugged. "I better see how Leo is doing."

He was waiting patiently in the cross-hatched shadow of a latticework screen. His shirt and trousers were loose on his shrunken body. He blinked up at me when we approached him, as if I planned to hit him.

"Cowardy custard," Kitty said cheerfully. "This is my new boyfriend. He's going to find the money and take me on a trip around the world. And you want to know what's going to happen to you, you poor old clown? We'll put you in a ward in the country hospital. And nobody will ever come to see you."

I walked out.

XXX

I DROVE BACK to Los Angeles. Stopped there for dinner during the twilight hour, and finished the trip to Montevista in the dark.

Vera answered the door of the Jamieson house. She was wearing her sunburst kimono, and her black hair was loose on her shoulders. It wasn't that late. The household seemed to be going to pieces in a quiet way.

"He's out in the guest house," she said, "with her." Vera seemed to resent another woman on the premises.

The guest house was a white frame cottage at the rear of the garden. Light spilled from its half-shuttered windows, reviving the daytime colors of the flower beds around it. Sweet unidentifiable odors drifted in the air.

It seemed like a place for an idyll, instead of the sequel to a tragedy. Life was short and sweet, I thought, sweet and short.

Peter called out: "Who is it?"

I told him, and he opened the door. He had on a bulky gray sweater and an open-collared white shirt which revealed the flabby thickness of his neck. There was a rather peculiar gleam in his eye. It could have been pure innocent happiness, it could have been euphoria.

I had similar doubts about the girl in the bright chintz room behind him. She sat under a lamp with a book on her knee, perfectly calm and still in a black dress. She nodded to me, and that was all.

"Come in, won't you?"

"You come out."

He stepped outside, leaving the door partly open. It was a warm night for May, and windless.

"What is it, Mr. Archer? I hate to leave her."

"Even for a minute?"

"Even for a minute," he said with a kind of pride.

"I have some findings to report, about her father's death. I doubt that she'll want to hear what I have to say. He wasn't a suicide. He may have died by accident."

"I think Ginny will want to hear about it."

Reluctantly I went in and told my story, slightly bowdlerized. Ginny took it more calmly than Peter. His foot kept thumping to a nervous rhythm. As if an uncontrolled part of him wanted to run away, even from a room with Ginny in it.

I said to her: "I'm sorry to have to dig this up and throw it in your lap. You've had quite a lot thrown in your lap recently."

"It's all right. It's over now."

I hoped it was over. Her serenity bothered me. It was like the lifeless serenity of a statue.

"Do you want me to do anything about Mr. Ketchel?"

Peter waited for her to answer. She lifted her hands a few inches and dropped them on her book. "What would be the point? You say he's a sick old man, hardly more than a vegetable. It's like one of the condign punishments in Dante. A big violent man turns into a helpless cripple." She hesitated. "Were he and my father fighting about me?"

"That was the general idea."

"I don't understand," Peter said.

She turned to him. "Mr. Ketchel made a rough pass at me."

"And you still don't want him punished?"

"Why should I? That was years ago. I'm not even the same person," she added unsmilingly. "Did you know we change completely, chemically speaking, every seven years?" She seemed to take comfort in the thought.

"You're an angel," he said. But he didn't go near her or touch her.

"There's a further possibility," I said. "Ketchel-Spillman may not have been responsible for your father's death after all. Somebody else may have found him wandering around the club grounds in a daze, and deliberately drowned him in the swimming pool."

"Who would do that?" she said.

"Your late husband himself is the best bet. I've got some further information on him by the way. He was a Panamanian who came out of a fairly hard school—"

She interrupted me: "I know that. Professor Tappinger paid me a visit this afternoon. He told me all about Francis. Poor Francis," she said remotely. "I see now that he wasn't entirely sane, and neither was I, to be taken in by him. But what conceivable reason could he have for hurting Roy? I didn't even know him in those days."

"He may have drowned him to get a hold on Ketchel. Or he may have seen someone else drown him, and convinced Ketchel that it was Ketchel's fault."

"You have a horrible imagination, Mr. Archer."

"So had your late husband."

"No. You're mistaken about him. Francis wasn't like that."

"You only knew one side of him, I'm afraid. Francis Martel was a made-up character. Did Professor Tappinger tell you his real name was Pedro Domingo, and he was a bastard by-product of the slums of Panama City? That's all we know about the real man, the real life that forced him into the fantasy life with you."

"I don't want to talk about that." She hugged herself as if she could feel a faint chill of reality through her widow's black. "Please let's not talk about Francis."

Peter rose from his chair. "I quite agree. All that is in the past now. And we've had enough talk for one night, Mr. Archer."

He went to the door and opened it. The sweet night air flooded into the room. I sat where I was.

"May I ask you a question in private, Miss Fablon? Are you calling yourself Miss Fablon?"

"I suppose so. I hadn't thought of it."

"It won't be 'Miss Fablon' for long." Peter said with foolish blandness. "One of these fine days it's going to be 'Mrs. Jamieson,' the way it was always meant to be."

Ginny looked resigned and very tired. "What do you wish to ask me?" she said softly.

"It's a private question. Tell Peter to go away for a minute."

"Peter, you heard the man."

He frowned and went out, leaving the door wide open. I heard him bulling around in the garden.

"Poor old Peter," she said. "I don't know what I'd do without him now. I don't know just what I'm going to do with him, either."

"Marry him?"

"I don't seem to have any other choice. That sounds cynical, doesn't it? I didn't mean it that way. But nothing seems terribly worthwhile right now."

"It wouldn't be fair to marry Peter unless you cared about him."

"Oh, I care for him, more than anyone. I always have. Francis was just an episode in my life." Behind her world-weary pose, I caught a hint of her immaturity. I wondered if she had grown emotionally at all since her father died.

And I thought that Ginny and Kitty, girls from opposite ends of the same town, had quite a lot in common after all. Neither one had quite survived the accident of beauty. It had made them into things, zombies in a dead desert world, as painful to contemplate as meaningless crucifixions.

"You and Peter used to go together, he told me."

"That's true. Through most of high school. He wasn't fat in those days," she added in an explanatory way.

"Were you lovers?"

Her eyes darkened, the way the ocean darkens under moving clouds. For the first time I seemed to have touched her sense of her own life. She turned away so that I couldn't look into her eyes.

"I don't see that it matters." That meant yes.

"Did you become pregnant by Peter?"

"If I answer you," she said with her face averted, "will you promise never to repeat my answer? To anyone, even Peter?"

"All right."

"Then I can tell you. We were going to have a baby when I was a freshman in college. I didn't tell Peter. He was so young, and so young for his age. I didn't want to frighten him. I didn't tell anyone, except Roy, and eventually Mother. But even them I didn't tell who the father was. I had no desire to be taken out of school and forced into one of those horrible teenage marriages. Roy was pretty let down with me, on account of the baby, but he borrowed a thousand dollars and took me to Tijuana. He treated me to the de luxe abortion, complete with doctor and nurse and hygienic atmosphere. But after that he seemed to feel I owed him money."

Her voice was toneless. She might have been talking about a shopping trip. But her very flatness of feeling suggested the trauma that kept her emotions fixed. She said without much curiosity:

"How did you find out about my pregnancy? I thought nobody knew."

"It doesn't matter how I found out."

"But I only told Roy and Mother."

"And they're dead."

A barely visible tremor went through her. Slowly, as if against physical resistance, she turned her head and looked into my face.

"You think they were killed because they knew about my pregnancy?"

"It's possible."

"What about Francis's death?"

"I have no theory, Miss Fablon. I'm still groping in the dark. Do you have any ideas?"

She shook her head. Her bright hair swung, touching her cold pale cheeks with a narcissistic caress.

Peter said impatiently from the doorway: "May I come in now?"

"No, you may not. Go away and leave me alone." She stood up, including me in the invitation to leave.

"But you're not supposed to be alone," Peter said. "Dr. Sylvester told me—"

"Dr. Sylvester is an old woman, and you're another. Go away. If you don't, I'll move out. Tonight."

Peter backed out, and I followed him. She closed and bolted the door after us. When we were out of hearing of the cottage, Peter turned on me:

"What did you say to her?"

"Nothing, really."

"You must have said something to bring on a reaction like that."

"I asked her a question or two."

"What about?"

"She asked me not to tell you."

"*She* asked *you* not to tell *me*?" His face leaned close to mine. I couldn't see it too well. He sounded wildly angry and belligerent. "You've got things turned around, haven't you? You're my employee. Ginny is my fiancée."

"She's kind of an instant fiancée, isn't she?"

Perhaps I shouldn't have said it. Peter called me a filthy crud and swung on me. I saw his fist arriving out of the darkness too late to duck it cleanly. I rolled my head away from the blow, diminishing its sting.

I didn't hit him back, but I put up my hands to catch a second punch in case he threw one. He didn't, at least not physically.

"Go away," he said in a sobbing voice. "You and I are finished. You're finished here."

XXXI

IT WAS A MORAL HARDSHIP for me to walk away from an unclosed case. I went back to my apartment in West Los Angeles and drank myself into a moderate stupor.

Even so I didn't sleep too well. I woke up in the middle of the night. A spatter of rain was rustling like cellophane at the window. The whiskey was wearing off and I was myself in a flicker of panic: a middle-aging man lying alone in darkness while life fled by like traffic on the freeway.

I got up late and went out for breakfast. The morning papers reported no new developments. I went to my office and waited for Peter to change his mind and phone me.

I didn't really need him, I told myself. I still had some of his money. Even without it, and even without his backing in Montevista, I could go out and work with Perlberg on the Martel killing. But for some important reason I wanted him to rehire me. I think in my nighttime loneliness I'd fathered an imaginary son, a poor fat foolish son who ate his sorrow instead of drinking it.

The sun burned off the morning fog and dried the pavements. My depression lifted more slowly. I went through my mail in search of hopeful omens.

An interesting-looking envelope from Spain had pictures of General Franco on the stamps and was addressed to Señor Lew Archer. The letter inside said: "Cordiales Saludos: This comes to you from far-off Spain to call your attention to our new Fiesta line of furniture with its authentically Spanish motif as exciting as a *corrida,* as colorful as a *flamenco* dance. Come see it at any one of our Greater Los Angeles stores."

The piece of junk mail I liked best was a folder from the Las Vegas Chamber of Commerce. Among the attractions of the city it mentioned swimming, golf, tennis, bowling, water-skiing, eating, going to shows, and going to church, but not a word about gambling.

It was an omen. While I was still smiling over the folder, Captain Perlberg phoned me.

"You busy, Archer?"

"Not so very. My client lost interest."

"Too bad," he said cheerfully. "You could do us both a favor. How would you like to talk to Martel's old lady?"

"His mother?"

"That's what I said. She jetted in from Panama this morning and she's screaming for us to release her son's body, also for information. You know more about the background of the case than I do, and I thought if you were willing to talk it over with her, you could save us an international incident."

"Where is she now?"

"She took a suite in the Beverly Hills Hotel. Right at the moment she's sleeping, but she'll be expecting you early this afternoon, say around two-fifteen? She'd make a nice client for you."

"Who would pay me?"

"She would. The woman is loaded."

"I thought she was from hunger."

"You thought wrong," Perlberg said. "The consul general told me she's married to the vice-president of a bank in Panama City."

"What's his name?"

"Rosales. Ricardo Rosales."

It was the name of the vice-president of the Bank of New Granada who had written the letter to Marietta telling her that there would be no more money.

"I'll be glad to pay a visit to Mrs. Rosales."

I called Professor Allan Bosch at Los Angeles State College. Bosch said he'd be happy to have lunch with me and brief me on Pedro Domingo, but he still had a time problem.

"I can drive out there, professor. Do you have a restaurant on the L.A. State campus?"

"We have three eating places," he said. "The Cafeteria, the Inferno, and the Top of the North. Incidentally our name's been changed to Cal State L.A."

"The Inferno sounds interesting."

"It's less interesting than it sounds. Actually it's just an automat. Why don't we meet at the Top of the North? That's on top of North Hall."

The college is on the eastern border of the city. I took the Hollywood Freeway to the San Bernardino Freeway, which I left at the Eastern Avenue turnoff. The campus was a sort of chopped-off hill crowded with buildings. Parking spaces were scarce. Eventually I parked in a faculty slot, and rode the elevator six stories up to the Top of the North.

Professor Bosch was a youthful-looking man in his middle thirties, tall enough to play center on a basketball team. He had a big man's slouch, and a bright disenchanted eye. His speech was staccato, with a Middle Western accent.

"I'm surprised you made it on time. It's quite a drive. I saved us a place by the window."

He led me to a table on the east side of the large buzzing room. Through the window I could see toward Pasadena and the mountains.

"You want me to tell you what I know about Pedro Domingo," Bosch said over our onion soup.

"Yes. I'm interested in him and his relatives. Professor Tappinger said his mother was a Blue Moon girl. That's the Panamanian equivalent of a B-girl, isn't it?"

"I guess it is." Bosch shifted his bulk in the chair and looked at me sideways across the table. "Before we go any further, why wasn't Pedro's murder reported in the papers?"

"It was. Didn't Tappinger mention that he was using an alias?"

"Taps may have, I don't remember. We both got excited, and we went round in circles for a while." His gaze narrowed on my face. "What alias was he using?"

"Francis Martel."

"That's interesting." Bosch didn't tell me why. "I did see the report of that shooting. Wasn't it supposed to be a gangster killing?"

"It was supposed to be."

"You sound dubious."

"I'm getting more and more that way."

Bosch had stopped eating. He showed no further interest in his soup. When his minute steak arrived he cut it meticulously into small pieces which he failed to eat.

"I seem to be asking most of the questions," he said. "I was interested in Pedro Domingo. He had a good mind, rather disordered but definitely brilliant. Also he had a lot of life."

"It's all run out now."

"Why was he using an alias?"

"He stole a pile of money and didn't want to be caught. Also he wanted to impress a girl who was hipped on French. He represented himself as a French aristocrat named Francis Martel. It sounds better than Pedro Domingo, especially in Southern California."

"It's almost authentic, too," Bosch said quietly.

"Authentic?"

"At least as authentic as most genealogical claims. Pedro's grandfather, his mother's father, was named Martel. He may not have been an aristocrat, exactly, but he was an educated Parisian. He came over from France as a young engineer with *La Compagnie Universelle*."

"I don't know French, professor."

"*La Compagnie Universelle du Canal Interocéanique de Panama* is the name de Lesseps gave to his canal-building company—a big name for an enormous flop. It went broke somewhere before 1890, and Grandpère Martel lost his money. He decided to stay on in Panama. He was an amateur ornithologist, and the flora and fauna intrigued him.

"Eventually he went more or less native, and spent his declining years with a girl in one of the villages. Pedro said she was descended from the first Cimarrones, the escaped slaves who fought with Francis Dr.ake against the Spaniards. He claimed to be a direct descendant of Dr.ake through her—that would explain the name Francis—but I think this time he was spinning a pure genealogical fantasy. Pedro went in rather heavily for fantasy."

"It's dangerous," I said, "when you start to act it out."

"I suppose it is. Anyway, the village girl was Pedro's maternal grandmother. His mother and Pedro both took the name Domingo from her."

"Who was Pedro's father?"

"He didn't know. I gathered that his mother didn't, either. She lived a disorganized life, to put it mildly. But she did keep alive the grandfather's tradition, even long after the old man died.

"There's a French tradition in Panama, anyway. Pedro's mother taught him French along with Spanish. They read together out of *Grandpère*'s books. The old man had been fairly literate—his library ranged from La Fontaine and Descartes to Baudelaire—and Pedro got quite a decent education in French. You can understand why the language obsessed him. He was a slum boy, with Indian and slave blood in his veins as well as French. His Frenchness was his only distinction, his only hope of distinction."

"How can you possibly know all this, professor?"

"I spent some time with the boy. I thought he had promise, perhaps very brilliant promise, and he was keen to talk with someone who knew France. I spent a year there on a traveling fellowship,'' Bosch added in a depreciatory tone. ''Also, in my advanced French composition courses I use a device—which incidentally I borrowed from Taps—the device of having my students write an essay, in French, explaining why they're studying the language. Pedro came up with a stunning piece about his grandfather and *la gloire*—the glory of France. I gave him an A-plus on it, my first in several years. It's the source of most of what I've been telling you.''

''I don't know the language,'' I said, ''but I'd certainly like to see that document.''

''I gave it back to Pedro. He told me he sent it home to his mother.''

''What was her name, do you know?''

''Secundina Domingo. She must have been *her* mother's second daughter.''

''Judging by her last name, she never married.''

''Apparently she didn't. But there were men in her life,'' Bosch said dryly. ''One night I gave Pedro too much wine and he told me about the American sailors who used to come home with her. This was during the war, when he was still quite young. He and his mother had only the one room, and only one bed in the room. He had to wait on the landing when she had visitors. Sometimes he waited out there all night.

''He was devoted to his mother, and I think that experience pushed him a little over the edge. The night I'm talking about, when he got high on my *vin ordinaire,* he went into a wild oration about his country being the trampled crossroads of the world and he himself the essence of its mud, Caucasian, Indian, Negro. He seemed to identify himself with the Black Christ of Nombre de Dios, which is a famous Panamanian religious statue.''

''He had Messianic delusions?''

''If he had, I wouldn't know. I'm not a psychiatrist. I think Pedro really was a ruined poet, a symbolizing idealizing soul who inherited too many problems. I admit he had some pretty weird ideas, but even the weird ones made a kind of sense. Panama was more than a country to him, more than a geographical link between North and South America. He thought it represented a basic connection between the soul and the body, the head and the heart—and that the North Americans broke the connection." He added: "And now we've killed him."

"We?"

"We North Americans."

He toyed with the dark meat congealing on his plate. I looked out toward the mountains. Above them a jet had cut a white wound in the sky.

I was getting a picture of Allan Bosch which I liked. He differed from an older type like Tappinger, who was so wrapped up in himself and his work that it made him a social eccentric. Bosch seemed genuinely concerned with his students. I said something to this effect.

He shrugged off his pleasure in the compliment. "I'm a teacher. I wouldn't want to be anything else." After a pause, which was filled with the interwoven noise of the students around us, he said: "I took it hard when Pedro had to leave here. He was just about the most interesting student I ever had here or at Illinois. I've only taught the two places."

"Your friend Tappinger says the Justice Department was after him."

"Yes. Pedro entered the country illegally. He had to leave Long Beach and then he had to leave here, one jump ahead of the Immigration men. As a matter of fact, I tipped him that they were making inquiries about him. I'm not ashamed of it, either," he said with a half-smile.

"I won't turn you in, Dr. Bosch."

His smile became wry and defensive. "I'm afraid I'm not a Ph.D. I failed comprehensives at Illinois. I could have tried them again, I suppose, but there wasn't much point in it."

"Why not?"

"Taps had already left. I was one of his special protégés, and I inherited a certain amount of ill will. What happened to him did nothing for my morale, either. I thought if it could happen to one of the most promising scholars in my field, it could happen to anybody."

"What happened to him at Illinois?"

Bosch went into a tight-lipped silence. I waited, and changed my angle of approach:

"Is he still a leading scholar in your field?"

"He would be if he had a decent chance. But he gets no time for his work, and it's driving him crazy. When the grants are handed out, they pass him over. He can't even get a promotion in a bush league school like Montevista."

"Why not?"

"They don't like the way he combs his hair, I guess."

"Or the way his wife combs hers?"

"I suppose she has something to do with it. But frankly I'm not interested in retailing faculty gossip. We are supposed to be talking about Pedro Domingo, alias Cervantes. If you have any more questions about him, I'll be glad to oblige. Otherwise—"

"Where did he get the name Cervantes?"

"I suggested it the night he left. He always struck me as a quixotic type."

I thought, but did not say, that the word applied more exactly to Bosch himself. "And did you send him to study under Tappinger?"

"No. I may have mentioned Taps to him at one time or another. But Pedro went to Montevista on account of a girl. She was a freshman, apparently quite gifted in languages—"

"Who said so?"

"Taps said so himself, and as a matter of fact I talked to her, too. He brought her up for our spring arts festival. We were putting on Sartre's *No Exit*, and she'd never seen a contemporary play in French before. Pedro was there, and he fell in love with her literally on sight."

"How do you know?"

"He told me. In fact he showed me some sonnets he wrote about her and her ideal beauty. She was a lovely thing, one of those pure pale blondes, and very young, no more than sixteen or seventeen."

"She isn't so young and she isn't so pure, but she's still a lovely thing."

He dropped his fork with a noise which merged with the continuous clatter of the room. "Don't tell me you know her."

"She's Pedro's widow. They were married last Saturday."

"I don't understand."

"If I told you all about it, it would only make you feel worse. He made up his mind to marry her seven years ago—perhaps the night he saw her here at the play. Do you know if he made any approach to her that night, or afterwards?"

Bosch considered the question. "I'm pretty sure he didn't. Morally certain, in fact. It was one of those secret passions the Latins seem to go in for."

"Like Dante and Beatrice."

He looked at me in some surprise. "You've read Dante, have you?"

"I've read at him. But I have to admit I was quoting another witness. She said Pedro followed the girl with his eyes the way Dante followed Beatrice."

"Who on earth said that?"

"Bess Tappinger. Do you know her?"

"Naturally I know her. You might say she's an authority on Dante and Beatrice."

"Really?"

"I don't mean that quite seriously, Mr. Archer. But Bess and Taps played comparable roles in their time: the intellectual and the girl ideal.They had a very beautiful Platonic thing going on before they had—before real life caught up with them."

"Could you be a little clearer? I'm interested in the woman."

"In Bess?"

"In both of the Tappingers. What do you mean when you say real life caught up with them?"

He studied my face, as if to read my intentions. "There's no harm in telling you, I suppose. Practically everybody in the Modern Language Association knows the story. Bess was a sophomore studying French at Illinois and Taps was the rising young man in the department. The two of them had this Platonic thing going. They were like Adam and Eve before the Fall. Or Héloïse and Abélard. That may sound like romantic exaggeration, but it isn't. I was there.

"Then real life reared its ugly head, as I said. Bess got pregnant. Taps married her, of course, but the thing was messily handled. The Illinois campus was quite puritanical in those days. What made it worse, the Assistant Dean of Women had a crush on Taps herself, and she really hounded him. So did Bess's parents; they were a couple of bourgeois types from Oak Park. The upshot of it was, the administration fired him for moral turpitude and sent him off to the boondocks."

"And he's been there ever since?"

Bosch nodded. "Twelve years. It's a long time to go on paying for a minor mistake, which incidentally is a very common one. Teachers are marrying their students all the time, with or without shotgun accompaniment. Taps got a very raw deal, in my opinion, and it just about ruined his life. But we're wandering far afield, Mr. Archer." The young man glanced at his wristwatch. "It's half-past one, and I have an appointment with a student."

"Cancel it and come along with me. I have a more interesting appointment."

"Oh? With whom?"

"Pedro's mother."

"You're kidding."

"I almost wish I were. She flew here from Panama this morning, and she's staying at the Beverly Hills Hotel. I may need a translator. How about it?"

"Sure. We'd better go in two cars so you won't have to drive me back."

XXXII

Bosch and I met at the desk of the hotel. I was a few minutes late for my appointment, and the clerk told us to go right up.

The woman who let us into the sitting room of the suite was fifty or so, still handsome in spite of her gold teeth and the craterlike circles under her eyes. She was dressed entirely in black. A trace of musky perfume hung around her like the smell of fire, giving her an aura of burnt-out sex.

"Señora Rosales?"

"Yes."

"I'm the private detective Lew Archer. My Spanish is not too good. I hope you speak English."

"Yes. I speak English." She looked up inquiringly at the young man beside me.

"This is Professor Bosch," I said. "He was a friend of your son's."

In an unexpected gesture of emotion, more hungry than hospitable, she gave us each a hand and drew us across the room to sit on either side of her. Her hands were those of a working woman, rough and etched with ineradicable grime. Her English was good but stiff, as if it had been worked over.

"Pedro has told me about you, Professor Bosch. You were very kind to him, and I am grateful."

"He was the best student I ever had. I'm sorry about his death."

"Yes, it is a great loss. He would have been one of our great men." She turned to me. "When will they release his body for burial?"

"Within a day or two. Your consul will arrange to ship it home. You really needn't have come here."

"So my husband said. He said I should stay out of this country, that you would arrest me and take away my money. But how can you do that? I am a Panamanian citizen, and so was my son. The money Pedro gave me belongs to me." She spoke with a kind of questioning defiance.

"To you and your husband."

"Yes, of course."

"Have you been married long?"

"Two months. A little longer than two months. Pedro was content with my marriage. He gave us as a wedding gift a villa in La Cresta. Pedro and Señor Rosales, my husband, were good friends."

She seemed to be trying to justify her marriage, as if she suspected a connection between it and her son's death. I had no doubt it was a marriage of convenience. When the vice-president of a bank in any country marries a middle-aged woman of uncertain background, there has to be a sound business reason.

"Were they business associates?"

"Pedro and Señor Rosales?" She put on a stupid mask and lifted her hands and shoulders in a shrug that half resembled a bargaining gesture. "I know nothing of business. It is all the more remarkable that my son was so successful in business, *n'est-ce pas*? He understood the workings of the *Bourse*—you call it Wall Street, do you not? He saved his money and invested cleverly," she said in a kind of rhythmical self-hypnosis.

She must have suspected the truth, though, because she added: "It isn't true, is it, that Pedro was killed by gangsters?"

"I don't know whether it's true or not, señora. The killer hasn't been run down."

Bosch put in: "You said you doubted that it was a gangster shooting."

The woman took comfort from this. "Of course, my son had nothing to do with gangsters. He was a fine man, a great man. If he had lived, he would have become our foreign minister, perhaps our president."

She was spinning a web of fantasy, to veil any possible truth that might emerge. I didn't feel like arguing with her grief, but I said:

"Did you know Leo Spillman?"

"Who?"

"Leo Spillman."

"No. Who is Leo Spillman?"

"A Las Vegas gambler. Your son was an associate of his. Didn't he ever mention Spillman to you?"

She shook her head. I could see no indication that she was lying. But there were sorrowful depths in her black eyes, depths below depths, like strata of history older than the Incas.

"You believe that Leo Spillman killed my son, is that it?"

"I thought so until yesterday. Pedro embezzled a lot of money from Spillman."

"Embezzled?" She appealed to Bosch. "*¿Que está diciendo?*"

He answered her reluctantly: "Mr. Archer thinks your son stole some money from Mr. Spillman. I don't know anything about it."

Her breath hissed through her gold teeth: "*Está diciendo mentiras. Pedro hizo su fortuna en* Wall Street."

"She says you're a liar," Bosch told me with a polite pleasure.

"Thanks, I got the message." I said to her: "I'm not bringing up these matters for fun, señora. If we want to find out what happened to your son, we have to go into the question of his money. I think he was killed for his money."

"By his new wife?" she said on a rising tone.

"That's a good question. The answer has to be no, but I'm interested in your reasons for asking it."

"I know women, and I know my son. He was capable of a grand—a great love. Such men are always deluded by their women."

"Do you know that Pedro was?"

"He suspected it himself. He wrote me about his fear that the woman he wished to marry did not love him. I intend to speak to the woman."

"It wouldn't be a good idea," I said. "Within the last

four days she's lost both her mother and her husband. Let her be, señora.''

She persisted stolidly. ''I have lost more than her—than she. I wish to speak to her. I will pay you well to take me to her.''

''Sorry. I can't do it.''

She rose abruptly. ''Then you are wasting my time.''

She moved to the door and held it open for us. I was just as glad to go. I'd found out all I was likely to, really all I needed, and I wanted no part of her black money or the black mourning that went with it.

''You were pretty rough on her.'' Bosch said in the elevator. ''She seemed quite innocent and naïve to me.''

''She can afford to be. It's pretty clear her husband's the wheeler-dealer. He's latched onto her and her money, and the U.S. government will never see a penny of it.''

''I don't understand. What did you mean when you said Pedro was killed for his money? His mother certainly didn't kill him.''

''No, and whoever did was probably unaware that the money had passed to her.''

''That leaves the field wide open, doesn't it?''

But Allan Bosch was a sensitive man, and he may have intuited the direction my mind was moving in. When we stepped out of the elevator he said good-bye and started away like a sprinter.

''I haven't finished with you, Allan.''

''Oh? I wasn't much help, I'm afraid. I thought we'd have a chance to talk to the woman.''

''We had our chance. She gave out more than I thought she would. Now I want another chance to talk to you.''

I steered him into the bar and maneuvered him into the inside seat of a padded booth. He'd have to climb over me to get away.

I ordered a coupled of gin-and-tonics. Bosch insisted on paying for his own.

''What is there left for us to talk about?'' he said rather morosely.

''Love and money. And Professor Tappinger and his big

mistake at Illinois. Why do you suppose he goes on paying for it twelve years after the event?"

"I have no idea."

"He wouldn't be repeating it, would he?"

"I don't quite know what you're getting at." Bosch began to scratch the back of his head. "Taps is happily married. He has three children."

"Children aren't always a deterrent. In fact I've known men who turned against their children because the kids reminded them that they weren't young themselves. As for the Tappingers' marriage, it's close to the breaking point. She's a desperate woman."

"Nonsense. Bess is a darling."

"But not his darling," I said. "I wonder if he's found another darling among his students."

"Of course not. He doesn't fool around with students."

"He did once, you tell me—"

"I shouldn't have."

"And it's a pattern of behavior that tends to repeat itself. I've had some experience in my work with men and women who can't grow up, and can't bear to grow old. They keep trying to renew themselves with younger and younger partners."

The young man's face puckered with distaste. "All that may be true. It has nothing to do with Taps, and frankly I find the topic slightly disgusting."

"It isn't pleasant for me, either. I like Tappinger, and he's treated me well. But sometimes we have to face up to unpleasant facts, even about people we like."

"You're not dealing in facts. You're simply speculating on the basis of something that happened twelve years ago."

"Are you sure it isn't still going on? Seven years ago, you tell me, Tappinger brought a girl freshman here to see a play. Were there other students in the party?"

"I don't believe so."

"Is it common practice for a professor to bring a girl student, a freshman, sixty or seventy miles to see a play?"

"It could be. I don't know. Anyway, Bess was with them."

"Why didn't you tell me that before?"

"I didn't realize it was an issue," he said with a trace of irony. "Professor Tappinger is not a sexual psychopath, you know. He doesn't require twenty-four-hour-a-day chaperonage."

"I hope he doesn't. You say you talked to the girl. Did she have anything to say about Tappinger?"

"I don't remember. It was a long time ago."

"Did you see them together?"

"Yes. In fact the three of them came to my place for dinner and then we all went to the play."

"How did Tappinger and the girl act toward each other?"

"They seemed to be fond of each other." For a moment his face opened wide—he'd remembered something—and then it closed up tight. He half rose out of his chair. "Look here, I don't know what you're getting at—"

"Of course you know what I'm getting at. Did they behave like lovers?"

Bosch answered slowly and carefully: "I don't quite get the implications of that question, Mr. Archer. And I don't see its relevance to the present. After all, we're talking about seven years ago."

"There have been three murders in those seven years, all of them connected with Ginny Fablon. Her father and mother and husband have all been killed."

"Good Lord, you're not blaming Taps?"

"It's too early to say. But you can be sure these questions are relevant. Were they lovers?"

"Bess seemed to believe they were. I thought she was imagining things at the time. Maybe she wasn't, though."

"Tell me what happened."

"It didn't amount to much. She got up and walked out in the middle of the play. We were all sitting together: Bess was between me and Taps and the girl was on his far side: and Bess suddenly got up and blundered out in the dark. I followed her. I thought she might be sick, and in fact she did lose her dinner in the parking lot. But it was more of a moral sickness than a physical one. She poured out a lot of stuff about Taps and the Fablon girl and how she was corrupting him—"

"*She* was corrupting *him*?"

"So Bess claimed. It's one reason I didn't take her too seriously. She was obviously pregnant at the time, and you know how women in that condition are sometimes crazily jealous. But possibly there was something in what she said. After all, Taps did fall for Bess when she was no older than the girl." Bosch flushed darkly, like a man being choked. "I feel like a Judas, telling you all this."

"What would that make Tappinger?"

Bosch sipped at his drink. "I see what you mean. He's not exactly a Christ-figure. Still, it's a long step from playing around with a pretty girl to murdering her parents. That's unimaginable.'

"Murder usually is. Even murderers can't imagine it, or they wouldn't do it. What time did Tappinger visit you the other afternoon, Tuesday afternoon?"

"Four o'clock. He made an appointment, and he arrived on the button."

"When did he make the appointment with you?"

"Less than an hour before he arrived. He phoned and asked me when I'd be available."

"Where did he phone from?"

"He didn't say."

"What was his state of mind when he arrived?"

"You sound like a prosecuting attorney, Mr. Archer. But you're not, and I don't think I'll answer that question, or any others."

"Your friend Pedro was shot in Brentwood Tuesday afternoon. Your other friend, Tappinger, left Montevista around one. Between one and four he had time and opportunity to do the shooting, and come over to cover himself with you."

"Cover himself?"

"He used his visit to you to explain why he canceled his Tuesday afternoon classes and made the trip to Los Angeles. Can he handle a gun?"

Bosch wouldn't answer me.

"He mentioned going to school under the G.I. Bill," I said, "which means that he was in some branch of the service. Can Tappinger use a gun?"

"He was in the infantry." Bosch hung his head, as if the

mounting evidence was tending to prove his own guilt. "When Taps was a boy of nineteen or twenty, he participated in the Liberation of Paris. He wasn't—he isn't a negligible man."

"I never said he was. What was his mental state when he came to you Tuesday?"

"I'm no authority on mental states. He did seem very taut, and sort of embarrassed. Of course we hadn't seen each other for years. And he'd just got off the freeway. That San Berdoo Freeway is really tough—" He cut himself short. "Taps seemed badly shaken, I can't deny that. He practically went into hysterics when I identified Pedro Domingo from the picture, and told him the basic facts about the boy."

"What did he say?"

"He didn't say much of anything. He had what you might call a laughing fit. He seemed to think it was all a tremendous joke."

XXXIII

Bess Tappinger came to the door with the three-year-old boy holding onto her skirt. She had on a torn and faded sleeveless cotton dress, as if she was dressing the part of an abandoned wife. Sweat ran down her face from under the cloth she had tied around her head. When she wiped her face with her forearm, I could see sweat glistening in her shaven armpit.

"Why didn't you tell me you were coming? I've been cleaning the house."

"So I see."

"Will you give me time to take a shower? I must look hideous."

"As a matter of fact you look fine. But I didn't come for the view. Is your husband at home?"

"No. He isn't." Her voice was subdued.

"Is he at the college?"

"I don't know. Won't you come in? I'll make some coffee. And I'll get rid of little one. He hasn't had his nap."

She led the protesting child away. When she came back, a long quarter of an hour later, she had bathed, changed her dress, and brushed her dark thick hair.

"I'm sorry to keep you waiting. I had to get cleaned up. Whenever I feel really bad, I get this passion for cleaning." She sat on the chesterfield beside me and let me smell how clean she was.

"What do you feel bad about?"

Suddenly, she thrust out her red lower lip. "I don't feel like talking about it. I felt like talking yesterday, but you didn't." Abruptly she got to her feet and stood above me, handsome and still trembling with expectancy, as if the body that had got her into marriage might somehow get her out of it. "You don't want to be bothered with me at all."

"On the contrary, I'd like to go to bed with you right now."

"Why don't you then?" She didn't move, but her body seemed to be more massively there.

"There's a child in the house, and a husband in the wings."

"Taps wouldn't care. In fact I think he was trying to promote it."

"Why would he do that?"

"He'd like to see me fall in love with another man—somebody to take me off his hands. He's in love with another girl. He has been for years."

"Ginny Fablon."

As if the name had loosened her knees, she sat down beside me again. "You know about her then? How long have you known?"

"Just today."

"I've known about it from the beginning."

"So I've been told."

She gave me a quick sidewise look. "Have you discussed this with Taps?"

"Not yet. I just had lunch with Allan Bosch. He told me about a certain night seven years ago when he and you and your husband and Ginny went to a play together."

She nodded. "It was Sartre's *No Exit*. Did he tell you what I saw?"

"No. I don't believe he knew."

"That's right, I didn't tell him. I couldn't bring myself to tell him, or anyone. And after a while the thing I saw didn't seem real anymore. It sort of merged with my memory of the play, which is about three people living in a kind of timeless psychological hell.

"I was sitting next to Taps in the near-dark and I heard him let out a little grunt, or sigh, almost as if he'd been hurt. I looked. She had her hand on his—on his upper leg. He was sighing with pleasure.

"I couldn't believe it, even though I saw it. It made me so sick I had to get out of the place. Allan Bosch came out after me. I don't remember exactly what I said to him. I've deliberately avoided seeing him since, for fear that he might ask me questions about Taps."

"What were you afraid of?"

"I don't know. Yes, I do know, really. I was afraid if people found out that Taps had corrupted the girl, or been corrupted—I was afraid that he'd lose his job and any chance of a job. I'd seen what happened at Illinois, when Taps and I—" She caught herself. "But you don't know about that."

"Allan Bosch told me."

"Allan is a terrible tattletale." But she seemed relieved not to have to tell me herself. "I suppose I had some guilt left over from that. I almost felt as if Ginny Fablon was re-enacting me. It didn't make me hate her any less, but it tied my tongue. I seem to have spent the last seven years concealing my husband's love affair, even from myself. But I'm not going to do it after today."

"What happened today?"

"Actually it happened early this morning, before dawn.

She telephoned him here. He was sleeping in the study, as he has for years, and he took the call on the extension there. I listened in on the other phone. She was in a panic—a cold panic. She said that you were hounding her, and she couldn't keep up a front any longer, especially since she didn't know what had happened. Then she asked him if he killed her father and mother. He said of course not: the question was ridiculous: what motive would he have? She said because they knew about her baby, that he was the father.''

Bess had been speaking very rapidly. She paused now with her fingers at her lips, listening to what she'd said.

''Who told them, Bess?''

''I did. I held my tongue until September of the first year. That summer when my own baby was born, the girl dropped out of sight, I thought we were rid of her. But then she turned up again at the *Cercle Français* icebreaker. Taps took her home that night—I think he was trying to keep her away from Cervantes. When he came back to the house we had a quarrel, as I told you. He had the gall to say I was interested in Cervantes in the same way he was interested in the girl. Then he told me about the abortion the girl had had to have. I was to blame, just because I existed. I was supposed to get down on my knees and weep for the girl, I suppose.

''I did weep, off and on for a couple of weeks. Then I couldn't stand it any longer. I called the girl's father and told him about Taps. He disappeared within a day or two, and I blamed myself for his suicide. I decided I would never speak out about anything.'' Again she seemed to be listening to her own words. Their meaning seeped into her eyes and spread like darkness. ''Do you think my husband killed Mr. Fablon and Mrs. Fablon?''

''We'll have to ask him, Bess.''

''You think he did, don't you?'' Even as she asked the question, she was nodding dolefully. ''Her mother phoned here the other night.''

''Which night?''

''Monday. Wasn't that the night she was shot?''

"You know it was. What did she say?"

"She asked for Taps, and he took the call in the house. I didn't have a chance to listen. Anyway, it didn't amount to anything. He said he'd talk to her, and went out."

"He left the house?"

"Yes."

"What time?"

"It must have been quite late. I was on my way to bed. I was asleep when he came in."

"Why didn't you tell me this before?"

"I wanted to, yesterday morning. You didn't give me a chance." Her eyes were wide and blind, like a statue's.

"Was anything else said on the phone this morning?"

"He said he loved her, that he had always loved her and always would. I said something into the phone then. It was a dirty word: it just came out. It seemed so terrible to me that he could speak like that to another woman with our three children sleeping in the house.

"I went out to the study in my nightgown. It was the first time I'd gone to him since our little one was conceived—our last happy time." She paused, listening, as if the three-year-old had cried out in his sleep. But the house was so quiet I could hear water dripping in the kitchen sink. "Since then our life has been like camping on ice, on lake ice. I did that once with Daddy in Wisconsin. You find yourself thinking of the ice as solid ground, though you know there's deep dark water underneath." She looked down at the worn rug under her feet, as if there were monsters swimming just below it. "I suppose in a way I was collaborating with them, wasn't I? I don't know why I did it, or why I felt as I did. It was my marriage, and she was breaking it up, but somehow I felt out of it. I was just a member of the wedding. I felt as if it wasn't my life. My life hasn't even started."

We sat and listened to the dripping silence. "You were going to tell me what happened when you went out to the study early this morning."

She shrugged. "I hate to think about it. Taps was sitting at his desk with a gun in his hand. He looked so thin and sharp-nosed, the way people look when they're going to die. I was afraid he was going to shoot himself, and I went to him and asked him for the gun. It was almost an exact reversal of what happened the night that little one was conceived. And it was the same gun."

"I don't understand."

She said: "I bought the gun to kill myself with four years ago. It was a secondhand revolver I found in a pawnshop. Taps had been out night after night with the girl, pretending to be tutoring, and I just couldn't stand it any longer. I decided to destroy all three of us."

"With the gun?"

"The gun was just for myself. Before I used it I called Mrs. Fablon and told her what I was going to do and why. She'd know of the affair, of course, but she didn't know who the man was. She'd assumed that Taps was merely Ginny's tutor, a kind of fatherly figure in the background.

"Anyway, she got in touch with Taps wherever he was and he rushed home and took the gun away from me. I was glad. I didn't want to use it. I even managed to convince myself that Taps loved me. But all he had in mind was avoiding a scandal—another scandal.

"Mrs. Fablon didn't want one, either. She made Ginny drop out of college and go to work for some clinic near the hospital. For a while I thought that the affair was over. I was pregnant again, with our third child, and Taps would never leave me, he promised he wouldn't. He said he threw my suicide gun in the ocean.

"But he was lying. He'd kept it all these years. When I tried to take it away from him this morning, he turned it on me. He said I deserved to die for using a filthy word in Ginny's hearing. She was absolutely pure and beautiful, he said. But I was a filthy toad.

"I took off my nightgown, I don't know exactly why, I just wanted him to see he. He said my body looked like a man's face, a long lugubrious face with pink accusing eyes and a noseless nose like a congenital syphilitic and a silly little beard." Her hands moved from her breast to the region of her navel, then lower to the center of her body.

"He ordered me out and said he'd shoot me if I ever showed myself in his private room again. I went back into the house. The children were still sleeping. It wasn't light yet. I sat and watched it grow light. Some time after dawn I heard him go out and drive away in the Fiat. I got the children off to school and then I started cleaning. I've been cleaning ever since."

"You say he isn't at the college?"

"No. The Dean's office called this morning to see if he was ill. I said he was."

"Did he take the revolver with him?"

"I don't know. I haven't been in the study, and I don't intend to go in. It will have to stay dirty."

I made a quick search of the study. No gun. I did find in a desk drawer about twenty versions of the opening page of Tappinger's "book" about French influences on Stephen Crane. The most current version, which Tappinger had been working on when I first came here on Monday, was lying on top of the desk.

"Stephen Crane," it began, "lived like a god in the adamantine city of his mind. Where did he find the prototype of that city? In Athens the marmoreal exemplar of the West, or in the supernal blueprint which Augustine bequeathed to us in his *Civitas Dei*? Or was it in Paris the City of Art? Perchance he looked on his whore's body in the massive cold pity of Manet's *Olympe*. Perchance the luminous city of his mind was delved from the mud of Cora's loins."

It sounded like gibberish to me. And it suggested that Tappinger was breaking up, and had been breaking up when I first walked in on him.

Besides the hopeless manuscript lay a rough draft of the five questions he had devised for Martel:

"1. Who responsible for *Les Liaisons* old and new?
"2. 'Hypocrite lecteur'
"3. Who believed Dr.eyfus guilty?
"4. Where Descartes put soul? (pineal gland)
"5. Who got Jean Genet out of jail?"

Seeing the questions as they had occurred to Tappinger, I realized their personal significance. He had used them, perhaps unconsciously, to speak of the things that were driving him close to the edge: a dangerous sexual liaison, hypocrisy, guilt and imprisonment, the human soul trapped in a gland.

If the questions had seemed oddly one-sided to me, it was because they were answers, too, forced out in a kind of code by Tappinger's moral and emotional conflict. I recalled with a slight shock that the answer to the fifth question had been Sartre, and wondered if, in Tappinger's queer complex academic code, it referred to the night at the play seven years before.

XXXIV

THE ABSENCE of the gun probably meant that Tappinger was carrying it. I went outside and got my own gun and harness out of the trunk of my car. Because there were children in the street, I retreated into the house to put the harness on.

"You're going to kill him," Bess said. She looked widowed already.

"I won't use this unless he forces me to. I have to protect myself."

"What will become of the children?"

"That will be pretty much up to you."

"Why should it be up to me?" she said in her little-girl voice. "Why did this have to happen to me?"

You married the wrong man at the wrong time for the wrong reasons, I told her silently. But there was no use saying it out loud. She already knew it. In fact she had been telling me about it, in her own queer inarticulate way, ever since I met her.

"At least you've survived. That's something to be thankful for, Bess."

She raised her fist in an impatient, almost threatening, gesture. "I don't want to survive, not this way."

"You might as well. The life you live may be your own."

The prospect frightened her. "Don't leave me by myself."

"I have to. Why don't you call one of your friends."

"We don't have any. They dropped away long ago."

She seemed to be lost in her own house. I tried to kiss her goodbye. It wasn't a good idea. Her mouth was unresponsive, her body as stiff as a board.

The thought of her stayed with me, poignant and unsatisfying, as I drove across town toward the Fablon house. Perhaps below the level of consciousness, down where the luminous monsters swam in their cold darkness, Bess was in love with her husband's love affair.

Ginny was home, and he was with her. His gray Fiat stood under the oak tree. When I knocked on the front door, they answered it together. He was red-eyed and sallow. She was shivering.

"Maybe you can make him stop talking," she said. "He's been talking for hours and hours."

"What about?"

"I forbid you to say." Tappinger's voice was hoarse and unnatural. "Go away," he said to me.

"Please don't," she said. "I'm afraid of him. He killed Roy and the others. That's what he's been talking about all day—all the reasons why he had to kill Roy. And he keeps giving different reasons, like he saw Roy kneeling by the pool trying to wash his bloody face and he felt so sorry for him that he pushed him in. That's the euthanasia reason. Then there's the St.-George-and-the-dragon reason: Roy was delivering me into the hands of Mr. Ketchel and something had to be done to stop it."

Her voice was savage and scornful. Tappinger winced under it. "You mustn't make fun of me."

"This is making fun?" She turned to me. "The real

reason was very simple. You guessed it last night. I'd been pregnant by him and Roy found out somehow that Taps was the father."

"You let me think it was Peter."

"I know I did. I'm not covering up for Taps any longer."

He gasped as if he had been holding his breath. "You mustn't talk like that. Someone might hear you. Why don't we go inside?"

"I like it here."

She planted herself more firmly in the doorway. He was afraid to leave her. He had to hear what she might say.

"What were you doing at the Tennis Club that night, professor?"

His eyes veered and then held steady. "I went there for purely professional reasons. Miss Fablon had been my student since February. I counseled her, and she confided in me."

"Did I not," she said.

He went on spinning out his string of words, as if it was his only support in a void: "She confided that her father, with the aid of a scholarship from Mr. Ketchel, was going to send her to a school in Switzerland. I felt that my advice as an educator would be useful to them, and I went to the club to offer it.

"I got there rather too late to be of use. I saw Mr. Fablon staggering across the lawn, and when I spoke to him he didn't know me. He stumbled into the pool enclosure, apparently with some idea of washing his face, which was bleeding, and before I knew it he had fallen in. I'm not a swimmer myself, but I tried to fish him out with a pole they keep for that purpose, with a paddle hook on the end—"

"You mean," she said, "you used it to hold him under water."

"That's a ridiculous accusation. Why do you keep repeating it?"

"Francis gave me an eyewitness account the other night. I didn't believe him then—I thought he was making it up out of jealousy. But I believe him now. He saw you push Roy in and hold him under with the pole."

"Why didn't he interfere if he was there?" Tappinger said pedantically. "Why didn't he report it?"

"I don't know." She peered up past me at the declining sun, as if it might abandon her, leave her in cold darkness. "There are a lot of things I don't understand."

"Did you take them up with your mother Monday night?" I said.

"Some of them. I asked her if it could be true that Taps drowned Roy in the swimming pool. I shouldn't have, I suppose. The idea seemed to throw her."

"I know it did. I talked to her after you left. And after that she talked to Tappinger on the phone. That was her last talk. He came here and shot her."

He said without conviction: "I did not."

"Yes you did, Taps." Her voice was grave. "You killed her, and then the next day you came to Brentwood and killed Francis."

"But I had no reason to kill either of them." There was a questioning note in his denial.

"You had plenty of reasons."

"What were they?" I said to both of them.

They turned and looked at each other as if each felt the other possessed the answer, the multiple answer. I was struck by the curious resemblance between them, in spite of their differences in sex and age. They were very nearly the same height and weight, and they had the same fine regular features. They could have been brother and sister. I wished they had been.

"What were the reasons for killing Martel?" I said.

They went on looking into each other's faces, as if each were a dream figure in the other's dream which had to be interpreted.

"You were jealous of Francis, weren't you?" Ginny finally said.

"That's nonsensical."

"Then you're nonsensical, because you're the one who said it in the first place. You wanted me to call the whole thing off."

I said: "What whole thing was that?"

Neither of them spoke. They looked at me with a kind of dimly comprehended shame, like children caught in forbidden play. I said:

"You were going to kill him and inherit his money, weren't you? But it's always the con artist who gets conned. You were so full of your own wild dreams that you believed his stories. You didn't know or care that his money was embezzled from an income-tax evader."

"That's not true," Ginny said. "Francis told me the whole story of his life last weekend. It's true he started out as a poor boy in Panama. But he was a direct descendant of Sir Francis Drake through his mother, and he had a parchment map which was handed down in the family, showing the location of Drake's buried treasure. Francis found the treasure, over a million dollars' worth of Peruvian gold, on the coast of Panama near Nombre de Dios."

I didn't argue with her. It no longer mattered what she believed, or said that she believed.

"And it isn't true," she went on, "that we planned to kill him, or anybody. The original plan was for me to marry Peter. I was simply to divorce him and get a settlement, so that Taps and I could go away—"

He shook his head at her in quick short arcs. His hair frizzed out like a woman's.

"Go away and study in Europe?" I said.

"Yes. Taps thought if he could get back to France that he could write his book. He'd been trying to get it started for years. I was getting desperate, too. It got so shabby, making love in the backs of cars, or in his office, or in a public motel. Sometimes I felt as if everyone on the campus, everyone in town, must know about us. But nobody ever said a word."

"You mustn't tell him all this," Tappinger said. "Don't admit anything."

She shrugged. "What difference does it make now?"

I said: "You originally planned to marry Peter and divorce him, is that right?"

"Yes, but I hated to do it to him. I only agreed because we were desperate for money. I've always liked Peter. When

Francis came here and asked me to marry him, I switched the plan. I didn't owe Francis anything."

"You were attracted to him." The words seemed to come out of Tappinger's mouth involuntarily, as if a ventriloquist was using him as a dummy.

"I said you were jealous of him, didn't I?"

He sputtered. "Jealous? How could I be jealous? I never even saw the man, until—" He shut his mouth, biting back the words.

"Until you shot him," she said.

"I tell you I didn't shoot him. How would I know where to find him?"

"I gave you the address. I shouldn't have. Francis told me after you shot him that it was you. He said it was the same man who killed Roy."

"He said that because he hated me."

"Why would that be?" I said.

"Because Ginny and I were lovers."

"You admit it, do you?"

His mouth worked, trying to produce the words that would support him over the void. "We were lovers in the Platonic sense, I mean to say."

She looked at him scornfully. "You're not even a man. I'm sorry I ever let you touch me."

He was trembling, as if her shivering chill had infected him. "You mustn't talk like that, Ginny."

"Because you're so *sensitif*? You're about as sensitive as a mad dog. I doubt that you know any more about what you're doing than a mad dog does."

He cried out: "How dare you treat me with disrespect? You were an ignorant girl. I made a woman of you. I admitted you to the intimacy of my mind—"

"I know, the luminous city. Only it isn't so luminous. The last dim little light went out Monday night, when you shot Marietta."

His whole body leaned toward her suddenly, as if he was going to attack her. But the movement was inhibited. I was there.

"I can't stand this." He turned away abruptly and almost ran into the sitting room.

"Be careful of him," Ginny said. "He has a gun in there. He was trying to talk me into a suicide pact."

The gun coughed apologetically. We found Tappinger lying on the floor of the room where he had shot Marietta. The revolver he had used on her and Martel had left a dark hole in his own temple. The briefcase of money stood behind the door, as if he hadn't dared to let it out of his sight.

I took the revolver, which still had three rounds in the chambers, and went next door to telephone the county police. Peter became very excited. He wanted to come back to the Fablon house and look after Ginny. He was the one who needed looking after. I ordered him to stay home.

It was just as well I did. She was lying on the sitting room floor face to face with Tappinger, their profiles interlocking like complementary shapes cut from a single piece of metal. She lay there with him, silent and unmoving, until the noise of the sirens was heard along the road. Then she got up and washed her face and composed herself.

ABOUT THE AUTHOR

"ROSS MACDONALD" was the pseudonym of Kenneth Millar. Born outside San Francisco in 1915, he grew up in Vancouver, British Columbia. He returned to the U.S. in 1938, earned a Ph.D. at the University of Michigan, served in the Navy during World War II and published his first novel in 1944. He served as president of the Mystery Writers of America and was awarded both the Silver Dagger award by the Crime Writers' Association of Great Britain and the Grand Master Award by the Mystery Writers of America. He was married to the novelist Margaret Millar. He died in 1983.